THE IRIDESCENT SOUL

THE IRIDESCENT SOUL

BOOK TWO:

"I MAY YET LIVE, BUT I DON'T
WANT TO REMEMBER."

C.E LAGERBOM

THE IRIDESCENT SOUL
"I May yet live, but I don't want to remember."

ISBN   979-8-218-40263-1 *Paperback*
        979-8-218-40264-8 *Kindle Ebook*

CONTENTS

AUTHOR'S NOTE

"Everything that is or was, began with a dream."
— LAVAGIRL

After book one got published I had several friends and family ask, "How do you do it? How do you choose to spend your afternoons and weekends writing words when you couldn't have been bothered to do a paper while you were in school?" Honestly, good question.

I love storytelling. It can be summed up to that in it's simplest form. It's where I find pure unfiltered joy and meaning to a life that otherwise feels pretty insignificant. It's how I feel I can contribute to society. By creating passion and inspiration as others have done for me. Passing of the proverbial torch, so to speak. What I'm not good at is being told what to write or what to do. I like to be able to have free reign to tell the story I want to, without any teacher telling me that's irrelevant or being forced into restrictive guidelines.

My friends will forever humble and remind me of my actual inability to form complete sentences in social situations and my constant typos of basic words. My editor has the patience of a saint. I guess this is my form of the American dream. A way of being my own boss. Creating my own worlds. My way of leaving something behind after I am gone. The ability to create something that will last forever. I suppose children are an example but hey, I'm only 23. I've got time. At the time of book two this is still most definitely a hobby.

In fact I was quite busy during writing the rough draft for the sequel. I'm amazed I got it done. I graduated college and packed up everything and left everyone I knew to move to the west coast to pursue the dreams of writing and cinema. It was a soul fulfilling, butt bruising, cross-country drive. I'm glad I did it. I definitely recommend everyone do at least once in their life. But those goodbyes were not easy.

Book two for me is a symbol of my independence. Not just stepping away from any publisher but also as a reflection of my growth in life. Learning how to do things myself without parental help. During the making of book two I did so many adulting things I never thought I could do. Fixed a flat tire, made a doctors and dentist appointment, learned how insurance worked, started and currently paying rent for an apartment.

I have to be able to look myself in the mirror, look past the impostor's syndrome and convince myself that I am doing a good job. Listen to others when they say as much. Some days it's hard. But as I write out this paragraph now I can truly believe it. I can be proud of this accomplishment. I can enjoy what is to come as a result.

I continue to explore and expand the world Isaac woke up in during book two. Learning how things have evolved or devolved since he's been on ice. Going deeper into the effects our neighbors had on major world religions and how dystopian governmental rule has suppressed humanity. How Isaac has been dealing with the death of his father and the relentless hunt from his mother. And finally, where is this all leading up to? If you are a returner from book one I hope you enjoy book two! If you're not, I recommend reading book one first.

Again I have no idea who you are. Where you are. When you are. Or why you are reading this book but you are. And that still blows my mind to this day that people would be interested in what I have to offer this world.

That's what I consider to be a successful writer. To have someone interested to read it. And I've already achieved that. Anything that happens now for the rest of my life is icing on the cake. Thank you again for opening this book and consciously choosing to read these words.

Dedication

For Uncle John. For all the noogies he gave me as a kid.

EPIGRAPH

"No matter what anybody tells you. Words and ideas can change the world."

—ROBIN WILLIAMS

PROLOGUE

Which life would you choose to live? If you literally had the choice? Unlimited options. I mean I guess it doesn't matter. You can live every type of life you want thanks to this technology. You can be a king and live in medieval times for a hundred years. Then for another hundred you can go live in Atlantis or visit the Library of Alexandria. At least our best representation of what we think it was like. Go live in the best mansions or build your own houses. Ever wanted a super power? Give yourself any or all of them. Invisibility. Super Strength.

Be a celebrity, slay a dragon, build a theme park, fly over mountains. Visit the center of the Earth. Build your own planet. Speak every language. Master every skill. Marry your dream crush. They wouldn't know, it would just be a fake version of them. How is it any different then owning photos of them? You can do anything. Oh? The real world? Who cares about that place? You can make your own world. So long as you can afford the monthly subscription.

The cost? Oh it's not bad. Certain chunks of your pay-check like anything else. Terms and conditions are so boring. The real world? Disaster. Everywhere you look. It's ugly. It's better to just shut it all out. Let it fade away. Plug in and live your own reality. Have regrets? Things you wish you did differently in life? You can re-do those mistakes in the machine. You can have your perfect life where you and everyone you know never get hurt.

Oh... You can't afford a subscription? That's okay because thanks to your government you can get three free months of service. Just sign these documents! Oh don't worry about what it says. Who ever reads the terms and conditions anyway? Let us take care of everything.

The same spiel I've seen and heard over and over again for months now. I can't decide what I hate more about it. The deception and lies behind it all? Or the fact that I am a hooked consumer of it. Of an addicting virtual reality paradise regulated by our countries' government.

Does anyone even wonder how you are able to live years in the timespan of days? Kanoa explained it to me. Essentially anyone starting off with a tier one subscription to T.R.A.C.I can experience any reality they desire but it moves in real time. The phrase went from time is money to money is time. In 2119, now you can buy time.

It's genius really. Someone will drop fifty thousand dollars to live fifteen years in a reality they design and to the perspective of the people in charge, he'll be right back to his shitty apartment the next day, or depending on how long he set himself up for. Kanoa's told me stories on how some people have signed waivers, forfeiting all their worldly possessions and agreeing to become test subjects for the rest of their life just to stay inside. However if you stretch out the amount of time you spend under, it wears out your brain more quickly. Your mind and body are two separate things but one cannot live without the other.

Governments are good...right? After all they are designed by the people for the people. They are meant to provide safety and security. But one of our fatal human flaws is greed and control. And this regime has a vice grip on the souls of their people. A trap that we walked ourselves into. We allowed this life to happen.

Eh, guess I don't really care to be honest. I don't like politics. I don't care about much these days. I just want to live my life. Or at least I used too. I wanted to go to college and now? Now things just suck. The only thing I enjoy is T.R.A.C.I. It's my saving grace. The thing I look forward too. Back in my day if we had this, my parents would tell me to go outside or something. But outside like I said is gross. Nothing but pain and suffering out there. And I am one human. Not really a lot I can do even in my current position.

I'm actually just in the way most of the time with these guys. Why did they think I would make a good asset? I'm a nuisance, a liability. It'd be easier if I just disappeared. So I'd rather just go back to my treehouse mansion I built with my dad. He always wanted to build a treehouse with me. We never got the chance.

Logging into encrypted T.R.A.C.I server #8456...

CHAPTER 1

NEXUS LOG 7.08.82

Abigail pushes past a sea of busy scientists and guards, arriving at a solid iron door. She takes out her card and slams it against the translucent white panel. A scanner pops out and scans her eye. A confirming beep rings as the doors glide open. She rushes into an office where a slightly younger version of the Prexy meets her. She is sitting down reading something on her computer at her desk. She looks up.

Her power reflecting in her attire. A white blazer to match her pants adorn her figure. Secured with a black belt and and fingerless work gloves that reach halfway to her elbows. Her pure black hair coiled up and held behind her head. The Prexy and Abigail have always been incredibly close in age. Both at this time looking to be around mid to late fifties.

The Prexy shows no sign of age or wrinkles however due to her rigorous skin care routine. Someone who is quite mindful of how they look. Abigail who's hurried and exhaust expression showing in her frizzled hair and not quite put together uniform. Her lab coat not buttoned all the way. Blue jeans secured with a brown belt. Her all black work shoes provide much more comfort then the extreme monstrosity her friend calls heels, that she is currently donning.

"To what do I owe this pleasure Doctor?" The Prexy says with her all-knowing attitude. Looking from her desk outside the window. The sunrise providing the majority of light into this office. Giving everything a warm glow to an otherwise tense conversation.

"Why are several containment vessels being moved from my lab?" Abigail asks, slightly panicked.

"We found the main resistance base. They tried putting up a fight before they could scatter. You are receiving new shipments of test subjects." Prexy says without skipping a beat, nonchalantly. "I'll need you to extract all the info they have."

"What is happening to the old test subjects?" Growing more frantic with each sentence. "Warehouse for whatever room we have left. The rest will be euthanized." She remarks, returning her focus to the computer.

"Some of those test subjects are still invaluable. They were the Rosetta stones."

She tries to reason with and regain her colleague's attention. "So go there yourself and pick the ones to keep." She dismisses the conversation and types away at her computer. Changing her mind, she stops and looks back up at Abigail.

"But I expect those new appointments to be successful."

"They will be." She says already walking out the door.

The fridge is an impressively massive, appropriately named location. A twenty story deep bunker built for one purpose only. Storage. Abigail reminisces on helping design it once it clearly became necessary. Her cryo-tech was one of Mercia's biggest achievements.

However she couldn't achieve everything she wanted to. So slowly more and more doctors and scientists at her and the Prexy's approval joined the program. Learning under her and being new fresh minds and extra hands.

With progressively more testing being conducted, Mercia needed a national cryo-bank vault for all of their willing and non-willing test subjects; the ones serving sentences. Those are specifically labeled with criminals' tags in their files.

As soon as her ride lands. Abigail races down the elevator to the lowest levels of the fridge, an enormous sublevel facility with seemingly endless pods lined up nice and neat. Being deep underground with all of this technology made it irritably cold. It had to be to preserve the subjects. She races across the airport-strip-long hallway, the roof about a mile up. Her steps echo with every impact. She gets to the workers unloading where most of the vaults have already been put into storage. Several remaining pods are scattered as the workers begin flipping levers and yanking cords.

"Stop!" She shouts

"I have to bring a select few back with me. They are still part of my research." She exhales out of breath.

"I was told to fill the fridge to the max. The rest get turned off." The grimy maintenance worker grumbles. His five o'clock shadow and annoyed attitude making her wonder if his loyalty is to his country or to his paycheck.

"Please." Abigail looks around at the remaining pods scattered around the warehouse floor. There are about half a dozen left. Her eyes go big as she reads the numbers on the side of one specific container. TS-0089 John Doe: Age 56. She looks around and freezes upon the sight of another containment pod. TS-0090 John Doe: Age 18.

"With all due respect, doctor." The worker tries to reason. "I saw the shipment coming in for you. You really aren't going to have much room-"

"I can hold one in my lab!" She exclaims.

"Okay, well pick the one you want and we will load them back up." The worker grunts.

Abigail tries to maintain her composure, looks helplessly back and forth at both of these pods.

"Put TS-0089 back on my plane." She says, trying to not to show emotion.

"Yes Madam Secretary." The head worker nods to his buddies as they grab the large tub-like container and wheel it away back to her aircraft. The head worker reaches for the main power plug to start removing the life support from the rest of the containment pods. Abigail grabs his arm.

"This one must be stored." She says with her cold emotionless glare. The worker gulps hard.

"The fridge is full ma'am. We can't hold any more." He says trying to not shit his pants.

"Then take. Another. Out. Please." She says in a sickly loving way. But nothing about her intent is loving. It is strong enough to send shivers down the toughest of workers. The worker, starting to tremble, frantically waves over a few more workers as they disconnect a random pod from life-support and let it fall to the ground. The screen and lights go dark. The pod cracks slightly from the impact.

"Load TS-0090 into the fridge and disconnect the rest. And clean this mess up now!"

She shouts, causing them all to frantically carry out her demands. She watches as they carefully install TS-0090 into the fridge network. Then as they disconnect pods on the ground, killing the subjects. She watches as all her former test subjects' faces go dark. TS-0094 John Doe Age 26, TS-0098 Jane Doe Age 27, TS-0103 [Redacted] TS-0115 Criminal John Doe Age 43. Abigail, now calm and collected, approaches the glass panel to look inside the one she saved.

"You'll be okay here." She whispers to herself. In a self-assurance way.

"You'll be fine. I'll bring you back when I can."

Suddenly there is a loud explosion as the whole room rumbles and shakes. Several men in suits approach Abigail. "Madam Secretary we are currently under attack. We are to deliver you to the Apex Mountain facility for further protection until this threat is over."

"It's those crazy aliens isn't it?" One of the workers yell over the rumbling. "Get out of here! I'm sorry Madam secretary we need to leave now!" The agent grabs Abigail's arm and drags her away. She looks back at the pod and allows one tear to shed as she wipes it away and goes with her protective detail. A loud crack and explosion as the lights momentarily go out.

"EMP. They're going after the servers." One of the agents says in a mic.

"The backup generators will protect them if they fail," Abigail reminds her guards as everyone leaves the area. As the lights blink on and off again. There is a sound of static as the long line of monitors for pods click off but then back on. Another explosion fills the air. TS-0090's pod manually reboots.

But due to the improper shutting down sequence the labeling has been changed. It is now labeled: Criminal John Doe Age 18. Another loud crash makes the entire facility shake. After a few minutes dozens of Neighbors swarm the facility. Chattering and screeching, they are all armed with various weapons.

They smash and destroy every pod they can find. One by one lights go out on people cryogenically stored. They make their way through the rows and hallways eradicating everything in sight. After a few minutes of this an automatic response rings out.

"Alien life detected. Human life not detected. Now initiating repellents." A female robotic voice rings out. The facility begins to fill with a deadly gas.

Some aliens near the vents get hit first and start gagging and yelling until their faces turn into a bloody mess. Once the fighting and horror is over. IHL soldiers sweep the place and do inventory. The head of the division walks down a hall, visibly nervous. So much so that people walking by comment that he looks like he is about to throw up.

Finally he reaches a set of double doors being guarded by two buff IHL soldiers. They nod and gesture that he may enter. With a big gulp this skinny scientist pushes open the doors into a dimly lit room.

"H-Hello?" The scientist's voice quavers.

"How many losses?" Abigail's voice bounces from the other end of the dark office.

"Ma'am. We lost 137 test subjects. Most of it was due to the overflow but we also have fifteen test subjects unaccounted for."

"What do you mean unaccounted for?" She says.

"Well they're just gone. Missing. There were no booths in fifteen fridge slots when we did inventory. We can't figure out how they were moved." The scientist says, trying his best to hide behind his clipboard.

"Let me see the list!" she barks.
Scared, the scientist hands the clipboard over. "I'm truly sorry ma'am. I noticed some of the missing test subjects initial freeze date. Some of those were your first ones weren't they?

"So TS-0090 survived. That's what I'm reading?" she asks, attempting to keep all joy out of her voice and only just succeeding at it. "Yes ma'am." She nods.

"Thank you, that is all. You may go." Abigail orders. The scientist nods and speed-walks out of the office. Abigail takes a moment to read the list of test subjects and her eyes go wide upon reading a certain number. She drops the chart onto her desk. "Where the hell did she go? She was Isaac's gift." She mutters.

CHAPTER 2

NEW WORLD

I wake up in a cold sweat. The room is still and silent.
I could see slivers of morning light shining in through the
partially closed door. I sit up, rub my face. I am drenched in
sweat. The window is the only thing providing any light in my
bedroom. I look over to my bed desk. My copy of Fahrenheit
451 is left open, slowly bending the book's spine. I grab it and
close the book only to have it slowly reopen due to the now-
bent spine. I slowly shuffle off of the mattress. I reach around
and fumble in the dark until landing my hand on the light
switch. A single exposed bulb does it's best to fill the room
with light. It starts to flicker.

"Great."

I rummage around the room, try to get myself together
while searching for a spare bulb. I open several drawers while
I dress. Carelessly, I trip over some loose clothing on the floor
and bang my knee into my bedpost.

"Fuck!"

I hold my knee. Suddenly the light bulb stops flickering
and glows brighter then I've seen it before. Then the bulb
bursts, sending a gust of glass and filament all over the room.
As I stare up in wonder and confusion there is a knock at the
door. I finish dressing and head downstairs.

I pass by dad's framed photo. It was a house warming gift for the light house. I stop and look, then quickly go by. He is happy in that photo. He and my mother are on a very early date. Before I was even thought of, much less around. He looks healthy and happy. So does my mother.

Finally I get down to the first floor, half-hobbling from my new bum knee. I open the door and see two gentlemen in officer uniforms. One clearly older then the other. The older one has short salt and pepper hair. The dark circles under his eyes make me think he hasn't yet had his coffee for the day. The other one looks practically like a kid. Fresh out of the academy. Bright and energetic, with blonde hair stuff up within his cap. The kid decides to talk first.

"Hello, I'm officer Caddel and this is Officer Barlowe. Are you Isaac Ashter?" He says.

"Yes." I say cautiously. "If this about the complaint, I've already hired a technician to come look at the bulb up there. I'm sorry for any delays this is causing."

"We're looking for someone. Have you seen this person?" The other officer says holding up a photo of a woman. She has shoulder-length black hair with a plaid headband on. It is a mug shot. She looks sad and hurt. I swallow hard.

"No officers. I have not seen that woman." Salt and pepper puts it away while I notice blondie move his hand to his waist over his weapon. "We received reports that she was last seen around this area." Salt and pepper continues.

"If you know anything-"

"I don't, so leave me alone." I cut him off and try to close the door. Blondie sticks his foot in. I slowly reopen it. The two officers now both share a look of serious intent. Their stares are grim and severe. They both now have their hands on their weapons. I scoff.

"Okay look before we do this, you should know I just banged my knee-"

Before I can finish the two officers rush me. Blondie kicks open the door and salt and pepper tackles me. I try and reach for the second officer's gun. But before I can he slams me to the ground, bouncing my head off the wood floor and takes out his taser and shocks me in the chest. I squirm on the ground in convulsions.

Blondie picks me up and handcuffs me. Once the shock wears off they seat me upright. They drag me further outside to my front yard. It is a bright day on the Cliffside. The lighthouse has had some major improvements done to it since I arrived. It's now fitted for multiple uses. The dazzling sun hits my face like a laser. I squint, try to look up at the policemen.

"I don't like handcuffs." I say.

"They know." I hear a familiar voice. I slowly open my eyes, allow them to adjust to see Kanoa. His long silver hair is back in a ponytail. His shoulder tech patch keeps his wound safe and clean. It's displayed over his uniform. He is wearing the standard combat attire of everyone in the resistance.

"Hey there." He says crossing his arms. He does not look happy to see me. "Howdy," I reply sarcastically. Great just what I needed. Why couldn't he just let me enjoy my time?

"Do you know why I'm here?" Hands now move to his hips. "Did you have to bring extra ones and zeros?" I look up at the now emotionless cops. Kanoa smirks and waves his hand. The officers start unraveling in a series of code until they blink out of existence. The handcuffs disappear. I stand and rub my wrists.

"When did you know?" Kanoa asks. "Can we just get on with it?" I ignore his question and reach for his gun. "Woah there hold your horses. We still have something to go over."

Kanoa successfully stops my arm. I draw back. I sigh in annoyance.

"Another one?"

I really don't feel like training right now. But knowing him I'm not in a position to make a choice. He's clearly bribed the tech I previously bribed to take control of my simulation. Jerk. Kanoa smiles and takes off his utility belt. He holds out his hand and suddenly a steel sword appears out of nowhere, flashing into existence. I hold out my hand and a similar sword appears.

"I'm getting better at these you know," I gloat. "Then show me." He grins. I crack my neck and stretch my arms. I run at Kanoa and swing my sword. He counters and parries my every move. Iron rings out with every clash as we fight. The world unravels around us in code as the scenery changes to the halls of a great cathedral.

"What year did our Neighbors arrive?" Kanoa shouts over the loud ringing of swords bouncing off the church walls.

"The Day of Discovery was on August 3rd 2030, America went to war two years later. Just after the Prexy took office. Mercia rose in the aftermath of World War Three." I dodge a lunge.

"What did our Neighbors bring to our planet?" Kanoa kicks me away, trips me over a pew.

As I hit the floor the area around us changes yet again. The cold stone of the cathedral turns into rough planks of wood. A strong scent of seawater and a gust of ocean breeze hits my face. The floor is uneven and rocks back and forth. All I can see around me is ocean for miles on end. Looking up I see a giant mast with a black flag waiving frantically. I regain my footing and catch Kanoa's advance, block his attack.

"War? Over-Population? Disease possibly?" I say sarcastically. "Stop reciting Mercia propaganda!" Kanoa says right in my face. I return the favor and kick him back, tripping him over a cannon as I head up to the top of the ship. As he gets back up I shout.

"They brought us Verve! An element not found on Earth. It's not able to be reproduced without using an ability provided by verve. Certain technology can interact with it to enhance it. Certain humans can interact with it to gain abilities. Because of Verve every major religion on Earth now believes that they have proof of their god's existence. The fact that our Neighbors believe in a higher power didn't help that either."

"People will always look for a reason to convince themselves they are not crazy." Kanoa says, catching his breath.

"You think believing in a religion makes someone crazy?" I ask sucking in air.

"I think people shouldn't let their guard down." Kanoa's eyes light up with a solid turquoise blue as he rips a fireball right at me. I jump out of the way as it slams into the mast of the ship! The sails catch like tinder wood. Quickly the boat ignites like a match. I scramble, throw myself off the deck. The water just a few feet below me vaporizes and instead of hitting sea I am now falling thousands of feet in the air. The earth now thousands of feet away from me.

As I begin to Accelerate, I close my eyes and concentrate and a parachute materializes on my back. I pull the chord and the fabric rips out of the pack and opens violently. I come to a slow descent. As I drift towards the ground, Kanoa soars in, pulls his chute.

"The three states of matter?" He raises an eyebrow. "Solid, liquid, gas," I repeat like a drone. "Why is that important?" Kanoa continues.

"Verve is a compound that takes all three forms at will. In the past people injected it as liquid to gain abilities but that proved risky. Inhaling it as a vapor is the safer form of integration. The element was first discovered by our Neighbors in a local white dwarf. Since then humanity has found ways to produce and distribute it through gained abilities. People can forge it permanently into one of the forms to use for specific purposes like tech and weapons."

"Correct." Kanoa nods.

"Name five technological advancements that have been made since you've been on ice." Kanoa shouts over to me, wind blowing all around us.

"Hovercraft technology. Artificial intelligence. The transfer from combustion to energy based weaponry. T.R.A.C.I..." I pause as I look off into the distance and see some clouds part to make out some kind of floating structure that looks familiar. I lose my train of thought as I simply mutter...

"Cryogenics."

Suddenly a body shoots right past us, falling without a parachute. I feel a sharp pain in my head as I grab my temple. I close my eyes and see Ramirez on the walkway right before he was killed. His body falls off of the loft and into the sky. I scream in pain and thrash around in the parachute until the pack glitches off of me.

I plummet, descending to the near-approaching ground. Just before splattering, I suddenly stop, frozen in midair and turned around by an invisible force to land on my feet. Kanoa touches down shortly after and removes his parachute. Concern and worry etched on his facial features.

"Are we done now?" I am exasperated and out of breath.

"What the hell was that?" He exclaims.

"They're just headaches." That's the truth. They are just these strange headaches I've been getting recently. I figure it's just from being inside the simulation for so long. Nothing to worry about though. However there had never been visions or anything like that before. I know he's supposed to be my mentor or whatever but I'm not about to trauma dump on him. There's been enough of that in our past.

"And this is just a magic trick." Kanoa says forming a fireball in his hand. I scoff. "Not one you can do anymore." I spit. He disperses the flame. His face now a mixture of anger and worry.

"Any notes, professor?" I continue sarcastically.

"You're doing fine with your studies. You've aced all the courses on history and on today's society. You've learned terms, phrases, laws. People wouldn't think you are from the past anymore. We still don't know why you carry Verve. If you had a power we would've found it by now but with every test, nothing comes up."

"It's like you said. Some people just don't get anything."

I am a bit bummed. We've known this for months now and I've just been waiting for a power to reveal itself. Except nothing has.

"There is no reason your eyes should be like that. Normally people have their normal eye colors and they only turn neon blue when they use their power but even then it takes over the entire eye. For you it's just your iris. We've never seen anything like it before. You swear they used to be hazel?"

"Can we please rise? I want to get out of here." I am not apart of this conversation. I start to twitch uncomfortably.

"I still need to know where you and Caleb have been these last few days." Kanoa says. My legs begin shaking.

"We were at the nether. You saw the letter." Kanoa taking note of my stress.

"But that wasn't your first destination." Kanoa presses.

"Alright. Enough." I am done with all of this. I don't want to be here anymore.

"Just wait!" Kanoa says. I grab his gun and shove him to the ground. I switch it to red, stick it in my mouth and pull the trigger. There is a flash of black then white then I hear the familiar sounds of a T.R.A.C.I booth as it brings me back to life.

I feel the headset slowly rise off of me as I open my eyes. I'm back in the training module where several T.R.A.C.I booths are linked together. There is a control room where people monitor the world we get put in behind bulletproof glass. I sit up and quickly escape the booth as I hear some of the tech's pound on the glass.

"Dammit Isaac!" I hear through the intercom system. The tech's look like they are about to burst a vessel.

"Stop hard resetting the system!" I ignore them and grab my jacket as I head out.

"Hey!" I hear Kanoa shout. Ignoring him I wave my hand on the sensor to leave. The doors whoosh open to a slightly busy hallway of soldiers and scientists busy with their own work. Pushing past some of them I ignore him as I head down the hall. Kanoa catches up and matches my pace.

"We're not done." Kanoa says grabbing my shoulder to spin me around. "What the hell is your problem?"

"You're going to have to be more specific." I roll my eyes. He lets go of me.

"What has gotten into you? You focus on your studies, especially T.R.A.C.I framework, but you have completely shut down in team training. That is when you decide to show up.

You haven't reported for almost a dozen sessions in the last month. Always running off with Caleb."

"Okay?"

"And I reviewed your T.R.A.C.I logs. You've stretched almost a year's worth of time in T.R.A.C.I in the last few weeks, Almost every time you've waken up you forced a hard reset."

"Get to your point." I am incredibly tired now. He is beginning to really get on my nerves.

"If this is about your mother-" Kanoa begins. I immediately shut him down.

"You mean the woman you can't wait to kill?" I fire back at him. He looks hurt at that. The hallway is now void of people.

"I know you must be bothered with the timing of-" Kanoa places his hand on my shoulder again, this time more gentle.

"I'm not." I continue to cut him off.

"Your father made his choice. You gave him that Isaac." I shake off his hands.

"I know." He then decides to go for a shove.

"So why are you killing yourself every night?"

I turn back around and head for my room. Kanoa doesn't follow me this time. Instead he shouts.

"Crane wants to see you. You better show."

I turn the corner and move through hallways, passing various rooms. The commissary, the armory, labs, offices. This new hideout makes the old one look like my cousin's room where I used to play GameCube games in. Crane told me that we have an extensive list of abandoned places. Once we pick a location to squat in we go into full montage mode of moving.

This group have taught me to stay mobile. We are able to pack up home and disappear within less then a day. It's probably how they've stayed alive against the I.H.L. We are roamers. I finally get back to my room.

A small room with everything needed to survive. A bed, a shower/toilet combo, a dresser and a desk. I rip off my jacket and flop onto my bed. I feel something crumpled up underneath my pillow. I pull it out and look at it, only to sigh and toss it to the ground. It is a newspaper article about my mother's latest achievement.

CHAPTER 3

PASCAL'S WAGER

A good hot shower can either start or end your day on a fantastic note, except when you obsess and worry over every seemingly abnormal thing about your body. Did I always have that mole? Have I gained weight? My showers are always the same. Using a mirror, I stare at the odd tattoo on my neck. Just as crazy as having verve in my system to wake up into a new world to.

According to Z and Kanoa it's a naturally forming birth-mark, so to speak, for every single member of their species. At first I thought it was an applied feature, but apparently every Neighbor is born with it. The versions humans put on themselves is an artist's rendition of the symbol. Earthlings eventually settled on a common well-liked version.

It's because of this tattoo I've been almost killed several times over. And I have no idea when or how I even got it. I've been offered the means to conceal it whenever we are out in the field, which I usually take. The shower, however, is the one place I can't stop thinking about it. A little bit later afterwards I pass Caleb in the halls.

"Hey!" I stop us in our tracks. "What's up?" He asks.

"Why are they called Techno's?" I point to the back of my neck. Caleb tenses, his mouth curves into a small frown.

"I've told you already. Do us both a favor and try not to use that word. It's bad luck."

Caleb continues on down the hall. I shrug it off, go on with my day. The days are usually filled with chores. Upkeep to keep us running. Crane implements a strict schedule to keep our efficiency up. Three different lunch periods a half hour apart. I enter the commissary to see the usual.

Lots of hungry workers and scientists, waiting eagerly for their turn. The job of the cook is cycled around like any other chore. No one here is a chef by any means. The line hugs the wall in an L shape, moving steadily. I wait my turn and grab my usual slop.

Food is something I definitely miss from my time. Luckily my lunch period is with a few of my friends. I find Mordecai, Kup and Kate chatting amongst themselves.

"Isaac." Mordecai nods to me. Kate waves. A unusual smile shines from her face. I sign back.

"You are in a good mood." I walk over and sit down.

"She's getting promoted. Captain of her own squadron. Answering only to Kanoa or Crane...and me."

Mordecai smirks. Kate punches his shoulder and shakes her head. "Congratulations!" I sign to her. Kup looks over to me mid bite.

"How is team training going Isaac?" "Oh you know... getting there. Hey I wanted to ask you guys. I won't say the name but can you guys tell me about them?" I point to my neck. Kate shakes her head. Kup clears his throat, excuses himself from the table.

Mordecai gives me a look like I just kicked a puppy and ushers me to lean in. He whispers.

"Isaac. They are bad people. That's all you need to know. People around here don't like it when they are brought up. Take the hint."

Even more confused, I devour my lunch, growing more curious. As we finish eating, Kanoa approaches.

"Come with me." Kanoa says, motioning for me to get up.

His eyes flare with that intensity I've seen on the battlefield and by my bedside that one time. I feel like I'm being sent to the principal for some reason. His face is calm, but stern. With a slight frown, he stands waiting for me.

I look around to everyone who have now grown much more interested in their lunch glop. "Why?" I ask. Not saying anything else, Kanoa heads out. I scramble out of my seat and race to catch up.

"Is it because I keep bringing up my tattoo?" I walk in tandem with Kanoa. He doesn't reply.

"I'll stop talking about it okay? I didn't mean to stress people out. I just want to know more about it. I was branded against my will, you know. It's not like I am actually one of them."

Kanoa leads me into the T.R.A.C.I. hub. Typically at this hour there'd be teams running training simulations but the room is unnaturally empty. I look over to the tech booth and only see a couple of techs instead of the dozen that usually inhabit there. Kanoa points to an empty booth.

"Log in."

He instructs setting foot into the booth next to mine.

"What are we doing? Where are we going?" As I clamber into the structure.

"You want to know more about that mark? I'll show you."

Kanoa says laying down, turning his head to look at me.

Excited but also a bit anxious, I lay down and allow the machine's IV's to stick into my arms. As I feel the program kick on, I close my eyes.

I find myself on the roof of a church. The slanted kind. In the middle of a bright day. I have to steady myself for a moment before Kanoa grabs my arm.

"Easy." Kanoa helps me find my footing.

He walks with ease on the slanted shingles to the edge and beckons for me to join him. Taking my time not to stumble, I reach the edge and look down to see people entering the church. The bells ring loudly. Being right next to them, I have to cover both of my ears. Kanoa doesn't react to the noise. He backflips onto the ground and looks up at me expectantly.

"Show off." I mumble.

I awkwardly scale the building and climb down. He's out of view, but I can't help grimacing as I hear Kanoa chuckle.

"You really think I'm at the point where I can do backflips?" I growl defensively. I know full well he could've spawned us on the ground.

"Only took me a month to learn how to do them." Kanoa says humbly. I feel exhausted as I reach the ground.

"Okay, why are we here?" Kanoa walks to the door.

"Let's go inside." Kanoa deflects from answering.

We walk in. The church is about halfway filled. Older folk sit sporadically in the pews. The priest at the front is delivering a sermon. There is organ music playing. Everyone seems happy.

"You were raised Christian, yes?" Kanoa asks.

"More or less. We hardly kept to a regular church service schedule. My mother didn't like it. She'd offer to take me to the park or candy store just so we wouldn't go. Made my dad upset. It was one of the things they fought about."

"Everyone in this room are proud Christians. Been that way their entire lives. They are true-believers. They live in a small community where everyone knows one another. They pitch in, help those in need. All-in-all, a decent place to live." Kanoa explains.

All the while we walk through the pews over and through people until arriving up on the podium next to the priest. It occurs to me that based on the simulation detail that this is a real world memory being played.

Suddenly the gigantic stained glass windows shatter as several deranged-looking humans jump inside the church. There are seven people who breached the windows. Every single one of them is dressed in these weird light-blue robes, all of their heads are shaved, and they have what appears to be paint on their face.

They have the symbol on their forehead but it grows and connects to their eyes, stretching all around their head. Creating a variable and intricate mask of paint. All of their eyes are dilated. Pupils the size of saucers. Kanoa freezes the simulation as the crazed people freeze mid-air. Their expressions while frozen still are terrifying to gaze into. Some of them were in the middle of some scream while others were smiling with malicious intent in their stare.

"Want to take a guess who these people are?" Kanoa says rhetorically.

"Techno's." I say. I manage to maneuver myself to look at some of their necks and I see the same symbol as mine. I rub my neck awkwardly.

"These people are about to kill every single person in this room." Kanoa says.

"But why?" I exclaim. "What's the point? For what reason?"

"What better reason do you need then your god made you do it?" Kanoa retorts.

"So they're fanatics. Extremists." I say.

"These people? They were living normal lives before our Neighbors arrived. Normal every-day jobs. They just so happened to be down on their luck and turned to their previous religions for guidance. When the Neighbors flew in on spaceships, the world had a religion shock that was unparalleled. At first, many couldn't cope that we are not alone." Kanoa continues.

"Plenty others rejoiced in it. We had a record-breaking amount of suicides with religion being the underlying factor. People's faiths crumpled in a matter of days. For others though they went in a different direction. After a while, once we discovered verve, people were so desperate to make their religion make sense they started creating their own conclusions. Denial ran rampant."

Kanoa paces around the podium as he talks, points to different religious ideology symbols within the church to further his point.

"Eventually New Churches started popping up. Revised versions of the Bible, the Torah and even the Quran came out with a latest edition to factor in our neighbors. Then one day, somebody had the bright idea to ask our Neighbors if they believed in a higher power. Communication with them wasn't like how it is now." Kanoa explains.

"According to the records, previous generations of neighbors talked about what we understand as a god. But their descriptions and sentences were vague. Hard to interpret. Speculation spread like wildfire. We had people suddenly claiming that the Neighbors were also visited by Jesus Christ.

So he must be real to have appeared on two planets with intelligent life! Others thought it was Allah. Or Yahweh. Or Vishnu. And once again debate turned into fighting which didn't help the war already being fought at the time. Once our ancestors all but excommunicated the Neighbors and hunted them, they clammed up about talking about their gods."

"So how did these guys enter the picture?" I look back at the time-locked crazed people.

"I have a few theories. But how does anyone fall so deep into a cult that they forsake everything and everyone? Control. These people before this felt that they had no authority over their lives. And that was before we discovered alien life. That they were subjects of the chaos of the universe. When presented with this choice, suddenly they felt like they controlled their world. They had a say in things. Suddenly, they were a part of something they believe is bigger then themselves."

"But killing?" I am flustered now; upset.

"To take another life? Why?" None of this makes sense.

"Ever since there have been gods, there have been sacrifices in their name." Kanoa shrugs sadly.

"If you believed whole-heartedly that you followed the correct religion. How would you feel against people who believed differently? To these people, Isaac?"
Kanoa gestures to the Techno's.

"These people believe they are saving them." I shake my head in disbelief.

"If you follow a religion that calls for killing and violence, then you need a different religion."

"I would argue that every religion that has ever existed has called for killing and violence at some point." Kanoa says.

"Texts have been misinterpreted throughout time." I argue defensively. "Religion isn't the issue. Humans are."
Kanoa raises an eyebrow.

"I think they would agree with that." Kanoa points to the Techno's. I grumble in annoyance.

"So do they all believe the same? Do they share a philosophy?" I ask.

"They all believe that because our neighbors exist that the one true god had to take many different names and forms throughout time to sow discontent and confusion so that the one true god may remain hidden."
Kanoa recites while summoning and pointing to paintings and depictions of Jesus, Allah, Hindu gods and goddesses. Greek pantheon gods and goddesses. Norse and Egyptian deities.

"They believe they are all the same god. And the ultimate test was to find the similarities within every known religion to unlock the true face of god. And their final piece to the puzzle lies on their home world."

"Which they have no way of getting to." I bite my lip.

"I wouldn't tell them that."
Kanoa ducks under a man who is frozen mid-brandishing a knife.

"It's kind of ironic really. This is a group of people with such insanely different beliefs. United thanks to our Neighbors. They actually did an amazing job bringing people together in that sense. Just in a way that no one wanted or expected. They idolize them Isaac. They look at Neighbors as demi-gods. Messengers and prophets of the one true god. This guy?" Kanoa approaches one of them.

"He was an accountant. He worked for a bank. No previous religion in his history. This woman?"

"She was a proud Hindu woman. This guy? A Muslim man. And this guy?" Kanoa stalks across the room.

"Let me guess, Jewish?" I ask.

"This guy went to this church." Kanoa says sullenly.
I stare at the guy lost for words. Somehow that hurt more.

"Everyone in here knows who he is. He was a choir boy. Not even a parking ticket on his record." Kanoa continues.
I look into the face of the man Kanoa is describing and I do not see a choir boy. I see a deranged, soulless, rabid animal of a human dressed in blue robes sharing my tattoo. I shake my head in despair.

"These guys aren't even the worst ones. It's the composed intelligent Techno's you need to watch out for. They organize the fanatics and send them off on holy missions like this. Make efforts to hide their mark and blend in with humanity. That's what we thought you were when we met." Kanoa explains.

"Okay. I get it. But again why the name Techno? Where did that come from?" I am dying to know. Kanoa shrugs.

"I honestly don't know. They started calling themselves that at some point. Maybe it has to do with their love for our Neighbors. They love everything about them. Verve. The technology they brought with them. I don't try to understand them any more then I already do Isaac."

"People think we are Techno's, don't they?" I turn back to face Kanoa.

"Well, we are actively against the government in charge. Our ideals are considered radicalized and we're not afraid to kill to keep our movement alive." Kanoa says.

"Okay, but we are not deranged. We're not killing people for no reason!" I argue.

"And I'm sure they think the same way!" Kanoa says, pointing to the Techno's.

"And I'm sure these people." Now pointing to the church members. "Wouldn't see anything different between us and them. It's all perspective Isaac. It's all about your own personal belief. And the problem is The Prexy has gotten a lot of people to think like her in order to keep their addictions supplied."

So we get lumped in with these people and that's why they don't like the word.

"That's why the guys don't like it when I bring it up." I realize.

"You were incredibly lucky to wind up where you are today. We usually don't take too long to engage with anyone with that tattoo. But your claims from being from the past were just, Intriguing to me." Kanoa says.

"I'm glad I trusted my gut." Kanoa finishes.

"Yeah, me too." I say. "Do we have to watch them murder this entire church?"

"No." Kanoa says shaking his head, smiling.

"I still want to figure out how I got this in the first place." I rub my neck again.

"Trust me, I do too." Kanoa initiates the wake-up protocol. The familiar feeling of waking up from a lucid dream hits me as everything dissolves and I feel that tugging on my ears like a vacuum.

CHAPTER 4

DUSTY MEMORIES

The buses in this city are different then I remember. To be fair I never really traveled as a passenger much so I have nothing to compare it to. However, I can tell something that was clearly invented while I was frozen. As it silently roars outside of the city into the outskirts, the towers of buildings give way to what remains of a suburban style.

There are more trees and grassy fields. The outer cities really did not fare well during the takeover. The battle of urban vs rural was waged and urban came out on top. Apparently according to Kanoa, about forty percent of the continent that I know as North America has become uncharted territory... again. I guess we will need trailblazers to return one day. Once we get to the furthest point the buses run, Caleb and I hike until we find an abandoned car. We hotwire it and head further north.

"You realize the odds are not good." Caleb looks out the window at old and rusted signs.

"Like the odds of us surviving The Loft?" I fire back.

"I'm just saying. Think of all the variables. She graduates. She moves on. Arrival Day. Day of Discovery.

World War Three. So much could have happened in those nine years alone. And no matter what she has to be long dead by now." Caleb says.

"Like me?" I repeat with similar attitude.
Caleb sighs, knowing he won't win this battle.

"She must've been really special."

"She was, is." I repeat. The drive lasts a few more hours until we get to a gravel backroad. The both of us tense up, keeping an eye out for anything. A ten minute drive seems to last an hour as we finally get to the end of this road. I park.

"Was this really the best time to leave the base?" I shoot Caleb a concerned expression.

"I needed to get out of there. And so did you I heard." Caleb says.

"Yeah, but it's not helping either of our cases."

"Well we're here now." Caleb stares at the house warily.

My shoulders are tense. They keep locking up. I crack my neck to try and relieve some of the pain. This is truly terrifying. The house is old. It wasn't anything like what I remember. They moved several times since I disappeared. Then again, when the war hit. The amount of searching through old and new countries' census records was intense.

But finally here I am. It's an old colonial house. Not many others around. It's rare to have a home on file in the outskirts of the cities. Usually those are abandoned or housing some form of resistance or outlaws. The structure is made up of gray wooden shingles. Making up not just the roof but all of the walls as well.

It's a kind of material I've seen used for treehouses, except this is a three-story, massive cube-shaped home. Battered and tested by the elements, it shows wear. A window or two seem clouded but not broken. You'd almost assume it's abandoned. There are no lights on.

With a hard gulp I put on the mask. After some chirps and beeps the device completely changes my facial appearance. My hair changes to a bright blond. The unique-ness of my face drops away and with the machine a completely normal-looking person who no longer exists appears before me. I look in the dashboard mirror. With a slight adjustment I decide to put a scar on my nose.

Fuck it, scars are cool. I get out of the car and go around to open the trunk. With a thud the back opens to reveal a long jacket and hat. I put them on and make my way up what remains of the front walk. As I get to the door, I take a big sigh. I knock hard. Every second feels like an hour until finally someone answers. An older woman. Jet black, shoulder length hair. I am rushed with emotion and memory.

"Clara?" I ask almost in a whisper.
Completely mesmerized. She looks just like her.

"I'm sorry?" The girl answers, rubbing her eyes. She seems like she just woke up.

"Um, apologizes ma'am. My name is Mason Ramirez. I am a detective. Is your great-grandmother Clara Hall?"

"What's it to you?" She becomes more alert and agitated.

"Is it true she disappeared August 4th, 2033?" I press.

"Probably." This girl says becoming increasingly uninterested.

"I don't know shit about my family. My good for nothing mother abandoned us when we were kids."

"I'm sorry, us?" I grow more curious.

"Honey, who is that?"

An old woman's voice comes forward. The door opens fully. An old woman in a wheelchair rolls up. She has heavily wrinkled skin with snow-white long hair pulled back in a single ponytail.

A wool cardigan and scarf envelops her snugly as her torso and legs are covered by a blanket made of similar material. Her wheelchair is advanced as she maneuvers with a joystick on one of the arm rests. It looks like she can carry things on the backside of her chair.

"Can I help you?" The old woman asks. Her attitude seems genuine and sweet. The younger girl not so much.

"Nana go back inside. Watch your shows." This woman says turning to her.

"Nana..." I mutter to myself realizing.

"Is your mother Clara Hall?" The woman in the wheelchair grows uneasy.

"Are you another well-wisher?" This old woman asks, worry clear in her voice.

"No-No. I'm a detective. I'm trying to figure out what happened to her." They both look surprised at this.

"That was almost a hundred years ago. Why do you care?" The daughter asks accusingly.

"Let him in Persephone!" The old woman barks. She turns in her chair and rolls to another room.

"We don't get company anymore. It'd be nice to chat to someone, anyone else before I die."

"Persephone..." I repeat, half mumbling. Clara loved Greek names.

"Yeah that's my name. What about it?" Her tune growing more aggressive.

"It's just lovely is all." I say awkwardly, fumbling with my coat as I enter.

The smell of mildew is a tad nostalgic as I look around to see a broken living area. Books and papers scattered every-where. Holes and chips in the wall. The weather outside is cold but inside is like a freezer. How do they survive in here without heat?

I push some stacks of paper out of the way and sit on a hard-cushioned couch. The old lady and Persephone excuse themselves to the kitchen. Eventually the old woman returns without Persephone. She re-enters with some tea and parks herself in front of me.

"My name is Dione." The old woman sweetly offers as she extends her hand. I lightly shake it and open my note pad.

"Dione. Pleasure meeting you." I try not to let my mind blow up at the implications of this.
I'm sitting down with Clara's kid. And she's old...she has grandchildren. Great grandchildren. Who did she end up with?

"So you are interested in what happened to my mother. I'll be honest, I am too." She says wittingly. She doesn't appear to have any negative emotion.

"To be plain hun you probably know more about her than me." Her heavily wrinkled face furrows in deep concentration.

"She disappeared a year after I was born. I was raised in the foster system until I was adopted. When I turned eighteen I inquired the foster home about my birth mother. They told me that she simply vanished. The police report was barely there, if at all. I was told theories left and right. She was a junkie, she was a terrorist. She tried to blow up The Central Zone. The one consistent thing I got from all my search was that she hated Mercia."

"She was raised before Mercia," I retort.

"That she was. It's all pretty hazy now. Please understand I was very young during the war. I've only known the life of Mercia. I don't care much for politics. As long as my family is protected."

The sound of a plate shattering in the other room rings out as Persephone yelps.

"Sorry, Nana!" I turn back towards Dione.

"Her mother. Your daughter. If you don't mind me asking..."

Dione sighs. She looks back towards the kitchen. She gestures to follow. Together we make our way through the house, down a dimly lit hallway to a locked wooden door; beaten and chipped. She shuffles in her wheelchair and takes out an old brass key. She unlocks it and wheels her way in. Inside is a messy office. A small desk covered with papers. Cluttered bookshelves collecting dust and cobwebs.

"Be a dear and grab that lockbox underneath the desk." Dione requests.

I maneuver my way across the room and bend down to retrieve the item, made of solid iron with a four digit turn-lock keeping it closed.

"6-0-2-5." Dione anticipates my need.

I turned the numbers and a satisfying click emanates as the box cranks open. Inside are several newspapers and documents.

"That was all I was able to gather about my mother. It's like she simply didn't exist." Dione says sullenly.
I sift through several newspapers about terrorist attacks and reports from private investigators looking for Clara Hall.

One that makes an impact is on the day Dione was left at the orphanage. Clara's High school Photo. I feel my throat tighten as I gaze at her face.

"That was the hardest thing to find, believe it or not. That photo is the only one I have of her. The only idea I have of what she looks like." Dione sighs.

"She is eighteen in this photo. If she had you a year before she disappeared then she is at least twenty-seven now." I blurt out, gritting my teeth. This is news for me.

"Oh Hun, you must know she is long dead by now."

"Of course." I recover, remember I am pretending to be a private investigator, not Clara's best friend from when we were young. I place the box on the desk. I find the last news article at the bottom. A story about a brutal car crash. The photo shows a flaming car wreck with a body bag being zipped up by an ambulance.

Confused, I hold up the article to Dione.

"Who was this?" I ask while dread fills my lungs.

Dione swallows hard.

"My daughter." Her voice cracks.

The first time I've seen her on the verge of crying. I put the newspaper back in the box. Seeing that paper must've brought a wave of painful memories.

"Do you mind?" She gestures to the door. I walk over and close it. She looks off towards the bookshelf, tears beginning to break away from her face. I put everything back in the box and lock it. I sit down in the office chair to face her.

"It was almost twenty years ago now." She says sniffling.

"Persephone..." I start.

"She doesn't know." Dione says shuffling in her wheelchair, still not meeting my gaze.

"Why not?" I ask. "I don't expect you to understand. It was a terrible time during the early days of Merica. When the vanguard was going town to town. Door to door. We had to hide to avoid being drafted. They were taking any able-bodied human to fight those aliens. It was a bloodbath. My husband died in service and I didn't stick around to hear their boilerplate apology letter.

I knew if they came around again they would take my daughter. So we ran."

I lean forward in the office chair completely enthralled by her story.

"Why didn't they take you?" I ask curiously. A smirk seems to break out from her despair.

"Because I was already in this chair."

She spins around, hits a button on her armrest. A compartment built large enough to fit a suitcase clicks loudly as it flips on the back of the chair. Inside are four delicately placed IV bags. I notice tubes running all throughout the chair in an intricate system that is constantly feeding her the contents. I look closer to see the bags' labels. They read Chemotherapy.

"I always found the irony to be quite a bitch. They didn't take me because of my illness. But my illness has taken more from me then I ever expected. At least this chair has some nice perks."

She spins around, shocking me by revealing a double barrel shotgun that now rests in her lap. It's pointed right at me. I never saw it coming. My entire body tenses.

"I—"

"The last person who asked about my mother threatened my daughter. Two weeks later she died in that crash going to pick up my treatments. Why can't you people leave my family alone! I will not let you take my granddaughter too!"

Dione shouts. I raise my hands.

"I'm not here to hurt you or your family. I just want to find out what happened to your mother."

I try to be careful, but I'm a jerk and my tone is too loud and clumsy to calm her.

"Why! Why is the government so interested in my fucking family? Whatever she did was for a country that no longer exists! We have followed every rule. Voted for the Prexy time and time again. We kept our heads down!"
She is breathing heavily. If she didn't have the chair to rest the gun on I don't think she could've held the gun up. Much less stand. Still, this was a delicate situation.

"And still you people pester us! Still you bother my grand-daughter. Take away every job and opportunity from her. Force us to live in this shithole!"
She trembles. I worry that if she fires that gun it'll kill us both.

"You don't understand..." I begin.

"No, I don't. But I'm not going to make the same mistakes twice." She says as she gathers her strength.

"Wait!" I shout. "I want to show you something."
She doesn't say anything. Her lip quivers from either anger or just the sheer emotions rocking through her fragile body.

"Please." I say softly.

"Move slowly," She keeps her finger on the trigger.
I slowly reach for the release switch on my mask. With a flip the mask deconstructs and I slowly peel off the tech on my face. I wipe my brow, drenched in sweat from the mask and the situation. Dione lets go of the trigger. Her eyes go huge.

"How?" She's seeing a ghost.

"I'm not a detective. I don't work with the government. I just really care for your mother and want to know what happened to her."
My hands resume their position above my head.

"It's you." Her face becomes very pale.
Confusion and wonder consume her facial expressions. She puts the gun into a secret compartment on her chair.

"I'm sorry?" Slowly, I relax and lowering my hands.

"You're the one in the drawing." Dione says, aghast.
She points back to the box. I reopen it. Shuffle around through it a tad less carefully now until I find a sheet of white paper with a pencil sketch of a face on it. It looks very much like me.

"Once I found out what school she attended I decided to pay it a visit," Dione remarks. "They had already changed a lot with the new countries' rules and all. But some teachers stayed who had been instructing there since she was in school."

"Who did you speak with?" My curiosity is exploding.

"A Mr. Lawson I think? He said how she was a brilliant mind and creative personality. And how she was very close to the student who disappeared."
She stares at me, bewildered. I take a big gulp.

"They showed me the portrait of the boy who vanished right before graduation. He looked exactly like you. Lawson then showed me drawings that my mother made. He had been given a few because apparently he was her favorite teacher. He gave me that one. He told me that 'she was the most heartbroken out of all of us when he disappeared. He worried it was going to affect her graduating but she finished with honors. But she was never the same after that. Always promising she would find him."

She pauses and moves over towards the bookshelf. She grabs a loose paper and hands it to me. It shows an obituary for one of my favorite teachers. His proud white beard and mustache sunken in a sad expression.

"He then died a month later from an apparent heart-attack," Dione finishes. My head pounds from all the information.

Learning about the fate of someone I had a conversation with less then a year ago. Well, for me, anyway.

"It's you isn't it?" She asks me in a straightforward, dead-pan voice.

"How would that be possible?" I try to deflect. Not even making eye contact with her.

"I don't know. But what I've come to learn is to expect anything."
She says taking deep breaths. Coming off her own adrenaline rush I imagine. I put everything back in the box.

"I think I should go now." I am eager to leave. I lock the box up and hold it out towards her.

"Take the box with you." Dione says. Her eyes growing watery.

"Are you sure?" I ask surprised.

"I know I don't have much longer." She taps the back of her chair.

"Persephone plans to sell this place as soon as I kick it. I've made my peace with the world. I've lived my life. I only worry what Persephone will do after I'm gone. We always say how we take care of each other." I gather myself and my gear together.

"Thank you." I say softly.

"If it's really you. And somehow a boy who disappeared almost a century ago is standing in front of me then maybe you're the best person to have that after I pass on. Lord knows Persephone won't care for any of this."

"Why won't you tell her the truth?" I ask. "That our family has been hunted by the government our whole lives and she should live her life looking over her shoulder? As far as I'm concerned she's safer not knowing. She's safer thinking her mother was a deadbeat.

Let her live her life away from this. Please."
I nod, not knowing if I fully agree with her or not. I get up and walk to the door of the room. I look back at her.

"You know they cured it right? You can enjoy your remaining time without cancer."

"I don't qualify for it." She doesn't turn to face me.
I awkwardly shuffle into my own bag while holding the box. I grab a metallic cylinder and toss it into her lap.

"I just reviewed your file. You qualify." I say, walking out without even seeing her reaction.
I take the box and reapply my mask. I make my way back to the car outside. I get to the door where Persephone is waiting impatiently for me to leave. She happily opens the door.

"Tell your boss I'm still waiting on my unemployment."
She says, spitting at me. Right before I walk through the door back out into the cold. I turn and gaze at her.

"Be kind to your grandmother. Enjoy your time with her."
She gives me a weird look then slams the door on me. I walk back towards the car and place the box in the trunk. I get back into the drivers' seat and sigh heavily.

"How'd it go?" Caleb asks.

"More questions then answers." I mull over everything.

"Let's go." I start the car up.

"So did you guys really call this body of water Lake Superior?" Caleb asks as we drive down the gravel road.

CHAPTER 5

THE CENTRAL ZONE

"There's more people than I expected," I remark as I pull a pair of sunglasses down onto my face.

The midday sun was shining brightly on an otherwise chilly winter city street filled with people.

"I thought overworld was practically empty?"

"It is." Caleb answers. "But in order for a species to spend all of it's time in a simulation you need some working on the outside to keep everything together."

Caleb explains as we walk down a city sidewalk. We pass by strangers left and right. I've never been to a city before. My Dad promised to take me to New York when I graduated. If only he could see what it's become. As we walk by a store I look at both of our reflections in the window.

"I know why we're wearing them but who are or were these people?" I ask.

"Does it matter?" Caleb dismisses me.

"I'm sure it'd matter to them." I take another, longer inspection of my own face. Before we entered the city, Caleb and I put on MK-Masks, otherwise known as Mankind Masks. The technology Mordecai used in Niagara. Caleb's head is bald and has wrinkles that make him look two decades older.

I have long strawberry blonde hair and my eyes are bright green. The face looking back at me reminds me of a stereotypical surfer dude from way back then. Do people still surf?

"You sure we won't stick out?" I jog to catch up to Caleb.

"Not as long as we have these!" Caleb sticks his arm up to show his barcode tattoo.

I look down at my own. Looking around at people as we pass them, I notice now that everyone does indeed have one.

"When do-?"

"At birth." Caleb says, apparently reading my mind. "It's applied almost instantly after. It has everything. Name, social security, criminal records. Some can even be laced with a trackable GPS. It's illegal to remove it." I study it closely.

"So then how come-?"

"Repent!"

A voice shouts as someone stops me dead in my tracks. I nearly knock into him. As I stagger backward I take in the sight before me; a man with long brown damaged hair dressed in blue robes tied with purple belts and ropes. His arms are visibly slashed and cut all over. He grabs me by my shoulders and shakes me hard.

"We have been given the light! The path to salvation lies before us. Do not deter from the righteous and succumb to the devilish temptations!" He shouts and points at a billboard advertising a T.R.A.C.I system.

"Get off me!" I shout, try to remove his grasp from my shoulders. Caleb hurries back and grabs him from behind.

"Ah, shit!" I hear him shout over this crazy guy's ramblings. Caleb knocks him hard on the back of his neck and he falls instantly. I brush myself off.

"What the hell is that guy's problem?" I gather my things which had toppled to the ground. I look around to see if he had drawn attention.

No one visible has looked over, even once. We are prac-tically invisible despite being on a sidewalk right out in the open.

"Look" Caleb says in a hushed whisper.
He points to the guys neck. My eyes widen as I see the all too familiar pattern of my neck tattoo donned on his body. Right in the same spot.

"He's a-" Caleb slaps his hand over my mouth.

"Quiet! People don't care about crazies but nothing draws I.H.L in quicker then a Techno. We need to move."
He removes his hand and I just stare at this sad, clearly home-less man. Nobody is doing a thing to help him. Once we get about a mile away I finally decide to ask him.

"So you thought I was like that?" Caleb looks at me.

"Yes and no. From the looks of it he was a variant. A wild-card. Probably a wannabe who couldn't get into the group."

"Arguably the only thing Mercia and us have the same. A common enemy. They're fanatics. They believe we are meant to travel to our neighbors home world and there we will meet the one true god." Caleb continues.

"Does this god have a name?" We cross a street. The con-crete jungle grows more massive the deeper we head in. Caleb kicks some litter out of his path.

"Not sure. Haven't spent long enough time with them to ask." Caleb retorts.

"And you thought I was one of them?" Thinking back to that day on The Loft. It makes a bit more sense now why they were so cautious with me.

"The Techno group started a few years after they arrived. We thought you were some agent sent into the future by them." I stuff my hands into my pockets.

"Yeah, I remember that fondly."

I think about life back on The Loft. Has it really only been a few months since we were there?

"What do the neighbors think of them?"

"Not sure, again contact and communication is not exactly standard these days. Not in the overworld. They have their own reasons for being hidden as do we. Look." Caleb points across the street where two individuals who look like police officers interrogate a couple.

"I.H.L" I remark.

They are indeed cops but they have this white pearlescent armor what shines in the sun.

"Disguised as peace-keepers. Truly weapons for destruction. Prexy's mindless drones." Caleb hisses.

"Except they're actually humans." I retort.

"Barely," Caleb snorts.

"You know now that I think about it. It's ironic. Techno's get casted as betrayers of humanity. Crazy? Yes. Terrorists? Depends on your point of view. But they believe they are acting in humanity's best interest."

"So are we. They are too, I guess." I reflect.

"Leave the politics for the politicians, what's left of them anyway. C'mon let's keep moving." Caleb hurries.

"Where are we even going?" I follow as quickly as my legs will take me.

"Giving you the grand tour!" Caleb says exuberantly.

Annoyed, I keep pace as he heads through this gigantic, yet seemingly vacant city. Seeing people every so often but never more than a dozen at a time. It's a weird feeling. It reminds me of stories my dad used to tell me about what the rapture could look like.

"So how many groups or factions or whatever you call them are out there?" I am genuinely curious.

Caleb sticks out his hand and begins counting on his fingers.

"Well, there's us. We work with other smaller groups all residing in the Nether."

"The Nether?" This is new. I am bewildered. How fractured is this place?

"I think in your time you referred to it as the underground? The black market? It's the last line of defense against Mercia's Prexy's oppressively choking rule. Problem is, they're disorganized, fractured. We're probably the best off out of all of them. So there's them, the Techno's, The ali-err... the Neighbors. I heard about one group organizing out on the West Coast. But anyone who travels across the desert has a death wish."

"Why is that?" We head into a street tunnel.

"The desert strip is the most dangerous area in the country. No form of civilization, just savages." Caleb's voice echo's off of the walls.

"You can't just fly over?" I echo back.

"They'd shoot you down. Savages with dangerous weapons, I should've added." Caleb remarks.

"Some rumors say they are holding onto a small supply of nukes."

"I thought they were all used in the last world war." Coming out the other side of the tunnel now. Into a market square.

"They were. Or so we thought. The ones that didn't detonate got dismantled but anyone who claims to have a log on those parts have been long dead. It's been nearly a hundred years now so people just dismiss it as fear tactics....shit." Caleb stops in his tracks. I bump into him and look over his shoulder to see lines of people waiting for turns with an I.H.L soldier in what looks like tollbooths.

"Checkpoint. Intel must've been outdated." Caleb grits his teeth. "Why is it a problem? We don't look like us!"

"Look closer." Caleb points. Everyone who enters passes through an odd-shaped arc. They are enveloped in a bright white light then move through it like nothing ever happened.

"It's a seer. It detects anything from verve to the smallest amount of metal you are carrying."

"So now what?" I growl, feeling the heat of my annoyance flair in my skin. Caleb scans around.

"Head back towards the square." We slowly turn around to walk away from the checkpoint when we hear a "Hey!" We turn back as a giant soldier approaches.

"Fuck. Do we run or not?" I am ready to move, but outwardly I try and maintain a posture of normality.

"We can't. Not here. We're exposed. Stay calm." Caleb hisses as he walks to meet the officer.

I follow. We're met by this six-foot five brick wall of a human. The uniform is a dark midnight blue with streaks of white. Standing out from the other armor I've seen. The Prexy's national symbol crested right above his heart. His utility belt is stocked to the brim with tools and a face mask. It makes me think he handles riots. He clearly is a superior of some kind.

"Can I help you both?" The officer asks.

"Help? Nope, no help. We just left something back at our place." Caleb speaks up. The guy stares at both of us.

"Don't you know what today is?" He asks expectantly. We both stay silent. My heart pounds in my chest.

"It's the Prexy's birthday! Per her gracious tradition she is offering free trials of the brand new T.R.A.C.I booths. Now with automatic waste disposal systems and a new cranial interface that is less invasive."

"That sounds great but I think we will have to pass today."
Caleb says. The officer looks bummed, then turns to me.

"You sure?"

"Absolutely. Thank you for the offer but we were in a hurry before we forgot something."

We turn around and start to walk away when he shouts

"Stop!" Caleb and I both flinch.

"Stay still." The officer orders.

Out of my peripherals I notice Caleb slowly reach for his waist. I lock in place as I feel the officer's hand on my shoulder. He moves my head down and brushes my hair away to expose my neck.

"Oh, um sorry." The soldier mumbles stepping back.

"Thought I saw something."

"You thought wrong." I say harshly trying hard to steady my breath.

"Sorry. Go about your day now."

The guy heads back to his post at the checkpoint. After a bit Caleb checks in on me.

"You okay?" I nod. "Yeah. Close one. Is the cloak fading?"

"Who knows. Let's just go." Caleb tugs at my sleeve.

"Well, now where are we gonna go?" Feeling more and more lost in this maze of buildings.

"I don't know about you but I need a drink after that."
Caleb sighs. "It's one in the afternoon." My tone is a little harsher than I meant it to be. Judgmental. Caleb smirks.

"Not that kind of drink," as he points to a small coffee shop. I raise an eyebrow.

"Really?" He laughs. "What, you never had coffee before?"

CHAPTER 6

JUST COFFEE

———

"Crane's probably wondering where we are." I agitate my coffee with a stir stick.

The familiar smell of espresso fills the air around us. The quiet murmur and chatter of about half a dozen patrons fill the shop in a calm manner. A few even are typing away on laptops. Caleb said that we are going to meet someone here. Someone who he thinks could provide some useful information about the current state of the city. For all the advancements I've seen since waking up. This little coffee shop reminds me of my time just a little bit. I guess some ways of life never change.

"Probably." Caleb says dismissively as he takes a big sip.

"Well I know why she hates me. Why does she hate you?" I lean back in my chair. He sits for a minute.

"It's complicated," he responds. His focus locked on his drink.

"That's an escape, not an answer." I retort. "If you don't want to tell me you don't have to." I'm not trying to pry anything here.

"Crane and I...we've been through a lot. I've known her longer then anyone else. And she doesn't hate you Isaac. She's just careful." I hum in agreement

"Were you two a thing?" I ask. He laughs.

"God, you really are senile. You really can't read the room can you?" He practically falls out of his chair. My eyes widen.

"Sibling?"

"You can call it that. We grew up together." He takes another huge sip. Almost finishing his coffee in two gulps.

"Is it really that bad?" Genuinely asking as an only child.

"You wouldn't know would you?" Caleb says in a self-realizing tone.

"I was supposed to. But according to my parents they lost her before she was born. My mother took it kind of hard." I remember that too. I was seven. My parents kept talking about how I was going to be a big brother. Got my old nursey all set up again. Dug out boxes of my old baby clothing. Then when it happened my mother just stopped talking and whenever I saw her she was red-eyed. She never was quite the same after that now that I think about it.

"Your mother is a piece of work," Caleb scoffs.

"At least she doesn't have telekinesis," I jab back. Caleb nods in agreement.

"To fucked up family." Caleb raises his cup to mine.

"To fucked up family." I clink his coffee mug with mine.

"So when is this person supposed to get here-" Suddenly I feel a bump on my chair. I look over my shoulder to see a little girl, no older then eight on the ground rubbing her head.

"Ow," she squeaks.

"Are you okay?" I turn to get out of my seat. Her mother, who is in the line for coffee, notices and comes over.

"Elizabeth I told you! Stay where I can see you!" She turns to me after scolding the girl. "I'm so sorry."

"It's okay. I just wanted to make sure she was okay." The mother kneels down to her level.

"Are you okay sweetie?"

The little girl rubs her head and nods. I thought she might cry but she toughs it out. It felt like a hard thump. As they return to the line I notice they are both wearing the same odd-looking necklace. A few others in the shop, even the barista, also wears one. It looks like some kind of choker or collar. It's silver with a dot of red in the center.

"They should be here soon." Caleb looks at his watch growing a little curious himself.

After a few more minutes Caleb's face brightens and waves over someone who has just walked into the shop. An African American woman with braided, seafoam green hair. No older then Caleb or I walks over. She is wearing a black leather jacket and I notice one of her hands is missing. Replaced by an advanced robotic hand. She walks over and Caleb stands to greet her.

"Cogs, you look better then ever." Caleb beams.

"And you look the exact same." She responds.

They both laugh and I join in just so I don't feel awkward. Caleb pulls up a chair for her and she sits down, removing her jacket. It's then I realize that it's not just a fake hand. But her entire left arm all the way to her torso is replaced by a pristine, regal almost looking bionic arm.

"Cogs this is Isaac, the guy I was telling you about." Caleb sits back down himself.

She looks at me and extends her still attached arm.

"The oldest man alive, it's an honor, Caleb's told me a lot about you." She has a warm yet confident smile that reassures me.

"Wish I could say the same. About knowing you that is." I blush a little.

"Well that comes to no surprise. Can't think of a reason why ol' dramatic would talk about your prior place of work." Cogs grabs Caleb's coffee and finishes what's left of it.

"C'mon Cogs you know Crane comes before those assholes." Caleb looks at his now empty coffee cup dejected.

"Which assholes are we talking about?" I chime in.

"My bosses. Your pal's old bosses. And we actually really should get going. I wanted to tell you but over the air is a little too risky right now. Pressure's building."
Cogs demeanor changes and her voice becomes a hushed tone.

"Reports of fanatic attacks are increasing." Cogs explains.

"We saw one on the way in. Are they a credible threat?" Caleb hunches over.

"Depends on your definition of credible and threat." Cogs leans back and looks around the store to the customers.

"I've been hearing chatter that they are getting their hands on more serious cargo. More then the sticks and stones were used too." Cogs begins to look a little worried as she is saying this.

"More and more eyes are watching, hell it was even hard to get here today."

Suddenly there is a loud crash. The sound of glass shatters as a football-sized metallic device is thrown into the center of the store. It beeps for a second then a blue gas sprays out of the strange object. Several folks shriek.

"Verve Bomb!" a patron yells.

All hell breaks loose. The Barista reaches under the counter, then a loud siren blares and a red light shines. People leap from their tables and rush the exit, trampling others in the process. Caleb, Cogs and I stand. "You got to be fucking kidding me!" Caleb groans.

"We're fine right?" I say as quietly as I can while trying to beat the yelling in the establishment. I pull my shirt over my nose to try and look believable.

"We won't be when the I.H.L swarm this place in a few seconds. Let's go!"

Cogs hurriedly grabs her jacket. Caleb reaches for his bag. I grab for my own when suddenly several peculiar whooshing sounds occur in the mist around the café. Doing my best to look through the blue fog, it is apparent that several people now have a bubble-shaped object around their heads.

When someone runs by I get a better look. It's a large glass-like dome. It looks like it grew out of those necklaces. Then I hear an ear-shattering scream. That little girl sits beside her mother, who lies on the ground, still. Did she get hit by the bomb?

"Isaac! Let's go!" Caleb screams.

The girl was now shaking her mom. Neither she nor her mother have glass domes and their necklace-collars lie on the ground a few feet from them. They must've fallen off. She is breathing in verve! I rush over and grab the necklaces. The girl's face is a mess of tears and snot.

"Mommy! Mommy, wake up!" She pleads.

I quickly try to put the necklaces back on them. I manage to get the mother's on and brief chirp and the glass dome safely protects her head. I manage to get the one on the little girl. Her screams become slightly muffled as she goes to hold her mother who is still not moving.

A loud crash forces my attention as the door is kicked open. Several I.H.L soldiers, weapons drawn, rush in. I recognize the one who we spoke to, not even a half-hour ago.

"Freeze!" They shout.

Before I can even react I feel my whole body grabbed and forced out of the store through one of the windows that hadn't shattered. I fly and tumble out, landing a hundred feet away. Groaning in pain, I roll over. Caleb and Cogs are a few feet from me. His shoes have smoke emanating from them. He painfully kicks them off, scrambles to his feet.

"Run!" He shouts, as he helps me up.

The guards chase us. I feel my heartbeat in my throat as we race down city streets trying to lose them. Bursts of blue energy fly by us. Stun rounds. We turn one corner, then another. Finally, we reach a back alley where we have a moment to catch our breath.

"Fuck. Our ride is on the other side of town, past that seer. I can't portal out right now." Caleb is visibly out of breath. As I also suck in air we hear the stomping of feet and the sound of a helicopter's propellers grow close.

"Don't you have some back-up emergency exit?" I ask, panting. Caleb flips me off and points to his now dirty and cut bare feet.

"That was it!" He exclaims. The sound of defeat is clear in his voice.

"I've got a way out of here. Follow me!" Cogs begins running.

Caleb nods and follows right behind. Right on their heels, Cogs leads us to a trash-littered alley. Boarded up doors and windows. Several rats scurrying across the pavement. An abandoned part of the city, truly.

"Right here. Be quiet!" Cogs orders.

She disappears into an abandoned storefront window and moments later, swings open the heavily barricaded door and hisses at us. We both dash into the building. It appears to have once been a food store.

Filled with empty glass displays, vacant shelves. I dive behind the counter. Caleb and Cogs do the same. Silence. All I can hear is my pounding heart. The seconds pass slowly. After a minute I hear the shuffling of feet and shouting. They continue on past the store. Silence again. She rises.

"Close one," she remarks. I spring up from behind the counter.

"Guess that makes us even now doesn't it?" Caleb perks up, smiling.

"Oh not even by a long shot" she replies, shoving him back with her robotic arm.
Caleb is clearly caught off guard by her unexpected physical prowess.

"Damn, what, did you upgrade that too now?" Caleb massages his sore shoulder.

"If I told you. You might try and steal it," she banters back.

"So Cogs. Where does a name like that come from?" I brush off dust and debris from my coat.

"Stick around long enough and you might find out." she winks.

"Cogs something is different about you. What is it?" Caleb says.

"Could be the arm tech. Or it could be..." Her eyes flash the all too familiar verve blue I've come to learn.

"You had a successful integration!" Caleb finishes. "That's fantastic, so what can you do?"

"I can see verve or anyone using or anything that has integrated with verve up to about a mile. Pretty neat, huh? Makes me pretty good at recon. Except for today." She looks down.

"City is getting more intense. The elections and these fanatics aren't helping." Caleb says.

"I think I owe you both an apology for that one. I noticed the group of fanatics near the shop."

"And you didn't see a large amount of verve being carried with that ability?" I say accusingly.

"No I didn't. I told you Caleb they are getting smarter. Someone is organizing them. They are becoming a serious threat. The shouters don't have the intellect or skill to create a device like that! Someone is funding them, leading them!" Cogs says to Caleb. He shakes his head.

"Add them to the list of shit to figure out. Your all good Cogs. Isaac didn't mean anything by that." He looks at me annoyed.

"They probably caught sight of me as I came in. They know I'm in the resistance so that's probably why they hit the store." There is a catch in her voice. "All those innocent people."

"You didn't know, so you couldn't act. It's not on you, I'm sorry." I say.

She nods, accepting my apology. These people are willing to bomb an entire store just to convert a few people? None of this makes sense. From my understanding those bombs are just meant to dispel concentrated verve into a vapor into the air. People who breathe it in either gain an ability, or a disability. Or nothing at all. What's the purpose of that?

"So anyway, what's your groups current status?" Cogs changes the subject and begins to walk around the store looking for something.

"We're mobile right now. Soldiers popped our three biggest hideouts." Caleb says.
He clearly trusts this woman to be blatant enough to talk about our movements with her.

"You could always come back into the fold. With Crane's numbers and tech we could be big enough again." Cogs offers.

"Big enough to fail miserably and almost lose the movement? Thanks, but no thanks. Crane still wants us as consultants not unified."

"Hey man, me personally I get it. But the council...they're a little tense right now. After all it's another election cycle and nothing major has really happened. Now I got to report Verve Bombs are back. The chatter was true." Cogs looks worried.

"Council?" I chime in. Cogs is moving around the place searching for something.

"The council can do what they always do and deliberate on the next appropriate step to dismantling a tyrannical dystopian empire. For now," Caleb reaches into his bag,

"Isaac and I need to get back to Crane. We have no clear path to our ride. I'm setting it to cloak and auto-pilot. It'll find it's way home. It'll be a few hours before I have enough energy to open a portal. We barely have enough verve to make up for what I'll need."

"Why don't you come down, then?" Cog says.

"Come down?" I ask. "Come down to where?" Caleb has a look of hesitancy.

"To the Nether." Cogs says. "It's better then this crap hole." Caleb reluctantly resigns.

"Okay, then!"

Cogs finally finding what she was looking for. A covered up hole, revealing a staircase leading straight down into the sewers.

"They'll probably want to talk to you though. Fair warning."

"Yeah, I know. I'll deal with them. Let's just get out of here." Caleb heads for the hole.

Cogs grabs a few things she had stored in here. She grabs a weapon, a crossbow designed in an X shape with the material being glassy and green.

"Pretty nice, right? Made it myself." Cogs gloats.

I am impressed at the unique design of this crossbow.

"Made it to match your hair?" Caleb scoffs.

"So what if I did?" She gets a little defensive about that.

"Follow me. We've got a long ways to go down."

She leads us down the staircase As we begin to head down, I nudge Caleb.

"Another part of the grand tour?" Caleb sighs.

"Unfortunately. I was hoping to spare you from this place."

As we descend into darkness.

CHAPTER 7

POLITICS & PERSONAL

———

The lab is dark. Only lit by some scattered fluorescent lights and computer screens. The air is clean. Much like setting foot into a doctor's office, the scent of sanitizer and sterilized tools fills the area. Abigail's work station is cluttered with papers and folders. Her hair is different now. A much shorter style. Her glasses, dirty and grimy. She has dark rings around her eyes. She closes her laptop and rubs her eyes, causing the glasses to fall to the table. Suddenly the PA system in the room blares.

"Madam Secretary. You have an incoming call."

"Tell them I'm busy." She groans. "I think you'll want to take this call, Madam Secretary."

The voice insists. She sighs in grief and grabs a remote. She hits a button and the entire side wall shifts in sections until a holographic panel appears. A female robotic voice calls out.

"Holo-panel connected. Network activated. Connecting." Suddenly, a woman materializes in front of Abigail. She has midnight dark hair tied up in Greek braids. A gray power suit adorns her body. Conservative but still shows off her figure. The display is so advanced Abigail can count the wrinkles on this woman's face, despite her attempt to hide them with makeup.

She stands with her arms behind her in an expectant stance. Her expression is neutral until giving a smile.

"Hello Abby." says the woman.

She walks around the room as if she is actually there. Only something passing right through her would destroy the illusion.

"Prexy." Abagail says.

"Oh please, Abby. It's just us. Call me Freida." Abigail tries her best to put on a friendly face.

"What do you want?" Abigail does not care for this conversation.

"I'm sorry. Am I interrupting something important?" The Prexy matches her attitude.

"I wouldn't want to disturb someone incredibly important unless it was a serious matter." Her tone grows cold, expressing a stern annoyance.

"I made this call, believe it or not, because I wanted to congratulate my colleague. It's not every day you cure a major sickness. One of the oldest ones as well. You must be very proud of yourself."

"Thank you." Abigail's throat tightens. "You know, under normal circumstances. You'd be praised, celebrated, possibly worshiped for finally curing cancer once and for all. You'd probably get the Nobel Peace Prize if that was still a thing." Freida stalks around Abigail's office like a predator taking in their surroundings. She's unable to pick up items as she walks through the desk to get from one side to another. Abigail stays silent and grows even more tense.

"Too bad the prize and that country no longer exists...probably." Freida says flatly, approaching Abigail.

The hologram gives off a slight heat signature, warming Abigail's face.

"I admit I am a tad curious." Freida says softer but in a more serious tone.

"You want to tell me why you were wasting both of our time and resources curing a disease that was actually helping us?" Abigail bites her lip.

"I thought The Grand Prexy was all about uniting her nation under peace, health and prosperity." She states this in a way as if she was reciting familiar commercials.

"The Grand Prexy can be about whatever she wishes when her nation is dependent on our technology. But when they hear about something good happening in the real world we begin to lose control. Have you seen the numbers for the last few months?"

"No." She's been too busy with other matters. She thinks to herself.

"Almost ten percent of all T.R.A.C.I users online times are down sixty-five percent!" The Prexy Shouts.

"Thanks to your little scientific miracle people are wanting to spend more time in this world!" "You mean your miracle? That was a pretty convincing broadcast you gave." Abigail counters.

"You forced my hand. If it got out I was withholding the cure to cancer we would've had another uprising. I'm getting sick and tired of those."
Abigail brings up footage onto the room's monitors.

"It's the resistances. They are the ones trying to take down what you've built." Freida looks at them them back to her.

"I thought it was what we built. You say that like the last decade working together was nothing." Abigail looks at her holographic colleague.

"The last decade for us was the last century for everyone else." She reminds her.

"All because of you." The Prexy smiles. Her presence completely dominating the room despite not actually being there.

"Look. I'm not one to hold grudges. You worked behind my back for something counter-productive to what we are trying to achieve here. I'm sure you had your own reasons. I don't care. What matters is crushing any possibility of an uprising. It's time we close ranks." Abigail's eyes furrow. She doesn't know what Freida means by that.

"I'd like you to meet Dr. Edward Kim." The Prexy gestures as the holo-panel connects another user into the call.

At a miraculous speed an adult male is pieced together until an entire body forms. He is slightly shorter then Abigail, Asian descent, late-twenties, dressed in a lab coat similar to hers. Thick round glasses rest on the bridge of his nose.

"Doctor." Kim extends his hand to shake. Abigail looks confused.

"You know I can't actually shake your hand right?" Dr. Kim retracts his hand. His face turns pink. "You will soon enough. Dr. Kim here will be joining at your facility for the time being." The Prexy announces.

"We don't need any more help here. We're doing fine." Abigail defends.

"Fine?" The Prexy points to the security footage.

"Those treasonous pests have gone from a nuisance to a considerable threat. Five facilities in the last three months? You assured me that you had it under control!"

"There were...extenuating circumstances behind those attacks. We were caught off-guard." Abigail says bitterly.

"Which is why I can't think of a better time to introduce my two top scientists to each other. I think you'll find Dr. Kim here has achieved a fair amount in his own field. I am excited to see what the two of you can create together."

The Prexy beams.

"And what would that field be?" Abigail's curiosity grows.

"It's an honor to meet you, doctor!" Dr. Kim says enthusiastically.

"I was raised idolizing and respecting your work. You've been able to preserve the smartest of minds for the future of technology. Now that it is here, we made great use of it!"

"How old are you?" Abigail asks.

This guy couldn't have been in his thirties. Dr. Kim laughs for a brief second.

"Like you, Dr. Ashter, I am also very well accomplished for my age." Dr. Kim says, bragging.

"Time is a precious commodity after all and I am trying to make great use of mine." Freida introduces him further.

"Dr. Kim is our leading neurosurgeon. Number one in the country! He has dedicated the last decade to studying human and alien brains."

"Your work with Virtual Reality and Cryogenics is un-paralleled!" He continues to praise her.

"Thanks to you, I had the perfect simulation rooms to conduct my experiments." Curious, Abigail engages more.

"What kind of experiments?" Abigail is genuinely intrigued.

"Dr. Kim has also made a recent breakthrough that rivals yours." The Prexy boasts. She and Dr. Kim look at each other knowingly.

"Which would be?" Abigail says expectantly.

"I'm sure you two will discuss in good time. I'm giving you both a deadline. We all know what's coming in the next month."

"Elections." Dr. Kim happily finishes her thought.

"Your breakthrough with cancer helped boost the Prexy's poll numbers. But we can't have these uprisings anymore. Every time we burn a nest we find a bigger one. If they keep recruiting they will eventually have an army and we will have another year like 2098." Abigail frustratingly agrees as she recalls the events of that year. Visible stress covers her face.

"That was the closest we've ever come to being overthrown. I will not have that again," Freida deadpan to Kim and Abigail.

"What is our assignment?" Abigail asks.

"Burn the entire tree instead of multiple nests." The Prexy says as Abigail's monitor boots up. On screen shows a female silhouette form.

"The Crane?" Kim is surprised. "I have a gift for the both of you. Consider it inspiration." The Prexy waves her hand and the silhouette shape fades to a crisp clear mugshot of a younger Crane.

"How did you-" Abigail starts.

"A discovery from a deep dive into some ancient terabyte hard drive records. We are the only three people alive with this photo." The Prexy says.

The younger Crane in the photo has a bruised eye and her hair is much longer and brown.

"So eliminate the leader, is the plan?" Kim asks. His brow furrows.

"Capture," The Prexy corrects him.

"This woman has been the mastermind behind every single attack we've seen for the last two years. Her connections to the black market rivals our own. She has invaluable information that could provide useful." The Prexy stares intently at the photo.

"Your assignment is to apprehend and extract. Dr. Kim will be joining you, Dr. Ashter, at your site in a few days to compile and share resources and knowledge. I want this done before elections. After they are over and my position is safe for another fifteen years then I will allow you to go back to sleep." Abigail's eyes widen.

"What would be my awake date?" Abigail asks.

"2257," The Prexy Says nonchalantly. "We need to end any possibility of uprising once and for all. Once we do and peace is secured. You can rest and Dr. Kim can continue your work. How close are we?"

"Weeks, Prexy. Once I'm situated it will only take a few more weeks." Dr. Kim responds.

"Good. So you have your tasks. Detain Crane. And help Dr. Kim reach his goal, Dr. Ashter. I expect to hear results." Suddenly a device on Abigail's desk starts beeping. She picks it up.

"Anything else?" Abigail asks. "That is all." The Prexy dismisses Abigail.

Not bothering to end the call, Abigail quickly leaves. The Prexy and Dr. Kim remain in the call.

"You fully understand the assignment, yes?" Prexy looks intently at Dr. Kim.

"I do." He nods. "And all of it's conditions and expectations?" The Prexy continues.

"Yes, Madam Prexy." Dr. Kim says seriously.

"Good. You know when they told me that a black market scientist turned agent had achieved what you did. I thought I misheard them." He blushes.

"I appreciate the flattery, Madam Prexy. You know it truly is a shame. That part about me being inspired by her work was real."

CHAPTER 8

SCARS DON'T HEAL

The air is stale and ripe of old mildew and discarded take-out food containers. As a man kicks open his crappy apartment door after several failed attacks. The door creaks open, crying out for oil. He closes it behind him and double locks it. Once at the door then slides the chain across. He flicks a switch and after a few struggling flickers the loud fluorescent tube light hums to life illuminating the limited space. A post it note falls from the nearby wall.

"Call landlord about shitty door."

The man grumbles and takes off his coat, hanging it up next to his other attire. A security uniform that looks untouched for months. Lines of dust beginning to gather around the shoulders. Along with a couple other coats and jackets. He walks over to his refrigerator and opens it. Only to slam it shut seconds later at the sight of it. Bare empty.

Next he moves to a sectioned off portion of his apartment which he has dedicated to as an office of sorts. A plastic desk with a massive cork billboard hanging on the wall. On it are dozens of pieces of paper, photos and receipts. String of red yarn connect paper to paper via thumbtack, to facilitate some vain attempt to make sense of the chaos on this wall.

Photos of Oakwood, Isaac, security footage of Crane's groups movements but no actual photos of Crane. Even various documents about Neighbors. He stares at the board intently, silently humming to himself. He grabs a warm, unfinished beer on the table and takes a sip. The phone in the corner rings. He sets the cup down and walks over to answer it.

"Hello, this is an automated voice response. Arthur Johnson. You applied for the security guard position at the Fantasia Supercenter." A small smile breaks through.

"We are sorry to let you know that we've decided to not move forward with your application. Thank you very much for your time. Have a nice day!" Click.

The dial tone rings out. The smile goes away. Arthur slams the receiver down and crumbles up a piece of paper lying next to it. Throwing it into an overflowing waste bin. He grabs his beer and collapses on the couch. His coffee table is buried in envelopes. Some stating past due.

Others being letters of termination. One specific one with the company header I.H.L peaks through on the top. He shoves all the paper off the table so he has room to put his feet up. His TV displays an ad.

"Don't forget to pre-vote for your favorite Madam Prexy and receive not one, not two. But three whole months of free, premium T.R.A.C.I service! Subject to credit approval." Arthur squeezes the remote and throws it at the screen, missing only by a few inches. The remote knocks off a photograph displayed next to the Television. The sound of glass shattering as the frame drops to the ground.

"Fuck."

Arthur sits up immediately and goes over to pick up the picture. It's a photo of him and a younger man, early twenties. Their shaking hands at some sort of ceremony.

He shakes out the broken glass and thumbs the image.

"I'm sorry." He says with a morose tone.

Suddenly the sound of bottles clattering and teenager laughter and hushes come from Arthurs window. He looks out his window over a graveyard surrounded by apartment buildings from three sides.

A group of three people snickering and hunched over. The sound of aerosol spray paint seeps through the air. Arthur's eyes go huge as he races out of his apartment.

The cold winter air cuts through his ragged jacket. As he clumsily tries to bundle up, he races out into the night. The south-west section of The Central Zone is very much a red-light district.

The homeless are in their highest concentration here and with that - crime, prostitution and all the amenities to follow. He takes a hard turn into a rundown, graffitied cemetery. No bigger then a basketball court. Several stones are cracked or have moss and nature overgrowing it. As though it hasn't been touched in years.

One stone, however, stands out from the rest. A recent addition that is clean and in perfect shape. Ripe for vandalism. As Arthur approaches his son's grave he sees three hooded figures spray painting the tombstone.

"Stop!" Arthur screams.

The hooded figures look up. One of them pulls out a pistol and fires. It is not an energy blaster; but an old fashion gun-powder-combustion model. Johnson ducks behind an already chipped tombstone. He fumbles with his energy blaster until getting a solid grip on it. He blindly sticks his hand out and fires a few shots.

"Oh fuck!" One of the young punks cries.

"He's packing energy. Let's get out of here!"

One of them attempts to run by him. With an easy shot, Johnson nails the kid in the back with a blue round and watches him fall face-first into the snow, completely stunned.

"Oh shit," one of his buddies yells in a panic.

Hearing bricks shuffle, Arthur peeks left. One of the young fools tries to climb the building's vines to get over the cemetery's back wall. With another bullseye, his stun round blasts the back of the poor teen as he tenses up and falls a few feet onto the hard snowy ground.

"Alright. Truce!" The final kid shouts.

"Throw your gun!" Arthur barks.

With a clatter, Arthur sees the old pistol slide a few feet in front of him. He stands up as the punk comes out of hiding holding his arms up.

"I'm sorr-" Before the kid can finish Arthur shoots him with a blue round right in the chest.

Like a domino, the kid falls on his back with a resounding wheeze from his mouth. Arthur approaches and kneels down beside him. He picks up the can of spray paint.

"Do you know who's tombstone you were spray painting?" Arthur asks. Unable to reply, the wannabe gangster looks scared.

"That's my son's." Arthur slams the paint can into the kid's temple.

"He was my pride and joy that boy. He was all I had. And he was murdered. By someone around your age." Arthur throws another punch with the metal can.

The kid's face bleeds as cuts and bruises form.

"Now if Ramirez was here, he'd be pulling me off of you by now. But he's also dead. Everyone I know is gone." Arthur upholsters the energy blaster and holds it above his victim's face.

"And do you know what my place of employment did when they learned about my son's untimely demise? They fired me. Said that I failed to act under pressure."

"This morning I thought about switching this lever here." And he does so. The cold blue energy switches to a fast-paced red fluid.

"And sticking it in my mouth to pull the trigger." Tears form in Arthur's wild eyes. The kid tries to shift and shuffle, but the stun gun did it's work well.

"But you've made me realize something. The fact that I dove out of the way of your bullet makes me sure that I'm not ready to die. I have wrongs to right. Business to take care of. People that need to pay. Starting with you." Johnson sticks the gun in the boy's mouth. Tears stream from both of their eyes.

"Thank you." Johnson says with a soulless gaze as he pulls the trigger.

Gunshots are common around this area. Johnson's shots blend into the ambient nature of the red-light district. Another night in The Central Zone. After two more muffled shots he drags the three bodies over to the far corner of the graveyard. Away from any streetlight or sight for anyone to see. He then walks back to his sons gravestone. He takes off his jacket, completely ignoring the piercing cold and begins cleaning the tombstone.

"I'll make them pay. I'll make them all pay." After about an hour, having to run back to the apartment for stronger cleaning supplies the tombstone is the nicest looking one in the whole area. It reads

"R.I.P Damien Johnson. 2095-2119. Beloved Son. Died in the line of duty. Died a hero."

CHAPTER 9

THE NETHER

——

Underground worlds. Don't lie and tell me you don't think about them. What do they look like, how do they operate? Is it as hard and rough as stories make them out to be? Well, yeah. People get inspired from somewhere. Not everything is made up on the spot. What I was not expecting, however, was the means of travel to arrive to said destination. After about two miles of walking through sewers, Cogs brings us to this abandoned underground bar. Old bottles and glasses still on shelves. TV hinges bare, hung from every free spot on the walls. There was a lingering smell of liquid courage in the air. Cogs jumps over the booth and heads towards the kitchen.

"C'mon, we're almost there!" Cogs waves us over encouragingly to the far back of the cookhouse.

Dinnerware littered the rusted and dusty counters. A once white-and-black checkered floor, now mostly grime, dirt and broken bits of tile. Cogs moves to a cleared area, then removes a giant piece of the floor to reveal a ladder going straight down into emptiness.

"Ladies, first" Caleb gestures.

Cogs smirks as she gives Caleb a mirthful look. Oh, I see. These two have a history. She slings her crossbow onto her back then slides down the ladder like a fireman. Caleb goes next. He pops his head up to look at me.

"Make sure to slide that back on after you enter." Caleb reminds me as he continues his descent.

More cautiously then Cogs, I grab the floor tile and position it above me. Once the tile is seated back in its spot, it is pitch dark. Some dirt falls past my nose and I feel a twitch.

"Careful," Cogs says. I feel the sneeze coming.

"Achoo!" It rings out and echoes down for what seems like a mile.

After about fifteen minutes of straight climbing, my body has grown quite sore. I can feel the muscles in my legs and arms burning. We finally reach the ground into a small circular room that contains...well, it looks like a submarine door because of the giant wheel in its center. Cogs slaps the door once and a slot appears at eye level. A pair of bright green eyes greets us.

"A perfect death?" The man behind the door asks us. It's some sort of code.

"One, that's my choice." Cogs replies.

"Color of the day?" The voice asks next.

"Indigo. Open the door, Markus." Cogs is clearly annoyed.

The slot slides shut and a loud click emits as it slowly opens. A huge man, six-foot-five with short black hair and over two hundred pounds of solid muscle. His tanned skin strikes me as unusual if they've been underground all this time. He has a massive weapon that looks like a cannon slung around his back. His getup consists of similar clothing to those from our group except a bit more rough.

A sleeveless, armored vest that looks to be made of mostly metal. A claw scar runs down his right shoulder. Cogs gives him a high-five then some sort of secret handshake.

"How's topside?" Markus asks.

"Techno's have gotten their hands on serious hardware." Cogs replies.

"I wanted to go after them but-" She stops mid-sentence and moves out of the way to show us. Markus eyes us up and down.

"Allies?" Markus asks.

"Constituents. Consultants from Crane." Cogs says.

"Crane? Council will be thrilled. Good news?" Markus asks looking at the two of us.

He seems familiar with Caleb but is eyeing me up and down.

"Depends on what mood the council is in today. Hey, Markus." Caleb high fives him.

"Caleb. Good too see you. Who are you?" Markus turns to me.

"Isaac." I hold my hand out to shake.

He does so. The guy could crush a marble with his grip.

"Integrated?" He asks me. I smirk.

"Is that your power too?" He smirks back.

"Nah, I'm just good at reading people. Mi mamá, she says it's a gift. C'mon."

We enter into a massive stadium-sized dome. It's miles wide and must reach several stories high. Several buildings and roads all interconnect. Giant oval-shaped doors equally separated run alongside the walls of this underground city. Beautiful, intricate mosaic tiles align the walls in patterns. Giant LED lights create some sort of fake daytime in here. The walls are covered with beautiful graffiti.

The city and streets are lit with these gorgeous lights. Glass balls in fishnets with some sort of warm energy radiate out of them.

"This is charming. How far underground are we?" I ask as we traverse the streets.

"Ah, maybe miles. Don't have an exact number for ya." Cogs replies.

"They stopped using a ton of the subway systems. The ones they left alone hardly get patrolled. However we have ways to hide if any ship comes through."
We pass by a rusted sign that reads "City Hall Subway Station."

All sorts of interesting businesses exist here. Bars and weapon smiths. There are training fields. People work with mind-blowing contraptions. A man with long, bright, ruby red hair, tied up in a ponytail, is wielding a spray nozzle like device. It's shooting what looks like paint. His clothes have various colored paint splatters staining his pants and shirt. The material he is firing is going up into the air then freezing.

He's creating unique 3-D shapes with different colors. He waves his hand and it all turns to liquid and pools together. Swirling together into this massive orb. It flows seamlessly through the air into a bracelet on his wrist.

"Generation before us dug out a lot of this town on their own." Cogs brags.

"I remember the stories," Caleb remarks.

"Some of the council members were there for it." Cogs says.

Passing a bar, I see a curious assortment of folk with mechanical enchantments. I can't tell if it's replacing their limbs or if it's attached on top of their arms and legs but there is a lot of metal covering their appendages, and even some devices on their faces.

Many of them glow verve blue.

"So you guys must have a decent verve supply?" I query.

"It cancels out. All we find and produce goes right back into improving ourselves and our machines. Anyone who can't integrate usually opts for a mechanical enhancement."

"Your telling me people choose to remove their own limbs?" I am shocked.

"You'd be surprised what people would pay for a superpower." Markus says. "Some of them didn't choose to lose limbs," Cogs chimes in.

"We've been fighting the same as you guys. We're just closer to the action. Not able to relocate at the sound of a bell." Cog says with a stern expression filled with concern and worry at Caleb.
Yes they are right underneath the city but they seem formidable. Are they really in that much trouble? I wonder.

"People these days are taking the best deals they can get their hands on." Cogs adds on turning back around.

"Where are we going?" I ask.

"Council will want to see you right away." Markus says.

"We're almost there." We walk a bit more until arriving at a huge municipal building.

Pillars stand. Armed guards scan us in. Walking through these halls it looks like it was once some kind of courthouse. My assumptions are correct when the four of us, along with two guards who escort us, bring us into a courtroom. Except it didn't look like any courtroom I remember. The judge booth isn't there. Six chairs with six people sitting in them fill the center.

"Were they expecting us?" I whisper to Caleb.

"They were alerted upon arrival." Cogs whispers back.
The six council members couldn't look more different.

"I hear we have some visitors from Crane's faction."

The fourth member stands up smiling and approaches us in greeting. He looks only a few years older then me. Short brown hair. He walks with a certain air of confidence. He has a charismatic expression. Dressed in a suit and tie, he has glowing verve tech bands around his legs and arms and a chest plate a similar to Markus. Overall a good looking fellow.

"Councilor Allahara. Caleb, as I'm sure you remember, and this is Isaac. First time here, they're both with Crane," Markus reports.

Allahara looks me over. He's sizing me up just as I am sizing him up. Both wondering who we are, what can we do, why are we here? He holds out his hand to shake.

"Isaac, a pleasure." I shake his hand in response. There is a brief strength contest until he turns to Caleb.

"I do remember you. Crane is your sibling. They must have an important message for us for you to be here."

"This is actually a matter of convenience. We were both in the city for other matters. Cogs saved us from getting grabbed." Caleb says.

"Hmph," Allahara hums.

"Tell me Isaac. What are you doing in the city? Surely, Crane is keeping members close to vest. What with the election and everything," Allahara asks.

"I'm searching for someone," I reply reluctantly. He stares at me for a moment. This guy is hard to read. He suddenly turns on his heel and heads back to his chair.

"This someone must be awfully important." He sits.

"Councilmen, I was on recon today." Cogs chirps up.

"I witnessed a Verve-Bomb attack." This gets the council's attention.

"Verve Bombs?" A councilwoman says. "There hasn't been a Verve Bomb attack in years."

Another councilman states.

"Who do we know has access to that kind of hardware?" Allahara asks.

"I witnessed a group of Techno fanatics right before the attack. We have reason to believe someone is funding and supplying them with serious gear."

"It's the election cycle. Those maniacs think making a little noise will do something." The oldest councilwoman groans.

She leans back in her seat. Her attire also matches this apparent black tie event going on in here. She is wearing a white and gold power suit. Her age apparent in the wrinkles on her face. She wears a headband with a couple gems incrusted within. The bags under her eyes tell a bit about the stress of this job. Her pearl white hair is done up in braids that complement the tiara.

"Can you blame them? Misguided and crazy as they are, they hate the Prexy as much as we do." A third members speaks up.

An African American man. Bald. He has a golden staff with a red gem handle on top resting against his chair. He doesn't appear to need the cane however. It might just be for show. He has a purplish blue suit on as well. Hided slightly by another set of power armor.

"If only they weren't religious nuts." A fourth member gets her word in.

A younger white woman, looks to be around the age of Allahara. He has long, straight, blonde, beautiful hair. Her dress being a mix of greens and blues makes me think of nature. She too adorns some sort of power armor over her fancy dress. The council begins arguing it's a fascinating sight. Allahara is writing something down. I look at Caleb awkwardly.

"Half of them think we could adopt them into our numbers. The other half think they are beyond saving." Caleb says quietly.

"At least this is democratic. Right?" Caleb doesn't respond.

Allahara raises his hand and they all settle.

"Forgive us, times are tense being an election year and all. We welcome you, guests of Crane. If there's anything you need during your stay here we'd be happy to oblige." Allahara says.

"Thank you." I bow. Not even knowing if that is the custom here. No one else bows.

"Just one thing." Allahara says as he finishes what he was writing, stands up and walks back over. He produces a letter and hands it to me.

"Could you do us a favor and deliver that to Crane?"

"They're not interested in coming back into the fold." Caleb butts in.

"Call it a matter of convenience." Allahara smirks.

I take the letter, a simple envelope with Crane's name written on it.

"Sure." I put it in my bag.

"Well, if you have nothing for us, then please, we were in the middle of a conversation. Cogs, Markus, show them the place." Allahara smiles innocently then returns to his seat. He flips a lever and the six councilmen and women start moving in their chairs. They rotate until they are all sitting in a circle and a dome of energy forms around them. It muffles their speech.

"Well. That's that. How soon can you bamf us back to Crane?" I ask Caleb.

"I'm still pretty drained. Unless you guys can spare some verve." Caleb turns to Markus and Cogs.

"We could. But what's the rush? You know O'Halloran is still kicking?" Cogs says to Caleb. He brightens up.

"Motherfucker. Are his drinks still as powerful as I remember?" Caleb laughs.

"Why don't we go find out?" Cogs grins at Markus. He takes a moment.

"Ah he owes me a few, why not?" Markus says.

"You're in for a treat hombre. O'Halloran's Elixirs will either give you the strength of ten men, or knock you on your ass." Caleb turns to me.

"That good, Isaac?" Caleb asks.

"What's one more night?" I want to get back but a place with a name like that is too fascinating to miss.
Stepping back outside, I get another look at this amazing underground oasis. After a brief walk we arrive at the rumored location. No sign, but none is needed as we approach a U-shaped outdoor bar attached to a rundown factory. A strange, colorful, mechanical device rolls along a frame above the bar. Glass balls are nestled right near the center fill the place with light.

It's lively. Several people chat and drink away. People as young as me and as old as that councilwoman I saw. They enjoy colored hair here I realize as I take in blues, greens, oranges. Eye pulling hairstyles with solid objects like automotive gears and machine parts intertwined that would've been a lot even back then. It's a variable explosion of rainbow down here. I almost forget these are mercenaries. The arm wrestling and fighting area next to the bar reminded me of that.

Everyone is wearing the same power armor I saw on the councilmembers. It's then that I realize that the people in this community have a brand. The power armor they wear has an insignia. A butterfly with six lines skewering through it.

"What does the butterfly mean?" I ask Cogs.

"It's our symbol for beauty and balance. What we want to bring to a world that has lost it."

"And the lines?" I add. Cogs smirks.

"True Neutral. We're neither good or bad. We seek the proper balance of power so no side may tower over the other." So does that mean if things were really good then they would be bad guys? Is that why Crane left? Caleb rolls his eyes.

"It's a breathing contradiction Cogs." Caleb spews. Cogs shoots daggers back at Caleb.

"It's a principle you and Crane used to believe in. You guys are lucky that our interests are aligned."

"For now." Caleb grumbles to himself.

The four of us take seats and I look over at the bartender serving someone. A spry old gentleman with frizzy white hair. A strange gauntlet on his left hand that I notice he uses to control the device floating above the bar. I watch with amazement as he uses it to create several drinks at the same time. Pipes extend and retract out of the machine, moving like tentacles, producing various colored liquids. After a few moments he makes his way over to us.

"Friendly and fresh faces? Will surprises ever cease?" He says in a sweet tone.

"What'll you have?" He asks excitedly.

"Calling in that favor Hal. I'll have my usual." Markus replies.

"Same here, Hal. On the usual not the favor." Cogs chuckles.

"Caleb," He speaks in a remembering tone.

"How are you, how's Crane?" He asks kindly.

"Staying safe Hal. I'll have whatever's popular tonight." Caleb says. Hal turns to me.

His facial hair is unkempt and grisly. He's wearing a pair of glasses that look more like goggles but shaped in wings. I introduce myself and we make a bit of small talk to get to know one another. After just a few minutes of it, O'Halloran treats me like an old friend. It's comforting and it's easy to see why this place is so popular, with a personable and social guy like him running the show.

These are the kind of people that I need to fight for. Being alone for so long in my lighthouse...I forgot that. But here I am, now, being treated to delicious liquor of a variety I've never sampled. It shouldn't feel normal. But somehow, it does.

"Do you have a signature drink?" I ask. Cogs laugh and Markus scoffs.

"Uh oh" He says.

O'Halloran's eyes light up and he cracks his one free hand. With surprisingly quick movement he makes gestures with his gauntlet and the machine drops four glasses onto the bar. Tubes and pipes lower down and with amazing speed three drinks create themselves in front of us. Mine doesn't get created completely. The machine fills my glass part way with some clear liquid then Hal takes off the gauntlet.

"Cue the fireworks." Cogs laughs.

Hal grabs a dusty bottle and a lighter. He pours a thick brown liquid into a separate smaller shot-sized glass. He uses the lighter to set the shot on fire. He quickly dons the glove, and, manipulates the machine to suck the ignited liquid in momentarily. It then unexpectedly shoots it hard back into my drink causing a small burst of flame. Once it settles, it retains a very dark blueish hue. Hal then puts a small umbrella in it.

"One Hal's Pal." He beams at his work.
The four of them eyeball me as I take my first sip, and they aren't the only ones.

It feels like I am suddenly on stage with a spotlight cast on me. Oh well, no turning back now. I literally asked for it. The moment of the first taste, it feels like a punch in the face! I stand and grip the bar. Everyone laughs.

"I'm impressed." Markus says. "Most people pass out after their first 'Pal'."

Caleb pats me on the back and I sit back down. Hal goes off to serve others. Regaining my focus, I come back to the conversation.

"So. You have a rep here. So does Crane." I say to Caleb.

"Crane was a councilmember" Cogs offers. "They were on the board for years until they left."

"Why did you leave?" I ask Caleb, but put it out in a way where any of my tablemates can answer.

Before anyone can answer there is a low rumbling noise above us. I look up to the ceiling miles above and see it shake. Everyone moves! Hal starts to shut down the bar. Lights blink off one by one. There are some panicked shouts as everyone scurries. The four of us stand.

"What's going on?" I shout over the noise.

The rumbling is gradually getting louder. Plates and mugs shake on the tables. Cogs looks at her watch and types.

"Markus, do you have any extra watches?" Cogs shouts.

"No, not on me!" He shouts back, drawing his weapon.

"We're too far from a checkpoint. Toss me an emergency stick!" Cogs shouts.

Markus produces a shiny translucent blue stick with a sharpened end and pitches it to Cogs, who makes an easy catch. Markus takes another out for himself.

"Okay, don't have time to explain just got to trust me." Cogs spins me around to face her.

"Trust you with what-" My breath halts as she stabs the stick into the top of my left shoulder.

I shout with pain as she leaves the stick there and steps back. I pull it out, and discover it is completely clear. Suddenly everything feels cold. I curl in. Cogs steps towards me again.

"Lie down and steady your breath. You're fine," she instructs me.

I listen...feeling overwhelmed...trying to process what is happening. Markus does the same to Caleb but he seems to understand what's happening. More lights wink out as the streets clear.

"Just lie here, and steady your breath. I know you're cold but try to be still." Cogs repeats.

"Markus turn yours on!" I watch as they both dive behind the bar. As the final streetlights go out I lie in pure darkness. My body shivers. The rumbling grows. The bright lights of an airship soar into the area from one of the tunnels. A search light shines and moves throughout the city. Did everyone actually simultaneously hide and make it look abandoned?

The light shines right on my face but then moves off. The airship hovers for a few more minutes then moves on through the shaft. Once the rumbling fades, the townsfolk emerge and the city illuminates. I struggle to my feet and approach Caleb. He's kneeling, and grasps his shoulder.

"You okay?" I help him to his feet.

"Yeah. I forgot the sting of those popsicle sticks. At least they fixed them." I hear Cogs over by the bar.

"Sorry!" Cogs pops out from behind the counter.

"Those airships use heat radar to detect life. Our watches shield us from it. We had to use an emergency method to lower your body temperatures temporarily. It should wear off in a few more moments."

"Isn't that dangerous?" I check my pulse.

"Typically. Hypothermia leads to shutting down organs and whatnot.

But when you slowly freeze to death the body draws blood in from your extremities, as you keep freezing more stuff goes." Caleb explains.

"But these..." Markus holds up a fresh stick. "...these create a sort of flash freeze effect over your entire surface skin. Completely undetectable by any scanning system. Usually doesn't go deeper than the muscles."

"Usually?" I need to know what the hell that means.

"Like with most inventions there was a trial and error phase." Cogs admits.

"You don't feel dizzy or weak do you?" She inspects me closer.

"Only like I just had the worst brain freeze ever, except it's my whole body. Like I was tossed in snow."
Suddenly Hal jumps in out of nowhere.

"Damn Prexy bastards! Trying to run me out of business!" Hal shouts as people return to the bar. I feel the warmth start to return.

"That packs a punch." I bandage my shoulder. "How often do they come by?"

"Enough," Cogs almost spits, spitefully. "Look it's late, how about Markus shows you guys to a place where you can sleep. I need to check on everyone." We nod in agreement.

"Let's go," Markus ushers both of us off.

After a few minutes we arrive at a motel. Its a building that says motel on it. It is inhabited. Markus pays for a room for us, then he leaves to go on more errands of his own. On the third floor of this cozy modern building I look out the window as the programmed sky suddenly shifts to a night time mode of sorts. Fake stars illuminate spots of the city.
"The leadership in this city is odd but isin't it a lot better then the Prexy? Why did Crane leave them?" I ask Caleb.

"It's too open. Vetting process isin't as strenious as what we do. Mole's are more likely to appear here. It wasn't always like this. Just remember they are our allies." Caleb reassures.

Again he evades the question. I suppose it's none of my business anyway. With everything that happened today I didn't feel like pressing further. Sleep comes fast and hard. The next morning I meet Caleb, Markus and Cogs by the bar. Caleb holds a few vials of verve.

"A boost to get us though. I'm still a little sore." Caleb shoots playful annoyed eyes at Markus.

"I didn't stab you that hard." Markus defends.

Caleb chuckles and holds his hand out.

"Glad you did it though." He high-fives him, then pulls him in for a hug. He then turns to Cogs.

"And you. Stay out of trouble." Caleb smiles warmly.

"Okay, next time I'll leave ya to fend for yourself against those suits." Cogs returns smugly.

She and Caleb hug as well.

"Hey, Isaac." Markus turns to me.

"Yeah?" Markus gestures to have a word. We step off to the side.

"It's another election cycle. Another year of nothing happening to dethrone the Prexy. People are tired." Markus says this more quietly.

"Crane has resources and technology. We have numbers. The last time we came the closest ever to an overthrow, we were all working together." He's being very open with me for some reason. Not sure why.

"So why did it fail? Why are we now separated?"

"There was a mole. We had a target, it got grounded and a lot of people died. A lot of good people.

Crane doesn't share our philosophy. Crane blames the council for allowing more lives to be lost then needed." This story coming out of nowhere was a little startling for me.

"What are you asking me, Markus?" His face is stern and intense. Realizing he is taking great efforts to keep Caleb out of ear shot of this.

"I just want you to know that a lot of us here, we still support Crane. We want to fight. But we need resources." Markus says. "Otherwise more deals are going to get made that won't help either of us."

"I'll see what I can do." Sort of shutting off this conversation. I'm still not sure what to make of this guy or this place. It's clear there are some unresolved issues thats for sure.

"You ready Isaac?" Caleb asks, but he isn't really.

He's already focusing as the familiar spark and hum of his power generates. I nod a goodbye towards Markus and Cogs. As Caleb's eyes flash, the portal grows. Caleb exhales hard. I jump through and help Caleb make his way across before it closes. We are back to familiar turf.

CHAPTER 10

INVISIBLE CHESS

The Crane. Leader of the resistance. Fearless and powerful. Today, she is dressed unusually in a gray tee and baggy pants. Her jet black shoulder-length hair now styled in a pixie cut. Looking like she just woke up. Walking towards the training room, she makes her way through the halls until arriving at a set of double doors.

She walks through to an open gym area. The air stale of rubber, metal and sweat. It is deserted all but for one person, Caleb, who is working very hard on his routine. He is on his back doing a set of reps. Crane walks up to him.

"Hey," she says. No response from Caleb.

"They tell me you've been logging a lot of time in here. It's basically the only place you go other than your room or the cafeteria." Still no response. Caleb continues working out.

"Can we please talk about it?" Crane leans over to look Caleb in the eyes.

"No." Caleb finally breaks the silence.

"They told me what happened. With the portal and Oakwood." Crane's voice is soft. Full of care. There is guilt riddled in her voice.

Caleb continues his set. He increases his speed and focus, clearly not wanting to be interrupted. Caleb starts to bring the bar down but suddenly find it is locked in air. Crane's face is concentrating on it. He groans and stops his workout. He sits up and gets off the bench.

"You believed the words of a traitor over mine. The team wanted to throw me off of the facility. Were you aware of that? My friends wanted to kill me." Crane is silent.

"I don't see why you're so worked up. It's not like this is the first time you wanted me dead." Caleb growls, spite in his voice.

Crane's eyes widen, her face shocked and hurt The bench press falls out of the air and clatters loudly into the rack.

"We were teenagers." Crane retorts harshly.

"You didn't care what happened to me. I overheard you before they put me under. You were fine with any outcome." Crane looks visibly hurt.

"We were starving, Caleb!" Crane tears up.

"And when I woke up? In a brand new body? Scared? Where were you? You were gone!" Caleb shouts.

"They told me you died." Crane utters as the tears break.

"Just go. I'm doing my rehabilitation, making my counselor appointments. They got this close to forcing me back into a wrong body to become a mindless drone. I would like to make sure that doesn't happen again."

"Conference room. Fifteen minutes. I'm not asking." Crane says regaining their composure.

As they leave they look back at Caleb who continues his reps not even acknowledging their leaving. At another end of the facility a lunch bell rings out through the halls. Workers, scientists and soldiers alike all line up for their second square meal of the day.

The overall buzz of chatter of people creates a strange white noise effect that is sometimes pleasing to tune out with. So much so I don't notice that I am next up. Kup seems to be on kitchen duty today again. He seems to like it.

"What's wrong there bud? You're looking gloomier then your usual self." Kup slides me a tray of the usual grub.
It's amazing how they've perfected the mass-produced meatloaf and potatoes in the 22nd century. If only it had flavor.

"Not now Kup. I'm not in the mood." I grab my tray and head to an empty table.
A few scattered members of the previous period finish up the last remains of their meal. I find this is the best time to grab a good seat. Kup exits the kitchen and joins me at the table. I intentionally don't look at him, but I can still tell he is staring, but not saying a word, which is odd. I look up annoyed to his concerned face.

"Meatloaf's pretty good today," I stuff my face. Kup continues to stay silent.

"Really loving the table ambiance you know." This is awkward. I fork the food into my mouth a little faster.

"You've been spending a lot of time in the booths," Kup begins.

"Yep. Anybody from my time would. Great technology."
As I shovel more potatoes into my face, Kup looks sad for a moment, then brightens up almost immediately.

"Well you know son I think if maybe we took a walk outside we could-"
I slam my fist onto the table stopping him. It takes him by surprise. A few people look over, then return to their food.

"Why do you do that?" I raise my voice.

"Do what?" Kup asks.

"That beyond cheery attitude and old-timey accent. It's like a gagging rainbow in an otherwise grim place.

It honestly annoys me more then the pitying. What the fuck do you have to be so up-beat about?" I shout.

Kup sighs and reaches into his pocket. He takes out a wallet. He opens it and thumbs though it for a second until pulling out a worn photo of him and two other people. He looks younger in the photo.

"Family?" I assume.

"Dead. Both of them. My wife and daughter. She was six." Kup says now in a serious tone. No more cheer.

"Dead family. Join the club." I do not care about this.

"My daughter died of cancer." Kup keeps my gaze with a piercing expression. That caught me off guard. I clear my throat and shuffle in my chair.

"I'm sorry." Thanks. Now I feel bad.

"My wife? Now she would've loved you. She was a history buff, just like Kanoa. She loved stuff from the past. She would read books from your time to our daughter. Even stuff before your time. Before, and after every chemo appointment."

"Kup I-" I begin but I'm not sure where I'm going to go next. Fortunately, he keeps talking.

"We were never the same after our little Anna died. I tried so hard to cheer her up. Do anything to allow us to move on, to grow. But losing your child leaves a hole you never can fill." I swallow hard.

"When Crane found us we were at the end of our rope. Pissed at this government. At this Prexy for not doing what they could to help our little girl. My wife died a year after we both came on. She died from an explosion from a weapon your mother made." I scoff.

"So you have an axe to grind with my mother too. Well, that you will have to get in line for."

"I feel bad for her." Kup states.

"Bad? Why on Earth do you feel bad for her?" I am bewildered.

"Because I know what it's like for a parent to lose a child."

I shake my head.

"She didn't lose me Kup. She froze me for a century! She ripped me out my life because she has to be in control. She took away both my father and my choice because she lives in her own world."

"I'm not saying I agree with her choices. But I can understand where she is coming from. If I could've cryogenically frozen my daughter until they cured it, I would've. Why do I use that accent and why am I so happy all the time? Because I made a promise to my daughter that I would go on living. She was remarkably mature even at six. She was worried for us, of all things! She didn't want us to die shortly after her."

The room around us seems to have emptied now as Kup is not holding back. This is a side of him I have never seen.

"Whenever it was my turn to tell her stories. I would use that accent and make up funny words to make her laugh. She loved it. So the reason you get annoyed at my attitude and accent is because I made a promise to my daughter to live life to it's fullest no matter how long or short. If you are not looking for happiness, you will never find it." I pick the photo off of the table and stand up.

Kup follows. I walk over to him and hand the photo back.

"I'm sorry that happened to you Kup. I'm truly, genuinely sorry for all of that. But my mother is not someone who can be saved. She lives in her own world. Unaware of ours."

Suddenly the PA system rings out.

"Isaac report to the conference room immediately."

"I should go. Thanks for the food." I walk off, leave Kup holding his photo.

Walking into the conference room feels a lot like walking into the principal's office. Crane is there waiting for us. Kanoa also in casual wear. His long silver hair is tied into a ponytail. Glasses rest on his face. His tree tattoo appears out of his left arm sleeve. I could see the bulge of the device on his shoulder. Caleb sits on the other end. I head over to join him.

"Okay. So?" Crane asks us.

She wants to know about our latest excursion.

"We were following a lead-" Caleb cuts me off.

"Don't blame him. Blame me." Caleb says.

"Lead. What lead? You're not on any active missions Isaac. You should still be in training." Kanoa says.

"A lead into my past." I state firmly. Crane sighs, frustrated.

"We don't have resources for personal missions. And you two have been using the hovercrafts recklessly."

"Recklessly?" Caleb interjects.

"We know how to use the hovercrafts." I retort.

Crane looks to Kanoa who hands them some sheets of paper.

"Isaac, your lessons with Kanoa have also brought up some concern." I sit back silently to listen.

"And per his recommendation I'm suspending you from all T.R.A.C.I use."

"What!" I shout, rising out of my chair.

"You will continue your lessons in the overworld until such a time you can prove you are not a risk to yourself or others." Kanoa finishes Crane's sentence.

I angrily grimace at Kanoa, who just has a look of sad concern on his face.

"This is not fair!" I shout.

"He has every right as your mentor. And as leader of this

organization if you have an issue on how I run things I will personally escort you to the memory booth." Crane's voice rises to match mine.

I walk out, slam the doors behind me.

"So what decision have you made for me?" Caleb asks.

"You're on recon duty."

"For how long?" Caleb is mad.

"Until such a time." Crane states angrily.

Caleb walks out. Crane sits back and sighs heavily. Kanoa heads for the exit.

"Stop." Crane barks to Kanoa

"I want to talk to you about Isaac." He doesn't turn to face Crane. He stays fixed on his escape route.

"He's dealing with a lot right now. Nothing you or I haven't seen."

"Why did you hold back?" Crane asks bluntly.

"What are you talking about?" Kanoa asks confused. This causes him to turn around.

"I talked to the T.R.A.C.I techs. You left out how he has been rebooting every time he goes under." Kanoa walks up to Crane.

"I'll handle it. He's my responsibility. Your words."

"He's reminding you of Luke isn't he?" Crane asks, concerned.

"He's not." Kanoa is starting to get annoyed, himself. Crane puts a hand on his shoulder.

"People are dropping on us left and right. Don't you start getting flaky on me now too. Neither of us can afford that." Kanoa brushes her off.

"I'll handle it." Kanoa leaves the conference room.

Crane goes back to her chair and starts organizing her paperwork when she hears a commotion out in the hall.

"What the?" She pops out of her chair to investigate.

CHAPTER 11

-1Z

"They're back!" I hear Mercedes shout from the hall.

Suddenly a flurry of footsteps fill the hall as dozens of people race towards the main doors. I join the crowd to see what the commotion is about. I shove my way to the front to see Mordecai and Kate. They are hurt. Bloodied and covered in bruises. Mordecai has Kate's arm around his shoulder. Kate is limping on one leg. They are almost immediately swarmed by nurses. But Crane is there first.

"What the hell happened?" Crane demands.

"Someone flipped. We got ambushed. Job was grounded from the start." Mordecai breathes heavily.

"Where is the rest of the team?" Crane looks behind them. Mordecai lowers and shakes his head.

"Where's Z?" I finally make my way to the front. Mordecai's eye is swollen shut and Kate has a deep cut on her leg right by her knee.

"She was with you guys on this one right? Where is she?"

"I didn't see-" Mordecai is interrupted as Kate taps him with her hand and struggles to sign with her free arm.

"Take- Taken? She was taken?" I try to make sense of her signing.

I have gotten pretty good these last few months but one hand down and shaky, Kate is struggling.

"That's enough. Mercedes, take them to the infirmary." Crane orders. "Make sure they weren't followed."

"We weren't. I made sure of it." Mordecai coughs, holds up his free arm.

The bandages drip crimson red. I step in to loop Kate's free arm around mine to provide leverage. Mercedes takes Mordecai, who staggers. Trying to find the middle ground between being careful and hurrying them to the infirmary we finally make it. I turn a corner through automatic sliding glass doors where they are already waiting for the arrivals. They must've been alerted when they got back. The head doctor, a mid forties man by the name of James. He has short salt n pepper hair by choice. He take my place as support and immediately begins barking orders.

"Aria, Matthew, take Kate. Were taking them both to the I.C.U." I follow and help out best I can.
Field medical training doesn't necessarily qualify me to be in the operating room but I'm able to run and get things they need. After some time I notice Crane arrive back at the infirmary. I was too busy tending to Kate and Mordecai that I didn't notice her at first.

"Tell me what happened." Crane's voice is softer as they walk over to us.

"It was the recruitment drive." Mordecai groans. "There was an agent hidden among the batch of recruits. It was a trap for us." I fetch more supplies.

"How come it's just you two?" I give Kate another pillow for her arm.

Kate points over to their gear lying in the corner of the room. Their bodycams, I realize, as Crane and I hurry over and rifle through their gear.

Most of it is charred and stained with blood. I manage to find the CF card in Kate's vest as Crane finds Mordecai's.

"Give it to me." Crane says.

I hand her Mordecai's card. I look back at both of them on the hospital beds. They're eyes are both closed now. Taking deep breaths. Their hands laying over their beds inches from each other. Crane walks to the conference room and inserts the cards into the computer. I join them a moment later.

"What do you think we're going to find?" I ask across the conference table. Crane doesn't answer.

Instead they project their screen onto the wall to enlarge the video. They play back the last five minutes of the camera's recording. From Kate's camera which, when wearing the vest, is positioned right in the center-high part of the chest. She is running. It's hard to see where they are since the camera is moving so rapidly. Mordecai is shouting.

"Keep moving!" We can hear various gunshots and screaming. They're running from a fight I think?

I notice train tracks on the ground as a locomotive whistle blows loudly. I watch as Kate and Mordecai sprint towards an oncoming railcar. They just barely leap across the track along with most of the crew, seemingly safe.

"Okay, that bought us a second." Mordecai says as Kate is taking a quick inventory.

Z stands among the group. Mordecai growls at everyone,

"We need to regroup back at-" He's cut off by a gunshot, and is struck in the shoulder!

He staggers towards cover as other group members are also hit. Kate scrambles to find cover, cracking the camera lens in the process. She manages to get behind cover to look out at who fell. Jake, a soldier I had gotten to know really well these last few months lies crumpled in a twisted heap on the floor.

I bite my lip as Kate's camera blinks, then shuts off. "Nothing." Crane is clearly frustrated.

"Play Mordecai's perspective." Kanoa requests as he enters the room from behind me.

His long silver hair is tied back in a single ponytail. His reading glasses have a bit of condensation from the cold. His casual wear consists of all black but he keeps his arm bracers on. Crane switches out the cards. Same situation, same train. Once they are over and Mordecai gets shot he stumbles behind his own cover. Groaning silent profanities, he looks at the ones who hit the ground. He spies Kate. He looks back one more time then starts to sneak towards her, managing to reach her. Jake and Z lie out in the open.

"Shit. Did you see the shooter?" Mordecai whispers to Kate. She shakes her head.

Suddenly the sounds of footsteps and shouting enter the area. Mordecai looks out to see people in power armor come out and stand over Jake, Z and two others. Not power armor I recognize. Not our groups and not the Prexy's minions either. They have a deep almost midnight purple coloration to them. They take out guns and shoot Jake in the head and the two others. As they raise their gun to Z someone yells

"Stop!"

"Who is that?" Mordecai whispers.
He looks out again to see more people come in.

"Oh shit. These were Crane's people. Boss ain't gonna like that." One of them say.

"Hey that's an alien. They got an alien working for them?" One of the suits remarks.

"Careful, watch it! It's still alive!" Another one shouts, jumping back. Everyone takes out their gun to shoot but that same guy yells again.

"Stop idiots. It's alive. You know how much aliens are worth alive right now? You three restrain it. The rest of you spread out, this wasn't the entire team. Better to have no witnesses to this fuck up."

"Let's go. We got to go Kate, c'mon." Mordecai tugs at Kate who hesitates, then moves. The footage ends there.

"The fuck?" I say. Crane stays silent.

She hits a button on the desk.

"Mercedes, Taylor. Please meet me in the conference room." As we're waiting I talk to Crane.

"They know you." I look at Crane. "They know who you are." Crane sighs in annoyance.

"I know who they are too." Crane says with disgust in their voice.

"Well, so who are they?" I ask.

"Neon." Kanoa is behind me.

I turn around to see him standing in the conference room doorway.

"Neon?" I ask.

"Zoom image." Kanoa shouts to the projector.

It closes in on one of the armors, to a logo on his jacket. A red and purple artist's rendition of the Leviathan Satanic Cross.

"Who are they?" I ask.

"Mercenaries." Kanoa walks by me towards Crane. Mercedes and Taylor enter.

"We need to send a team to talk with Neon about this. This is not going to fly." Crane is angry.

"What about Z?" Kanoa asks.

"He'll want to sell her. I'd rather just take her back but turf wars with Neon are the last thing we need right now." Crane is annoyed. "How many boats are operational right now?" Crane gazes in Taylor's direction.

"Only three." She says hesitantly. "We've lost five in the last few months. Keeping the Prexy off our tail has not been without some sacrifices."

"And now we have to deal with Neon!" Crane mouths off to everyone.

"So what's the play?" Kanoa asks.

Crane looks about the room to all of us. You can see the gears turning in her brain.

"Mercedes, help the nurses. Get Mordecai and Kate back to one hundred percent as soon as possible. Taylor, prep a boat. We're going to pay Neon a visit."

"If we use the printer they can be ready by tomorrow, maybe the day after. They have burns, deep cuts and bullet wounds." Mercedes says. Crane nods. Mercedes exits.

"We're flying into The Central Zone as soon as those two can move." Everyone nods in agreement.

"Yes, Crane." Taylor leaves.

"What can I do?" I ask. Crane and Kanoa look at each other.

"You're serious." Crane is surprised.

"You banned me from using T.R.A.C.I not from field missions." I argue.

"And you suddenly care for the interests of the group. Or is it just because it's Z?" Crane fires.

I stay silent at that. I don't have a good reply.

"Well? Am I wrong? Didn't you two have some fight or something?" Crane questions me.

"I want to help." I say flatly.

"You'll be heading the mission, Kanoa. I trust you to pick your crew." Crane grabs a jacket and heads out the conference doors. Leaving only Kanoa and I.

"Are you going to be an asset or a liability?" He folds his arms.

"It's Z, Kanoa." I try to reason with him.

"That's not helping your case." Kanoa says. "Can I trust you?"

"Yeah. Yes, you can trust me." I reply earnestly. Kanoa sighs.

"Field mission, Isaac. Not T.R.A.C.I. No resetting." Kanoa repeats. I've heard him say that a million times. Kanoa and I walk back to the infirmary. Mordecai and Kate hold hands. When they notice us enter the room, they let go.

"You already look better." Kanoa tries to brighten Mordecai up. They have them locked down like I was months ago. Printing new skin on their burns. Their cuts and bullet wounds are dressed and they look a lot further now from death's door.

"Told you I'll outlive you." Mordecai smirks. Kanoa pats him on the shoulder. I sign to Kate.

"You look like crap." She scoffs and signs back.

"Did you mean shit? You look like shit?" I smile back. Must've used the wrong sign.

"Right, whoops." I say out loud.

"Get better quick. Both of you. We're going to save Z." The next two days pass slowly. A change of bandages, a good night's rest and all the information compiled on Neon and next thing you know I'm waiting in a seat on what I like to call a hovercraft.

"A thousand yard stare. Don't get existential on me." Mordecai says as he steps on board. Kate is right behind him, bags in tow.

"I'm about a hundred years too late for that." I remark.

One by one, everyone boards. Kanoa and Mordecai take the pilot and co-pilot seats. Kate settles in the row behind me.

That girl Taylor is joining us as well. I haven't really spoken with her a lot these last few months. A repair tech for the hovercrafts, I met her a few days after Oakwood. I just nod at her as she walks by and sits next to Kate.

"Everyone accounted for?" Kanoa shouts back to the four of us. "Alright, let's go!" I feel a lurch as the ship moves forward and up.

We hover and zoom right past our security and into the night sky. It's raining hard so we already have great cover. After a bit, I rise and walk to the cockpit.

"So this Neon guy. Where is he?" I ask.

"He works in The Central Zone. In the Red Light District near the river." Mordecai replies.

Kanoa is focused on piloting.

"He's an ass." Mordecai adds.

"Great. So how are we going to get close enough into the city to park?" I ask.

"The Nether has a landing pad. As long as we stay cloaked." Mordecai continues.

Kanoa looks unusually angry. He has a tense stillness while driving. I walk back to Kate.

"Do you know anything about this Neon guy?" I sign to her.

"Only that he used to be with us. Years ago. Back when Crane and everyone that supported them split from the Nether." I nod taking in this information.

"What happened?"

"Kanoa happened. I don't know the story, only that those two could not work together if their lives were at stake." Kate closes her eyes to try and sleep a little. I look ahead to the cockpit, wondering what happened between them.

CHAPTER 12

THE NEON DEVIL

"What is this place?" I am concerned.

For the last half hour I've been guided down various back alleys and hidden paths to get to the building we are standing in front of. It's name is displayed proudly in an arrangement of neon animated colors and gestures to suggest this is a place of drinking and sex.

"The Neon Devil?" I read. The sign illuminating the quickly darkening area due to the rapid sunset.

"We're going to have to make some deals if we want to find her," Kanoa rummages inside his backpack.
He leads us to the unmanned door. A numeric keypad flips over for a code.

"Code Please," an automated voice commands.

"Do you know it?" I ask. Kanoa not saying anything, punches in a three digit code. The red light switches to green and a confirmation chirps as the locks disengage. The door glides open and instantly I am hit with a musky smell. The air is hot. As we step in, my senses are overwhelmed at the loud music and flashing lights. The ever-present scent of alcohol and smoke dominate.

"What kind of business did you do with this guy?" I shout over the noise.

I notice the large amount of security all around the main area. There are bodyguards every few feet.

"Mutually beneficial," Kanoa remarks.

He looks uncomfortable, like he is reliving a bad dream.

"What did you sell?" I try to get past his dodgy answers.

"At first just Verve. But he wanted a more...diverse portfolio." Kanoa looks at the stripper pole where a woman is dancing. She looks unhappy.

Sweat drips down her face as various large grimy men throw money at her. She has a shiny choker bearing the club's logo.

We make our way through until arriving at a door labeled "staff." A woman, about my height, sturdy with short blonde hair, stands guard.

I notice a bright red stripe down the center where her hair parts. She has strange geometric patterns tattooed on her face. A circle around her eye connects to squares and triangles. I am bewildered at the sight. I can't figure out if she is security or a dancer, as a tight black sleeveless top shows off her impressive form. She's wearing floral fishnets with tight black shorts. No heels like the rest of the dancers. That leads me to believe she is a watchman. I wonder if she is enhanced.

"Sure is shit out there," she doesn't even make eye contact with us. She clearly has a slight attitude.

"It'd be nicer if I was dead." Kanoa replies.

She looks up, surprised at his answer. Her eyes widen.

"It's been a while since you've been here." She says judgmentally. She clearly knows Kanoa.

"I'm not happy about it either. We need to speak with him Scrape." Kanoa replies. She opens the door and gestures for us to enter. Once we head in she also enters, then closes and bolts it.

She leads us down a crowded hallway cluttered with boxes and lockers. It's a short walk until we reach a private lounge. There is a smaller stage, currently occupied built for one dancer to perform on with a single viewing table, round, with one side furnished as a booth.

The circular booth holds six people. Almost everyone is dressed like they just came from a reception. Business suits and ties. They have pieces of technology around their waists, shoulders and arms. It's mismatched and clashes with the formal attire. One guy is bald.

A heavyset individual who is currently inhaling a plate of shrimp. Two others are in the middle of what appears to be an argument. Annoying the forth guy to their left. He and the other two are trying to enjoy the show being put on. We walk right up, and I take a guess at who the one in charge is.

He has a triangular face. It makes me think of a rat. His black hair is slick and styled with product although it only runs halfway to his shoulders. He has rings on every other finger and sits in the center. What's most notable is a J-shaped scar that runs from his eye to the top of his head until it's hidden by his hair. Kanoa confirms my guess.

"That's the Neon Devil. Neon for short." Kanoa whispers to me.

He is joined by other men of similar caliber. Each one looks like they have at least a dozen pending charges against them. Although to be fair I thought the same of Kanoa and Mordecai when I met them. Still, seeing Kanoa stress out is only adding to my own anxiety. The gentlemen stop when Scrape strolls up to their table and whispers something to the guy in the center. He looks past her to us. I provide a some-what comical half-wave. He pushes the table forward to create an exit route and approaches.

"And here I thought I'd never see the day." This guy locks onto Kanoa. He is about Kanoa's height.

They both have me beat by half a foot. He reeks of booze and I can see some blue liquid dye under his nose, in his mustache, like a stain.

"I thought you were too good for this place." This gentleman is reading Kanoa.

I recognize the stare. He's seeing how much of a threat he currently is. Their history is apparent. He is bathed in a cologne that makes my nose twitch. An odd mixture of cinnamon and mothballs.

"We need to talk," Kanoa does not flinch.

"I know. You should know I got an anonymous tip there was a cargo shift going down. I had no idea you guys were there."

"After killing Jake and Ryan, and-" Kanoa lists angrily before getting cut off. Neon looks over Kanoa's shoulder, at me.

"Who's the runt?" I straighten my back.

"He's a part of my team. None of your concern," Kanoa says.

"For now." I interject. He smiles.

"I don't believe we've met. I'm the guy who is allowing you to stand in his private entertainment room. I'm the guy who owns this place. I'm the guy who can kill you where you stand and no one would do anything about it."

"That's a bit of a mouthful. Got like, a title or a nickname?" I meet his eye-line.

Maybe I should tone down the arrogance. But this guy is rubbing me the wrong way. He clearly annoys Kanoa as well. His smile vanishes, changes to a stern look as he points to one of the neon signs displaying the club's logo.

"So you are the neon devil? I thought it was just a catchy club name. Or even a drink."

I try to size up this man. Maybe I should stop pushing it. There are a lot of unknowns here. Something about him rubs me the wrong way. The blonde chick hasn't taken her eyes off of us since settling here. There is a momentary tense silence.

"It's all three!" He shouts, turning on his heels, causing me to flinch slightly.

He walks to a fridge with a see-through door and a faint blue glow. He rummages through it, locates a bright blue glass bottle. It has a bold red and purple design of his logo wrapped around the container. He uncorks it, pulls a few more out of the fridge, then shuffles back.

"Want one?" He asks.

Before I can decide, he walks back to his buddies and gives them all one. There are none left after he finishes handing them out.

"We're not here to drink or fuck around." Kanoa starts. Before he can continue, the dancer on the stage trips and falls hard on her knees.

"Dammit, Harmony!" Neon shouts, extremely agitated.

"I'm sorry. I'm sorry. Please, don't!" She shouts as she grabs at the metallic choker around her neck.

Neon grabs at a remote on the table and presses a button. A sharp clicking sound rings out as the dancer screams and thrashes. She tries to pull off the choker, to no avail.

"Apologies. They know better than that." As he sets the remote down, I am completely shocked.

Kanoa has a look of bitter rage that he works hard to suppress.

"Don't worry. It doesn't leave marks. Can't be damaging the product now." This bastard smiles with the smuggest grin I have ever seen. He puts his feet up on the table. I step forward but Kanoa stops me.

"Don't." Kanoa says quietly.

"Hello!" The Neon Devil sits back upright. "Twig over here has some fire in his step." Kanoa's arm holds me back.

"You said you'd try to stop human trafficking." Kanoa grits his teeth but still holds me back.

"And I did...try. But the business is just so good right now." He puts his feet back up on the table.

His friends either watch this conversation unfold or return to their original entertainment.

The dancer looks to be on the verge of crying as she resumes her routine.

"A country that can't keep their shit together. Incomplete census records. Scarce resources. Poverty through the roof. Over-population. You wouldn't believe what some people would do for a meal these days. And that's nothing compared to the internet. Have you seen some of the sicko's on there? They'll pay anything to...live out their desires. Normally you'd just perv out in a T.R.A.C.I booth but some people prefer the real thing." He turns back towards Harmony. I push Kanoa off.

"So where are they then? Where do you keep your product!" I demand. His eyes brighten.

"You're after someone in my possession. Aren't you?" Kanoa nods.

"Do you keep people here?" Kanoa asks frustratingly.

"I keep many things here. You should know." He says.

"What are you looking to pay?" Kanoa grumbles and pulls out his bag.

"The resistance is willing to let go an amount no less than-" I interrupt Kanoa, "Release her." Staring right at this businessman.

"Quiet kid, the adults are doing business." Neon barks.

"Release that dancer," I shout. Kanoa's face bends in surprise. Everyone at the table stares at me.

Some of them look astonished as well. A couple of people laugh but others look tense and ready to attack. Some reach for their waistbands, but their leader stops them.

"I knew it." He says in a soft, yet intense voice.

"Bright eyes." He practically whispers.

What just happened? Why did Kanoa and everyone suddenly grow surprised and tense? Did my eyes shine through my contacts?He pushes the table away from himself again, knocking over a few drinks. He stands up, approaches. I ready myself and it seems like a fight is about to break out. He grabs my chin with one hand, and holds open my eye with his other hand.

"Contacts. Those are the eyes of an enhanced individual." Neon's breath reeks of booze and shrimp.

"He's a techno." Scrape finally speaks up. "I saw his mark as we came in."

He spins me around and moves my hair. I push off of him

"Let go of me!"

"A rare variation techno..." He says as if he just found the holy grail.

"Most people who successfully integrate with verve can hide their integration. It's rare to meet someone who is unable to hide it." Suddenly my mind flashes back to the Loft with Desolate.

He had two different colored eyes. Was one of them fluorescent blue? Did he have an ability? Just how much trouble was I in at that facility?

"What's your ability, runt?" One of his lackeys from the table chimes in, now unsure if his boss is in danger. Kanoa steps in front of me.

"Not even an option."

"Funny, he's now looking like the only option. I have money, but you!" He points at me.

"You are very, incredibly valuable. Eight? Possibly nine figures on the black market. The value of a terrorist, add in the value of an enhanced ability, plus a genetic variation. Jack-pot."

"Alright, enough. She's probably not even here Isaac let's go." Kanoa clearly wants to make a swift exit.
I don't want to leave without the dancer, but I can't take on everyone in this facility. I move with Kanoa.

"You're looking for an alien, aren't you?" Neon shouts. We both turn back.

"How did you know?" Kanoa growls.

He grabs that remote again and this time turns on a nearby monitor. It shows several storage rooms as he flickers through them. Half a dozen rooms of various product. Money, drugs, cargo, until finally arriving in the biggest room. Large human or alien-sized cages line the area. Some humans, disheveled and malnourished, are caged together. They wear matching collars with the same logo on those glass bottles.

One of the cages holds neighbors. I walk closer to the TV to look at the faces in the cage. There! Sitting down among them, there is no mistaking it. It's Z.

"She came in with some of your guys' gear. Didn't know you are working with them now. What is she to you?" Neon asks.

"None of your business." My throat tightens. "So can we have her or not?" Neon smirks.

"Put your money away." Neon says to Kanoa. "How about we have some fun?" Kanoa tenses.

"Crane would rather we just make this trade quickly and quietly." Kanoa pleads.

"Well, I'd rather have some fun." Neon says. "And I'm the one in charge around here." I step in front of Kanoa.

"So what do you do for fun around here?" I ask. He grins and looks at me.

"How good a fighter are you?"

"This is stupid, Isaac." Kanoa tries to butt in.

"Let the man speak for himself Kanoa! Clearly he's mature for his age." He glances me over.

Did I win some respect by challenging him? Maybe that's how it is around here.

"I had to grow up quick," I retort.

"Good. I have just the game then. Scrape!" He looks to Scrape, who walks forward now growing a similar shit-eating grin.

"Here's the game. It's simple. First one to tap out or die, loses." He says confidently.

Scrape cracks her knuckles and punches her hand. I hesitate for a moment.

"Oh, I get it. You want to know if she's enhanced. Go ahead. Show him what you are capable of." Neon instructs.

Scrape cracks her neck. Her eyes illuminate a full bright blue and her blonde hair turns a bright red. The red stripe inverts to blonde and her body seems to almost glow and vibrate as in the blink of an eye she does a lap around the room and downs an entire bottle of Neon Devil.

"I showed you mine, now show me yours." She says confidently.

"I don't show all my cards right away." I try to sound confident.

The truth is we still do not know why my eyes shine a bright blue. Several blood tests confirmed it. I do carry verve but we still have no idea when or even how I interacted with it. I'm not sure what made my eyes go almost a full bright state but that's what clearly happened. That has to be why they reacted so strongly.

"So, a fight?" I ask.

"You win, you get your alien and Harmony because I'm feeling confident." Mr. Neon says.

"And if you win?" Kanoa asks.

"I get your golden boy here." He says, with greed in his eyes. He holds his hand out to shake.

"No." Kanoa says. "Deal." I shake his hand.

"Isaac!" Kanoa shouts, red-in-the-face irate.

"Dan, gather everyone. Start taking bets. We have a new exhibition match." Neon glares happily at me.

Everyone moves at once. Some goons head out to gather a crowd. Others clean up the room and grab needed gear. Neon grabs his remote and presses another button. Suddenly the bookshelf in the room separates to reveal an elevator door.

"A secret door, in a secret room, at a secret club." I say in a stupor.

"VIP has it's privileges." Neon gestures for me to enter first, Kanoa staggers behind, in tow. Then the Neon Devil and Scrape enter the elevator. Together, the four of us descend into the depths.

CHAPTER 13

EXHIBITION

"Why do you feel the need to piss me off like this?" Kanoa paces back and forth as I sit on a hard metal bench in front of him. "You don't know your ability. You're hardly combat trained-" I cut him off.

"I can take her." I say confidently.

Kanoa turns to face me. He looks like he's about to burst a vein. "And that!" He shouts.

"That is the worst of it. You have an incredibly cocky behavior."

Once we reached the bottom most floor the elevator could go, we are lead down a hallway. The smell of iron and metal is incredibly strong down here. In the distance I could hear shouting and bells ringing. One of Neon's associates took us aside into this waiting room of sorts. Various lockers and benches are stuffed into the corners. It's slightly damp with everything having a thin film of water over it as if we are in a sauna. There is a considerable amount of warmth down here.

"He was torturing that girl, Kanoa." I argue.

"The other people he has are not our concern. We are here for Z." I am given some wraps for my hands. I begin wrapping up my hands like a boxer.

"Slavery is wrong. Period." I state. "We can't save everyone." Kanoa exclaims.

"Isn't that what we are trying to do?" I begin to fumble with finishing my knots for these hand bandages.

Kanoa sighs and walks up to me and gestures for me to stand up. He begins helping me tie on the wraps.

"And if you can't beat her? What then? Were you able to think that far ahead?" He jabs me in my chest.

"What do you care about how I end up?" Before he can reply there is a knock at the door.

"They're ready," one of Neon's grunts bellows over the sounds of cheering and chanting.

I shove Kanoa off and walk steadily towards the egress.

"If I lose...just buy back Z and forget about me." I don't look back. Kanoa grinds his teeth and sighs as I continue forward.

I am immediately overwhelmed by the bright stage lights and roaring sound of people as I approach the circle-shaped cage in the center of this massive place. Much like one of those old pro-wrestling arenas back from my era, there are rows of audience looping all around the stage.

There is a balcony with another row of people above. Bright colorful lights blind me as they trace the rows in a preset pattern, all ending in the center of the stage. Huge monitors magnified the view for those further out. Loud music blasts through massive speakers, controlled from a DJ booth nestled neatly in the corner next to a small, simplified bar. How many spots to acquire liquor are in this place, I wonder. A man, white, early thirties, with a reverse mohawk dyed bright red. Someone who appears to work here, opens the door to the cage. I step in and they lock it behind me. Addison stands on the other side, cracking her knuckles. Neither of us changed into any other attire.

We'll do it as is. She also wears hand wraps and a confident smirk as a voice booms through speakers around us.

"Ladies and Gentlemen! We have a very special treat for you tonight. An exhibition match between our beloved Scrape and a newcomer. A Techno!"

The Neon Devil's voice dominates the crowd. There is a roar of boos and hisses towards me.

"Now I know how you all feel about traitors, not just to our country but to our own species. I assure you he will learn what happens to all Technos when caught!"

A giant cheer erupts. Kanoa joins the crowd quietly. He folds his arms and settles in to watch.

"You know the rules! Only one! What is it?" Mr. Neon asks. Everyone chants in unison.

"Tap out or die!" It sounded ritualistic.

"Everything else is fair game," The Neon Devil says slowly, for dramatic effect.

I look at him. He stands behind a podium three levels up. He hits a button and a loud buzzer sounds. Almost suddenly, I am knocked to the ground on my back. I cough and sit upright. She stands over me. She scoffs in a "are you for real?" kind of way, and kicks me in my side.

"Get up. At least make this entertaining." She holds up her fists. I scramble to my feet, try to punch her, only to be met with a blur of motion and several jabs to my side.
I fall to the ground again only to see her lean against the far side of the cage nonchalantly.

"Fuck." I mumble, climb back to my feet.

A series of blows riddle me as all I see is flashes of light and movement. I can hardly see her as she uses me as a punching bag. Kanoa shifts and moves slowly through the crowd until getting to a less crowded room corner. He focuses on his hand, tries to summon a fireball.

The veins on his head bulge as his hand slowly heats up. His bright blue tattoo shimmers. Tree branches shine in the neon light until suddenly the device on his shoulder chimes and he loses his focus. He grabs his head in pain as the flame fades.

"Fuck," he mutters.

I can hardly keep track of Scrape as she delivers one attack after another. It ends with a trip. I slam hard into the ground! I see spots. The crowd erupts into cheers. I look up to see several of her. Is she moving super fast or is my vision really that blurry?

We aren't in here alone. At the edge of the fight pit, inside the cage with me and Scrape. I see a figure standing perfectly still. Some gentleman in a police officer uniform. How did a cop get in here? Before I can make out his face the figure drops, lifeless to the ground. I don't see the body thud. Instead something small and metal rings out as it makes impact. It's a golden security guard badge.

"No," I mumble.

I quickly scamper to my feet, stagger. My head feels like it's splitting apart. I hold my head in my hands while trying to stay on my feet. Kanoa watches this unfold, with a worrying expression he nudges his way to the back of the crowd and turns on a device.

"Mordecai, be ready to grab us. We need to cause chaos." Kanoa whispers.

"Copy." Mordecai whispers back through this tiny device. With a look of regret, Kanoa flips a switch. The device reads "Encrypted." Kanoa dials a number.

"Prexy Local Division Zone Three Security. Name your emergency and section." A stern male voice states.
Before Kanoa can respond a goon grabs him by his other arm.

"No phones allowed in the fighting pit." A huge security guard says.

Kanoa twists his arm and shoves him to the ground.

"Trace this number if you wanna impress your boss." Kanoa hisses into the device, then hides it under a table. He then dashes to a fire alarm and pulls it. A loud ringing roars as everyone looks around. I look up from the arena floor to see people race to leave.

"What the-?" Scrape notices what's happening. Next thing I know, she's gone in the blink of an eye. Kanoa runs towards me. He tosses me my bag and gun.

"What did you do?" I ask.

"Saved your ass. Can you still fight?" Kanoa shouts.

"Yeah...yeah, I can." I clutch my battered ribs. Together, instead of running, we head deeper into the storage halls. We run by crates and cages filled with all sorts of contraband.

"How deep does this building go?" I shout ahead to Kanoa.

"All I know is it's connected to the underground subway system. That's how he moves cargo. It's also our new exit!" Kanoa hollers back.

After a minute of running we enter a large open area underground. Off to the side I see tracks. Further ahead right at the edge of the area is a tunnel. A train is parked right at the mouth of it. Several cages are already loaded onto the train. Kanoa and I arrive just in time to see Neon and Addison loading more.

"Never could play fair, could you?" Mr. Neon shouts across to us.

"Never liked playing in the first place." Kanoa raises his energy gun. I do the same, but it gets ripped out of my hands. Kanoa's goes flying as well. Scrape reappears next to him, holding both of our firearms. They both step into the subway and the doors close. As it starts up I see the crates they loaded. One of which has a bunch of neighbors looking terrified.

"Z!" I shout as I race towards the subway.

With a loud swoosh it takes off at incredible speed. The air almost knocking me down on my feet.

"Fuck!" I shout. "Dammit!" Kanoa shouts as well. I turn towards him.

"Now what?" I am irate at this point.

"H-hello?" A weak voice rings out. Kanoa and I turn around to look at the crates and cages they didn't have time to take. There was one cage left with humans in it. A woman, frail, skinny, clearly hasn't eaten in awhile owns the voice. Walking closer I'm hit with a stench of filth that makes me want to turn away, but there are two kids in the cage. A boy and a girl. The woman is protecting them, holding her body over them.

"Please let us out," she begs.

"Kanoa?" I am unsure how to proceed.

"I don't see a key anywhere." Kanoa looks around.

After a few minutes of searching we both hear the shouts of soldiers making their way down the building.

"Shit," Kanoa hisses. He runs back towards me.

"Isaac we got to go. We'll have to run down the tunnel on foot." Kanoa says. I ignore him, run back to the cage.

"Okay, we can't find a key, we'll have to cut it open. We'll get you out of there!" I try to reassure her. Her kids look frightened.

"Isaac, we don't have time. They're making their way through the facility. We got to move!" Kanoa says louder. I can hear the footsteps above.

"Just give me a few minutes!" I rummage through my bag, looking for anything to cut through the metal bars.

Suddenly I feel a sharp pain in my shoulder and everything locks up. I can't move my arms, my legs, anything. Kanoa grabs my bag and slings it over his shoulders.

"I'm sorry, but we're going. End of discussion." Kanoa reaches for me and picks me up like a fireman, then starts dashing through the subway tunnel.

"Please, please don't leave us. At least take my children!"

The mother shouts using all of her strength to hold up her children. Her face red with tears, her voice strained. Her two chidren cry helplessly trying to hold onto their mother. Not wanting to be seperated from her. All I can do is watch from my trapped position at the now sobbing mother and children as they grow progressively further from view.

CHAPTER 14

INTERFERE

———

Kanoa has been carrying me for a while. We traveled miles down this subway tunnel until we finally arrive at an unmarked door. He kicks it open effortlessly. Inside is some sort of maintenance room. The layers of dust indicate no one has been in here for years. He lays me down against a pipe as he closes the door behind him. He rummages through his bag. Drops of sweat fall from his forehead. He takes out a radio.

"Mordecai, come in. What's it like up there?" Nothing. Just the sound of static.

"Mordecai come in...Dammit!" Kanoa throws the radio back in his bag.

I am regaining feeling in my jaw and legs as I try to shuffle to my feet, much of my body still paralyzed. What the hell did he hit me with?

"Stay down," Kanoa barks.

"It's just a mild, temporary paralytic. It should wear off soon." He frantically searches around the room for something to bar the door with.

Grunting loudly, he pushes a cupboard in front of it. He then places his ear against the wall to listen.

"Shhh!" He hisses at me as I ignore his command to stay put. I'm now able to fully flex one of my arms.

I try to wake up the other one by slapping it around. Kanoa steadies his breath as a low hum quickly grows until it sounds like it's right outside the door. The room rumbles a bit until it passes by harmlessly.

"Another subway. I don't think they saw us. They would've shut the tunnel down if they had. I think were in the clear now. Z's train went this way so as long as we stay on this track..." Kanoa turns around to meet my fist as I punch him as hard as I can.

He stays on his feet and shoves me back to the ground. Some muscles are still stiff. I fall, not able to fully catch myself.

"What the fuck was that for?" Kanoa holds his nose. I try to climb to my feet again, only to have him kick them out from under me.

"Why did you do that?" I shout. Feeling more blood flow, now I get to my feet. I feebly throw another punch that he dodges easily. He grabs my arm with no effort. I try to throw another punch with my one free hand that he catches and pushes me back.

"What, save our lives? We would've died if I didn't do that!" Kanoa shouts. I let him have it, my vocal chords strain,

"I needed just a few more seconds. I could've had that cage open!" Tears begin forming.

"Then what? Were they going to join us? Did you think that far ahead? They would've only slowed us down. The soldiers were right behind us!"

"You have no right to make those decisions for me!" Tears streak down my face. Kanoa slaps me hard. I wince.

"How dare you. Your actions affect everyone back there! Being in our organization comes with responsibility! You know that. What if you got captured and they learned of Crane's location? Or the powers we have at disposal? It's not just for you and your self-pitying soap opera bullshit!"

"Is that what you think this is about?" Rage consumes me.

"You tell me." Kanoa matches my anger.

"I'm sorry for whatever the fuck my generation did that brought us to where we are today. But in case you forgot, I wasn't a part of that generation. I lost everything. I was ripped out of time. The one thing I have is this amazing technology that lets me live whatever life I wish." Kanoa shakes his head.

"And like so many people, once they start spending more time in there then in the real world they start to forget what is real. I think you have an issue separating them Isaac. Ever since Oakwood, you've been moody and distant. Logging more and more time inside T.R.A.C.I. Running off with Caleb on insane one-in-a-million chance missions. Reckless quest after reckless quest!"

A sharp pain slices through my skull. I grab my head as it begins to pound from all the emotion and adrenaline coursing through me. As the adrenaline wears off the extent of the last hour crashes over me. A strong ache from my ribs grows. I double over clutching myself.

"And those. Don't think we're ignoring that. Ever since last month you've started having headaches, haven't you? I've been putting it aside. But what I just saw in that fight pit..." Kanoa is genuinely worried.

"They haven't been happening in the real world. That was the first time." I am admittedly now feeling a little scared. That felt exactly how it felt inside of T.R.A.C.I.

"Why are you spending so much time in T.R.A.C.I when it's doing that to you?" Kanoa asks.

"It's the only way I can still see him." I choke on my words.

"Isaac, it's not real." Kanoa says softly.

I scowl as I gaze at him. He doesn't know what any of this means to me.

"Says who? Says you? Crane? My mother? I don't care. It's real enough for me." Finally regaining full mobility I turn to face away from him. I'm an ugly crier. I don't want him to see that.

"Isaac, listen to me. I've been where you are. I know how you feel."

"No, you don't! You have no idea what it feels like to be responsible." I could feel my blood boiling, my face getting hot.

"It would be so much easier if Crane would just wipe my memory already." Kanoa has a look of shock.

"You want to forget." Kanoa is surprised. I sit down against the wall, giving up my attempt to hide my face.

"You've been using T.R.A.C.I to numb yourself." Kanoa realizes as he approaches.

"Why won't she just boot me already?" I breaking down with tears. "I'm no help to anybody. I can't fight a war. I couldn't even save my dad. What more do I have to do to get Crane to erase my past? Why won't she do it?"
I look up at Kanoa, my face a mess. Kanoa looks sad as he sits a few feet away.

"It's because of me." Kanoa says. "What? Why?" I stop sobbing for a moment.

"I chose to watch over you. I wanted to be your mentor. Crane gave me full authority over you," Kanoa continues.

"So why, then?" I ask.

"Because I don't think you should forget, Isaac." Kanoa states.

"Why? Because I'm a historian's treasure?" My nose sniffles.

"Because I don't think that's what your father would've wanted for you. I think you should honor your father's memory." Kanoa tries to reason with me.

"Oh, like you know what my father wanted!" I toss it out with an extra helping of spite.

"No, I don't know what he would've wanted. But I know honor. You can't just erase pain." Kanoa reflects.

"Maybe not in my time. But your time has some pretty advanced stuff." A shaky laugh escapes my lips.

"This is your time too. Whether or not you accept that doesn't make it any less true. This is your time now Isaac. Erasing pain now, comes with a price." I rub my face.

"Why do you care?" I turn to face him again. "What?" Kanoa asks.

"Why do you care so much about me? Why go to all this trouble? Why choose to be my mentor. Why look out for me?" I wipe the tears from my face.

Kanoa stays silent then suddenly the radio hums. We scramble to our feet, the moment lost.

"Mordecai! Mordecai, you there?" Kanoa shouts into the radio.

"...Ka......the......away.....base.....change..." While Mordecai's voice tries to get through, the device starts to smoke and spark. Kanoa drops it as he winces. It fizzles, screeches, then stops.

"Great."

Kanoa stomps out the small fire before it becomes dangerous. Guess we're on our own until we can find them. If we got grounded on this job, that means Crane will move the base into the wind.

"But you know where we we're moving next right?"

"I know of a few possible locations. The point is, we need to move." Kanoa walks over to the barricaded door and reaches up with his bad arm.

He winces in pain as he uses his free arm to knock the device embedded in his shoulder.

After a few light hits he regains full mobility in his arm. He pulls the shelf down and opens the door. The subway is dark, only being lit by guide lights alongside the roof and floor of the tunnel.

"Let's move," Kanoa orders. I reluctantly follow.
The tunnel is long. A subway passes every fifteen minutes or so. When we hear it coming we duck into a crevice or service closet. After what feels like hours of walking we both make out a point of light at the end of the tunnel.

"Daylight?" I ponder aloud.

"Just how long have we been walking?" Kanoa doesn't respond. We both pick up the pace.

Once we get closer we have to squint really hard because we have been in darkness for a long time. Once our eyes adjust, we can see where this tunnel led us. It exits to an intricate metallic gate. The subway continues onto a bridge. I can make out a few buildings. But what's surprising is that there is a lot of trees.

"We must be in the Southern district. Neon's place was somewhat close to here. Seems like we closed the distance," Kanoa remarks.

"How do we get through this?" I eyeball the circular gate before us.

"It's on a timer. It opens and closes automatically for the subways. We'll have a short window to climb out after a subway has gone through," Kanoa explains.
I look back the way we came.

"Closest spot to hide is about a hundred feet," I say.

"Guess we'll have to sprint it." Kanoa retorts.

"Just try and stay on the bridge. Don't fall." We head over to the hiding spot and wait. It only takes a few minutes. As we hear the low rumble, We position ourselves on both sides of the track.

As the tunnel shakes several lights flash near the gate. A loud horn blares, and the gate rescinds into the walls. The train comes flying in fast. I have to hold onto the wall to keep my footing. The moment it passes, Kanoa shouts,

"Now!"

We book it with all of our might towards the gate. Kanoa easily beats me. The bag on my back flies around wildly but stays strapped to me. As we close half the distance I hear the same loud horn ring out as the gate slowly reveals itself. Kanoa gets through before the bottom portion assembles. He looks back, and yells

"Run, Isaac!"

I feel my muscles burn. I go as fast as I can. As I get about fifteen feet away I realize I'm going to have to leap over it or I won't get through. I throw my backpack over it and with the last bit of energy I have I launch myself over the forming gate. I slip though just as the final pieces set in place. I throw my arms out to brace for the fall but Kanoa catches me. I knock him on his back from the sheer force of my dive. I roll off of him.

"Ow!" He laughs. "You're a bony ass dude. You need to eat more!" I laugh too.

"Neon wasn't the first person to call me twig in my life." We both laugh harder. After a good few seconds we gather ourselves and our things.

"Oh, wow!" I gaze out to the cold winter morning. "That's the Brooklyn Bridge." I point out just a short distance away towards the now broken and fallen historical sight. Its mangled but I can identify it because one of the bridge markers is still standing.

"And that...is a forest." I am bewildered. Looking past the Brooklyn Bridge, all of the city that used to be there is now tall, fully grown trees and grass.

There are a few buildings still standing but they have nature overgrown all over them and are heavily damaged. Truly a sight to behold.

"Yeah it's a beauty. Also a deadly forest. Rumors of Techno's and wild Neighbors live out past that river over there." Kanoa points off into the distance.

"The further we are from that the better." Kanoa states. Kanoa pats me on the back.

"Let's go. With any luck I can get in contact with Crane before nightfall." We sprint steadily along a high subway bridge overlooking the greater part of the city and this newly grown forest.

"There are a lot more bridges around New York then I remember!" I yell up to Kanoa.

"Ninety odd years. Even though there was a war, plenty of things can happen!" Kanoa shouts back.

I chuckle as I look ahead. This particular subway bridge is connected to an impressive series of new bridges that all seem to stem from an island near where Lady Liberty used to be. Governor's Island, I think it used to be called. Now it has that massive structure I saw when I first arrived; Prime Center.

A giant white marble building that reaches far above the clouds. I'm bewildered by the sight, how it doesn't even have a bottom. The center building is supported from four similar towers circling it.

So close to the forest it must be a fortress. Good thing we are heading away from it. We are walking north up the bridges back towards the city when suddenly I hear a faint chirping. Not like a wild animal. This sounded strangely familiar.

"Kanoa!" I shout, but he doesn't hear me.
He's gotten pretty far ahead while I was admiring the structure. I hear it again. Whooshing. Like the air starting to move really quickly.

I look up just in time to see a blur swoop down from above and football tackle Kanoa. He is thrust right off the bridge with the figure still holding on.

"Kanoa!" But then it's my turn. I am tackled hard against my side by an unforeseen force. I fall. Right before I hit the water I am stopped, held in place by something...invisible? I get an angle of Kanoa, in an identical predicament. As two young-looking Neighbors enter my field of view, their screeching and chittering echoes in my ears.

"Neighbors." I mumble.

"Friends! Allies!" I shout, but whatever they trapped us with is blocking any sound.

The younger of the two gets close to my face. His eyes are a different color then Z's. I thought they all had the same eye color? The older one screeches, pulls him back. He points off somewhere I can't see then he produces a blindfold.

"C'mon," I am annoyed now, as the older one puts a blind-fold on Kanoa then heads my way.

"Neck, look at my neck!" If he hears me, he ignores me. Nothing. I am blindfolded, then a hard pain across my temple. Everything goes black.

CHAPTER 15

THE FLOWER ROOM

A quiet knock on the door snaps Abigail out of her deep thought. She shakes her head and walks over. Peering through the peephole, an excited and slightly exhausted Dr. Kim waves from the other side. Abigail hesitantly shifts the bolt to unlock the door. With a cautious open, Abigail greets her new scientist. Dr. Kim is shorter than her.

With short black hair and similar rounded glasses. He is wearing a jacket with the Infinite Horizons Logo embroidered on the front. He is strangely sweaty and out of breath. He has a laptop bag slung around his shoulders and is lugging a small suitcase.

"Come in," Abigail rubs her temple.
Dr. Kim enters, sets his bags on the couch in the corner and turns back to face Abigail.

"It is an honor to finally meet you!" Kim says with a big smile as he holds out his hand to shake. Abigail reluctantly does so.

"The Prexy assigned your lab in the east wing," she says dismissively.

"Oh, I saw. Remarkable work area. I just wanted to stop by and meet you in person.

I have to say your work with cryogenics is what inspired me to become a scientist. I am a huge admirer of your work."

"Thank you." Abigail tries to sound polite. She wants nothing more than for him to leave right now.

"As I'm told, you also have work that I'm sure is inspiring others." Dr Kim suddenly remembers something.

"Ah, yes! Another reason why I am here. The Prexy asked us to pool our information and knowledge so I'd like to show you something I have been working on!"

Dr. Kim sits on the couch and grabs his laptop. He puts his feet up on the glass coffee table and begins typing away excessively. Agitated, Abigail walks over.

Suddenly the TV comes to life with a security camera feed of a room with brown walls, and a cast iron bed with a bare mattress. A man is lying in the bed. He is tossing and turning. Clearly uncomfortable, sick almost. Only one other thing is in the room. A circular table with two items on it. A vase with one single flower and a gun. Another screen shows the same man inside of a cryogenic pod.

"This is a TRACI simulation." Abigail studies the two scenes on the monitor.

"Yes!" Dr. Kim exclaims, excitedly.

"You see. While your work, doctor, is brilliant, there was always a part of it that bothered me. Why do subjects wake up when they die?"

"The brain can't take the trauma of death. Even simulated to the level the system provides. It doesn't matter if it's the real or virtual world. Killing a subject in TRACI causes the system to dump all of the data it's collected and reboot the program so that the subject's brain may be saved. A round of anesthesia is administered at the moment of death in TRACI so the system can disconnect from the subject's electrical signals without harm."

"Exactly. That is very kind and humanitarian of you, Doctor. And S-Transfers I assume are the same principle? The receiving subject has to be dead?"

"Forty-Eight hours after, or a comatose patient, yes. We've been processing more transfers then ever. They wind up being our most elite soldiers due to the reconditioning factor." Abigail reflects on her part in making that technology possible.

"Exactly. Essentially a backup drive for a human brain." Kim says.

"Technically...immortality." He hints at.

"Not quite." Abigail corrects. "I've never seen a subject survive a second S-Transfer. The brain takes enough toll adjusting to a completely different body than the one it grew in. That second body will still age and die. We can extend an individuals life but not make them immortal. After all we have to take the entire brain." Kim shifts gears.

"Doctor. Have you ever considered what TRACI could be capable of if you take bigger risks?" He hits a button and shows the same room but with a different time stamp. The display reads: Day Eleven. The man in the bed suddenly shoots out of his disturbing slumber. He is an extremely skinny human with dark circles around his eyes, wearing a shirt with the number 187. He stumbles around the room, delirious.

"What we consider reality is simply our brain responding to five simple senses. T.R.A.C.I allows someone else to control those senses. And what do you call someone who controls every aspect of one's reality?"

"A God." Abigail mutters as Subject 187 screams his head off.

He looks to the gun, grabs it, and shoots himself in the head. The screen freezes, then cuts to the guy back asleep in the bed. "What just happened?"

Abigail asks confused as the guy wakes up. His face looks mortified. He screams as he jumps out of the bed and suddenly bashes himself with the gun, which he takes off the table.

"The program should have brought him out of it. How is he still in there?" Abigail asks.

"This is his sixth iteration in the Flower Room. A program I designed to make the subject lose all concepts of reality."

"He's died six times in the program?" Abigail eyes grow big.

She stares into the monitor while the guy sobs uncontrollably and pulls the trigger again ending his life yet again. He falls to the ground limply. The screen flickers and like replaying a tape, he is back in bed. He wakes up almost immediately and bashes his head against the wall, screaming in agony and frustration. Abigail notices two separate stop watches in the corner of the screen.

"He's been in a booth for over a month straight!" Abigail is amazed.

"A hundred and thirty-seven accelerated days T.R.A.C.I time." Kim is impressed with his own work.

"How? His lactic acid should be through the roof."

"Oh it is, he is severely malnourished and dehydrated. Good thing he dies just about...now."

As Kim says this a warning buzzer and flatline ring out around the pod as the monitor goes dark. Dr. Kim smiles eagerly at Abigail.

"I started studying the brain at a very young age, doctor. Thanks to your work I was able to realize the next steps in human evolution."

Kim puts on surgical gloves, reaches into his bag and removes a translucent bright blue orb shaped item.

"Please," He gestures to a second pair of gloves. Abigail puts them on. He hands the fragile piece of equipment to her.

She inspects it closely. It has a glimmering, iridescent shimmer to it with zeros and ones flicking around inside.

"What is this?" Abigail asks. Dr. Kim smiles.

"Test subject 187."

Abigail's eyes widen again. "You mean?" Abigail starts.

"You are holding a person's consciousness." Kim beams.

"How?" Abigail asks amazed. "Anyone can be a god. You just have to perform a miracle." Kim states emphatically.

"This is a portable, fully alive human that has the ability to be plugged into a T.R.A.C.I booth with ease. We no longer require massive booths and expensive machinery to sedate and tame the human body."

"Where did the last hundred and eighty-six test subjects come from?" Abigail asks suspiciously.

Kim doesn't reply. Nor does he need to as the item in Abigail's hand is capturing her full attention. Guess it doesn't really matter anyway.

"An active, alive human brain. In my hand." Abigail's mind races at the world implications and possibilities stemming from this singular object in her palm.

"How much digital space do you think a human consciousness takes?" Kim asks.

"I'm assuming you know the answer to that now." Abigail says almost in a whisper.

"Five Petabytes. Half for all of the potential memory of a human brain. The other half is for the software needed to interface with the T.R.A.C.I system. A decent bit but manageable. The trick is moving the data. The thought patterns, the brain chemistry. One surgical procedure while the subject is in a specifically designed program within T.R.A.C.I and I can extract and remove their consciousness, leaving behind a body for S-Transfers, doctor."

"This subject remembered all their previous iterations? What are they feeling right now?" Abigail holds up this baseball-shaped object.

"No idea. I like to think they are dreaming." Kim shuts down the monitors. Abigail stares deeply into the orb.

"The Prexy is already made aware. She wants us to perfect this process before the election." Kim reports.

"What? Why?" Abigail snaps out of it, placing the ball back into it's case carefully.

"C'mon, doctor, you are smart. You know as well as I do election times are the most intense. The Prexy wants more options available," Kim explains.

"If I have anything I'll let you know. Thank you, doctor." Abigail dismisses Kim.
Reluctantly, he gathers his things and leaves. Out in the hall he opens a phone and dials a number.

"No. No I'll need more time." Kim heads back to his office. He stands in the hall away from passing scientists and soldiers.

"If she is hiding something it will take time as I'm sure you can understand. You have put us under a serious deadline here. I am balancing a lot of plates as it is." He takes a moment to listen to what the other person is saying.

"Uh-huh. Yeah. No, I understand it's just-" He stops and looks at his phone to see the caller has hung up.

"It's just you want your cake and to eat it too." Kim mumbles to himself, resuming his walk down the hall.

"Politicians." He mutters, annoyed.

CHAPTER 16

ENEMY OF MY ENEMY

On the shivering-cold streets of The Central Zone, a bundled-up man is walking down a empty street. His several layers give the impression that he is unaffected by the current weather. The north end of the city is the closest to the forest. As such, that is where the biggest walls and defenses are located. Invaders from the west and north are the most common to The Central Zone's residents, so that is where the biggest police and I.H.L presence are.

The man shuffles past a few beggars asking for any food or money. The clothes they wear are soaked with oil and dirt. Faces cut and bruised from fighting over scraps and warmth. He looks up. The sidewalk ahead has a police barricade checking I.D's and only allowing certain people to pass. The man grumbles and takes a detour down a grisly-looking alleyway. Broken glass and various splotches of unknown substances freeze over the pathway. He covers his nose to avoid any possible odor. He walks for a bit until coming by a door that opens from the inside, no handle visible.

He knocks on it five consecutive times. After waiting a bit, they door opens, but only a small crack.

"Sure is shit out there." A quiet but clear and concise female voice beckons from within.

The voice on the other side of the door says. The man looks down at a crumpled, folded piece of paper, then looks back up.

"It'd be nicer if I was dead." He replies. The door opens fully now showing Scrape.

"I'm here to meet The Neon Devil." The man removes a few layers of protective clothing, showing his face and revealing Arthur's poorly-maintained five o'clock shadow.

"This way." Scrape holds the door for him.

He enters and she closes and locks the door behind him. Inside it is almost pitch black. The only source of light is several random neon signs emitting a soft buzz. After walking a bit of a ways, Scrape steps in front of another secondary door.

"Strip." Scrape orders.

Confused, Arthur squirms for a moment. "I don't even know your name." He tries to crack a joke.

"Addison but people call me Scrape. If you're carrying any weapons it's in your best interest to hand them over," Addison explains.

Arthur, still grumbling, fumbles with his jackets until Addison grows impatient and uses her ability to frisk him at lightning-fast speed. He is only able to process it after it's over.

He pats his sides looking for his blaster. But she is holding it, along with the rest of his belongings. The kid's M1911 pistol, a knife and wallet.

"How did-?" He is amazed. She cuts him off.

"You enhanced?" she asks.

"Enhanced?" Arthur replies. "I don't understand." He shakes his head.

"Never mind." Addison takes out a device that looks, and in fact is, a scanner. With the press of a button she sweeps Arthur. At first, he doesn't understand what is happening, and is unnerved. The device finishes and beeps twice.

"Negative for any Verve. Okay, you're clear to pass." Addison unlocks the door and opens it.

Arthur nervously proceeds. His coats are now beginning to betray him as the interior is properly warmed inside. As he unbuttons a few layers a voice calls out to him.

"What's your business?" The Neon Devil steps into view. Arthur eyes him up and down.

"Are you The Neon Devil?" Arthur asks.

"You must be Johnson. Except your file says your legal name is Arthur Powell, if my informants are truthful?"

"They are. I never liked the nickname." Arthur grumbles.

"I'm sure you earned it for a reason." Neon scoffs.

"We've been arranged to meet due to a common interest." Arthur attempts to move on.

"And what would that be?" Neon is intrigued. Arthur reaches into his pocket before realizing. He turns to the woman who escorted him in.

"Can I have my wallet back?" He asks.

With no expression she hurls his wallet back to him. He catches it and pulls out a physical photograph of Isaac, pulled from one of the security cameras at Oakwood. Neon's smug smile turns to an angry frown.

"How do you know him?" Neon asks. "How do you know him?" Arthur fires back.

"That punk caused me a lot of grief. Shut down one of my locations." Neon grits his teeth. Arthur smiles.

"Then your informant deserves a raise. I'm looking for him." He explains.

"What would you do if you find him?" Neon asks.

"That's my business." Arthur states flatly. Neon shifts gears.

"Have you ever killed before?" Neon asks. Not fully surprised at that question. Arthur wastes no time.

"When necessary."

Neon picks up the pace of his questioning.

"How recently?" Arthur not even flinching.

"Two weeks ago." Neon folds his arms. "I can tell. You have the look. Personally I would like to see this kid cease breathing. Him with a few others he's running with who've crossed me." Neon says.

"He's one of two targets for me." Arthur says. "Who's your other target?" Neon asks.

"Madam Secretary." He says nonchalantly. Neon does a double take.

"Are you high? Secretary to The Prexy? You got some sort of death wish?" Neon exclaims.

"Something like that, yeah. Can you help me or not?" Neon rubs the back of his head.

"She's the bigger target for sure. That one will take a bit longer. I for one like living. It suits me. And I am quite profitable under her and the Prexy's regime. Perhaps I feel a tad loyal." Neon proclaims. Arthur looks unimpressed.

"The kid however, he's a bit easier. The group he's running with? They're people I used to work with. I still have some old contacts and favors to call in."

"So what's stopping you?" Arthur pushes some buttons. Neon scowls, somewhat annoyed.

"Take a look around. We're in-between locations." Neon spreads his arms to show off the shabby, hastily-put-together area.

"I can get you some supplies. Some of my old access codes still work for a few warehouses I know the locations of." Arthur offers. Neon grins.

"Beautiful, limitless government spending." Neon chimes.

"I'll be honest with you when they told me a disgraced ex-officer was looking for me I just thought it was another recruiting drive." He says amused.

"We can look for the kid. The Secretary? Don't hold your breath." Neon continues now changing tone.

"It's a start, then." Arthur says as he holds out his hand to shake. Neon accepts it.

"Looks like we're in business." Neon says. Addison brings in a metal briefcase. She sets it on a table in-between them and stands off to the side.

"What's this?" Arthur asks. "A gift. To celebrate this partnership." Neon replies.

After a series of locks and clips, Addison opens the case. A bright blue florescent glow fills the area. Arthur picks up the vial of Verve.

"Verve is getting too risky to move right now with the elections coming up. Security is stepping up their game. And this was my last dose anyway," Neon explains.

"Is it true it gives people abilities?" Arthur asks.

Neon smirks and nods to Addison. In a blur she returns all of his items onto his person, then she blinks right back into place where she was. Arthur notices his items back as he pats himself down.

"Amazing," He remarks.

"The trick is to integrate with it properly. Those religion-obsessed freaks ingest it. Says it gives them visions." Neon laughs.

"So, what is the right way? Inhaling it?" Arthur asks. Neon scoffs.

"Intravenously."

He holds out his hand to ask for the vial. Johnson hands it over. Addison hands Neon an auto-syringe.

Neon takes the vial and sticks it into the device and shakes it. The verve shifts radically into liquid form.

"It's more intense to be introduced straight into your bloodstream. More potent for your brain to begin to reproduce." Neon explains as he tosses the auto-syringe now filled with Verve back to Arthur.

He stares at the magical liquid in the tube. Its bright blue glow shimmers and sparkles in the container.

"Don't you want an ability?" Arthur offers it back to Neon.

"I was part of the unlucky group. Body wasn't built for it." Neon explains, tracing the scar on his face.

"So, it's a gamble." Arthur realizes.

"Get a cool power, or nothing, or be disabled or damaged like this." Neon gestures to himself.

"Although, I have to say I think I pull off the scar quite well." Addison rolls her eyes.

Arthur looks back down at the device. He slowly brings it to his arm and aims. Then fully committing, he plunges the needle into his arm. The verve drains from the cylinder. Johnson drops it and with a sudden burst of energy, he jumps off the ground.

"Wow, that's brisk." He says.

His heart begins to race. Unsure if it's from the Verve or his adrenaline. A cold fuzzy feeling climbs up his arm, up his neck until the freezing feeling reaches behind his eyes. He grabs his head.

"Worst brain freeze ever" He remarks.

"Remember, powers aren't guaranteed. If you're gonna get one it can take as long as a month to show or as soon as tomorrow." Neon reminds.

"Yeah, yeah, sure." Arthur looks all around him. His vision begins to blur a bit as his pupils dilate.

"It feels amazing!" He practically shouts.

"It's also not something meant to get hooked on." Neon cautions. "It's meant as a one-shot. This stuff is incredibly valuable. What you are feeling right now is temporary."
Neon puts a hand on his shoulder. Arthur looks back at him and nods.

"Addison will show you around. There's still enough sensible business folks under me that we can still run the majority of this city." Neon proclaims.

"Tomorrow you will show us those warehouses." Addison opens the door for Arthur.
He makes his way out and follows her into their main area for their temporary base.

"What's your beef with the kid?" Addison asks.

"My business." He says rather rudely. "Why do you want him dead?" Addison presses.

"What's it to you?" Arthur walks past her.

"I'll find my way around, thank you." He brushes past Addison and explores around the main area.
An annoyed Addison heads back to Neon's office. She opens the door without any warning.

"I don't like him." Addison says.

"You don't like half the people we work with." Neon barely pays attention to her. He is face down in documents.

"Half the people we hire turn on us." Addison says bluntly.

"Hazards of the business." Neon finally pulls his gaze from the paperwork.

"What's really bothering you?"

"Something's off with him. He's rubbing me the wrong way. I don't think you should've given him that dose." Addison says.

"It was about to expire anyway." Neon says carelessly.

"The odds of him actually getting an ability were less then fifty-fifty.

That particular dose made his chance more like one in ten."

"And the odds of him getting hurt from it?" Addison asks. Neon just shrugs and does a motion with his hands imitating balancing scales.

Arthur walks around for a little. This warehouse appears to have been an old manufacturing plant. Creating what he has no clue. Conveyor belts snake through the facility like an intricate maze. The floor office has been repurposed into a makeshift commissary. A couple people nod acknowledging his presence.

Others pay no interest. After awhile he decides to step aside into a broom closet. He sets his pack down and notices his photos. One of him and his son Carter, arms over the shoulders. Then he sees the security shot of Isaac. Holding the still, Johnson's blood pumps. His anger grows.

He begins to crumple the photograph, as he does so a porcelain paper weight on a desk, made to look like a bird begins to rattle and shake. Pieces of porcelain chip and fly off it. Not even noticing it, he rips the photograph out of sheer anger. The figure shatters into pieces, startling Arthur. He approaches, and picks up the head of the bird in sheer astonishment.

"Woah." He says, amazed.

CHAPTER 17

THE COMMUNITY

———

Any doctor worth their salt would tell you it's not a good habit to be regularly knocked unconscious. Unfortunately, the last doctor I saw tried to kill me so I don't really trust them right now. But I'm not a fan of waking up with a splitting headache either. Something just as bad as rousing with a throbbing head? Being tied up.

Can't believe some people pay for this experience. I wouldn't recommend it. When I first come to, the first thing I notice is wood. Lots of lumber around me. I smell mothballs. The taste of iron staining my mouth. It looks like a shed. My arms are bound, crisscross-style around a cast iron frame. It looks like it was part of a bed once. It's loose. I'm able to shuffle to my feet but I can't hold my pounding head.

There is a wooden door on the other side of the room. I drag the bedframe towards it. I'm trying to find my footing. Finally I manage to get a foot from the door when in walks in a Neighbor. He is hulkingly large. His eyes are bright neon green and he is wearing a type of armor I have not seen before. At first I think it's leather but then I note the strange colorations around the chest and back.

Various parts of the getup seem to be furry almost. As if this chest plate was made up of a dozen different animals. It's wild looking and makes me guess at their intelligence. Are they like Z? Or are they more primitive?

"I could use a hand here." I jiggle my arms.

He scowls and unsheathes a knife. I lock up as he approaches. He cuts my binds and the bedframe falls to the ground with a hard slam. Rubbing my wrists, I try to look past him towards the door but he moves to block my vision. With an ear splitting screech he points towards a brown sack lying in the corner of the room. Guess he doesn't trust me yet.

Not surprised. I stagger over, keeping my eyes trained on him and grab it. Inside is a small question mark shaped device. It looks like a hearing aid, but nothing from my generation. The bag is filled with them. I hold one up to the guy.

"I don't understand," I say.

He screeches again and points to his ear. So I was right. It's an ear piece. For what I haven't the slightest. I fiddle around with it until awkwardly placing it inside my left ear. Thinking I did it right. It shoots out a quick puff of air, startling me, then it settles into a low buzz.

The gentleman who is built like a tank stands off to the side of the door. In walks another alien, a lot smaller - around my height. Skinny. He address me directly.

"I've been instructed to communicate with you using your language until you meet with our leader. Do you understand?" His voice shrill, yet elegant. Almost like a butler.

"Where is my friend? You grabbed two of us." I ignore this shrimp's question. He hisses and raises a hand to signal Tank, who subsequently grabs me by my arm and begins escorting me out. It's nighttime. I immediately get a whiff of fresh air. We are outside. Looking around we appear to be in a forest.

It must be the one Kanoa and I saw from the bridge. We are standing on wooden logs and planks. It's some kind of network of treehouses. Our sources of light being woven all throughout this place via lanterns and old building fixtures. Anything that is built to give light is here. It's an impressive collection of illumination.

Tank and his English-speaking friend lead me through several paths until arriving at what looks like the center of the wooded city. A massive hut is built around a hulking, thick tree. We are the last to arrive, as apparently my arrival was meant to be a city-wide event. Several hundred Neighbors are here, either on the main platform with us or watching from other, smaller platforms. Some hang from trees or using makeshift ropes and ladders to create new pathways to view.

"Holy..." I mumble.

Arriving at our destination I see four Neighbors sitting outside the big hut. They strike me as the ones in charge. I look to my side where Kanoa stands ten feet away. He is also being constrained by a big Neighbor.

"Kanoa!" I shout. The Tank escorting me jabs me in my side and Kanoa looks over with a face that says

"Shut up". I've learned that one well. One of the four leaders, an older male, stands. Everyone silences themselves and bow. I'm forced to my knees. The older male raises his hand. Everyone who is sitting rises to their feet in proud unison.

"Humans. We caught you both entering our territory." Kanoa and I share a look of oh shit.

"Per our conditions any human caught wandering our lands would normally be executed upon sight." He wears a scary, emotionless glare.

"However. My daughter has informed me that you two are the reason she is alive."

"Wait, what?" I exclaim. I see movement behind them as an all-too familiar neighbor steps forward. She is dressed like everyone else in various animal furs and leather.

"Z!" I shout happily! "We've been monitoring those vessels that travel along our borders. Rescuing any of our kind as we see them. Can you imagine my delight to happen upon my own flesh and blood?" He says as Z approaches the four elders. They must be her family.

"And then! She tells me to stick around for you two. Apparently you were trying to rescue her. Is this true?"

"It is." Kanoa speaks up. The Neighbor seems to smile and turns to Z. He places both hands on her face and screeches in their own language. Their species language reminds me a lot of how birds talk to each other. They do have scales after all. What exactly are they in comparison to humanities understanding of the animal kingdom?

"Then you are not trespassers. You are friends. You have my welcome." He screeches out to the entire city listening and everyone erupts into some communal timed screech. Kanoa and I cover our ears during some of it. After that everyone watching seem to depart off to their own duties. The only ones that remain are Z, her family, and Kanoa and me.

"Perhaps we should introduce ourselves. My name is Baix. This is my wife Norx. And these are our two youngest, Hillo and Nax." Baix says gesturing to everyone. The two other Neighbors, both young in age, jump out of their seats and chant.

"Guests, guests, guests, guests!" They begin circling Kanoa and me.

"Apologizes they are easily excitable." Norx explains.

"It's okay." I assure. I bend over to greet them when the device falls out of my ear and onto the ground.

"The devices disrupt your brain's signal for detecting

verve. Renders any ability you might have moot. It was just for our safety. You no longer need to wear those. I'm sure you understand." Z's father explains.

"We do." Kanoa takes his out and pockets it. I do the same.

"Z." I approach her but she recoils and retreats back into the hut.

"She is still a little strained from the events of today. Please, it would be our honor to have you as our guests." Norx says.

"Of course." I don't wait for Kanoa to tell us what we'll be doing next. He politely but begrudgingly nods in agreement.

"Perfect!" Norx claps. "Please," she gestures for us both to enter the hut.

Inside I am amazed at the complete tree house vibe these guys are rocking. Almost everything is made of wood except some cooking instruments. They have a fireplace. It's well-built and protected with rocks and clay. They funnel the smoke through a skylight above us.

I look around and see various bits and bobs of random things. Guess that's something our species have in common. We hate throwing stuff away. I see a book in some language I don't understand. I look at it when the mother calls out again.

"Dinner's ready. We've had it ready for you for a while now. Sorry for all the cloak and dagger." She says cheerfully.

"Trust me, we get it." I say walking over to their table. They have an actual dining room table. Kanoa and I sit next to each other while the neighborly five circle around us into the rest of the seats.

"Thank you. Not just for dinner but for rescuing us and Z." Kanoa and I then introduced ourselves as well. Baix asked us about our roles as resistance fighters. We gave him as little information as possible without insulting him, which I'm sure he understood. Then he told me about himself, and his story.

Apparently Z's family and this whole community have lived on earth their whole lives. Baix tells us about how he was the first generation to be born here. His father arrived on the ship. He was told story after story about their home planet and I grew increasingly interested.

"So it's true then? You all want to return to your homeward?" I eventually ask. I notice Z shuffle awkwardly.

"Well, I don't presume to speak for my entire species. While yes at one point our numbers here were beginning to grow again, we've long since had changes of opinions range amongst us." He is a bit more sullen as he reflects on this last point.

"Which is why I wanted to ask-" Baix is abruptly cut off by his wife.

"Leave it alone," she says rather sternly.

"No, it's okay. Ask us what?" I say. His eyes light up he leans forward in his seat.

"Do you know where our ship is?" He asks excitedly.

"Your ship?" Is he asking me about the one his whole species arrived in?

"Yes. The one my father's generation arrived in. Our community — we've stayed alive by staying out of sight. We thought we might find salvation here but have only been given hardship and practical re-extinction. We challenged your natural food chain."

"Why do you want it back?" Kanoa asks.

"Well for starters, it's our property. After the culling we lost several of our major inventions and vehicles we brought with us. Your people seized everything we had, left us for dead." He gets angrier. "What would you do with it?" I ask. Baix sits quietly for a moment.

"We would like to return home." Baix reaches out and holds his wife's hand.

"We're sorry we ever invaded your world. We've only brought pain and suffering to us both. I do not wish the extinction of who we are. None of us do. We would like to leave in peace." She says sweetly.

"Z is one of our strongest soldiers." He gazes at her. "If things continue as they are, Hillo and Nax are to follow and become just as strong as her. I do not wish for my children to fight in a war. I do not wish to bury my children."

"Unfortunately, we have no idea where your ship is being stored." Kanoa says. This prompts Z to storm out of the hut. Everyone looks confused.

"I'll go talk to her." I excuse myself from the table.
I follow Z outside to see her looking out at all the treehouses. Being deep into the forest you'd think you would only see trees but due to the height of these treehouses I can make out the city skyline It twinkles softly in the night sky, creating an artificial star belt along the horizon. Prime Center acting like a smaller moon. It stands out.

"You're alive." I say, relieved. She stays silent.

"We saw the video of that botched recruitment drive. I thought you were honestly dead." I continue. Still no response. "You can't still possibly be mad at me." I use our telepathic link.

"Except I am!" She shouts out loud.

How? This was months ago now! It was a few days after Oakwood. When I was debriefing everyone about what I had learned from my mother. When I mentioned what my mother said about how their world is un-returnable, Z became enraged. Saying how it's not true and it's just another one of my mother's tricks. Sometimes though I am able to read my mother. She uses genuine expressions sparingly so they are easy to notice. I don't want to believe her. But I had trouble believing she is lying.

"You of all people should know you can't blame me for my mother's actions." I shout trying to bring the conversation back to some privacy by using our telepathy.

"I did everything for you and your father!" Z quotes my mother's logs from our interaction in T.R.A.C.I. Z is not interested in talking unless it's out loud.

"I didn't ask for this!" I defend myself.

"Your mother has killed millions." Z states rather coldly. "What sort of punishment do you think she deserves?"
I stare at her in disbelief. "That's not my call to make."

"Then whose is it? She made the call to lock me in there! To torture me, experiment on me! You know we don't get reasons as to why we get locked up in your flying fortresses. With humans at least it's because they did something. Committed a crime or something. The only thing we ever did was search for a new home!" She turns back to stare at the city skyline.

"You still haven't told me what she did to you." I try to console her.

"It wasn't always her." Z clarifies. Backing off a bit. "There was someone else a couple times. Some man. I don't remember much about my time with them. Only that whenever I came to, I was nauseous, my head was in terrible pain. They kept finding new reasons to hurt me over and over again. Only to bring me back less every time."

"I'm sorry." That sounds terrible. What could possibly be the purpose of all of that?

"You can't tell my parents what your mother said. It would kill my father's hope and that's all we have going for us here. Don't take away what little hope we still believe in." Z pleads.

"I won't. C'mon, let's go back inside." I gesture.

We enter together. The rest of the meal goes by as well as you'd expect, when you meet parents for the first time. Despite being wanted criminals and different species of animals. After the dinner Kanoa stands.

"Thank you for your generous hospitality. But Isaac and I really should be getting back now." Kanoa insists. I give him a look. Are we not bringing Z?

"Oh, I'm sorry. It's too unsafe to travel at this hour. We are about a days' distance from the city. Our next group won't be heading out for a few days." Baix says.

"You're more then welcome to stay until it's safe again." Norx adds. Kanoa and I look at each other, unsure.

"Crane knows we're in the wind. What's a few more days?" I croak. Kanoa groans, and steps out of the hut. Z follows him.

"I'm sorry. We're all a bit strained. Thank you." I stand.

"You're free to explore the area and any of the structures on the ground. Find someplace comfortable." Norx nods and Baix smiles. I exit and look for my companions, and spot them.

"You could be a little kinder to them you know. They did save our lives." I say.

"They dragged us into the woods away from Crane and everyone." Kanoa bickers.

"They could've killed us, now we're allies. That can only be good for us." I cross my arms and join the watch party. The city in the distance gleams in the night like sparkling diamonds.

"Maybe." Kanoa begrudgingly agrees. "I just don't want to spend any more time in this jungle then we have to."

CHAPTER 18

OUR WAY OF LIFE

———

We call ourselves Dimechions. It's as synonymous to me as Isaac is to being called a human. It's the name of our race. Our planet was called Trikatta. Or so I'm told. I wasn't raised in a world where I was the dominant species on the planet. Hearing the stories of how we used to be on another planet. It's easy to understand why I dreamed about my home planet most nights. What was the atmosphere like?

The land masses? What did our cities and infrastructure look like? Father says our current home reminds him of stories his father told him about some smaller communities we had on Trikatta. Isaac calls it the best treehouse mazes ever constructed! It's simply an interconnected network of various huts and houses all supported, lofted up about fifty to a hundred feet from the ground. But we have some structures on the floor-level as well.

Our entire camp is as big and wide as the Staples Center, Isaac tells me. I don't know what a Staples Center is. But it's outside and wide open. It was amusing to watch him walk around in amazement. These are multiple story houses made of wooden planks, with windows crafted from randomly-found assorted glass. Lights are strung and woven through the railings and buildings all over.

The daily routine is simple. Training. Mentor and teach the children. Tend to and aid the public. Everyone pitches in on every job here. That way we all learn to take care of everything and everyone. We're taught how to grow and clean food. How to properly manage store and distribute it. We are taught basic electronics and how machines factor into our survival. How to properly set up our solar panels.

We have an impressive display that peak out of the trees. Cleverly hidden enough to not be noticed but still in direct enough sunlight to provide a sufficient power source. Lastly we are taught how to fight. That wasn't a necessity on our world. But ever since arriving here. Everyone is trained in one area of combat.

Today however I am showing Isaac and Kanoa around. I'm happy they came to rescue me. This however has created some problems. It's not like I didn't want to find my family. I did! However knowing what I know now changes everything. Our home world is un-returnable, I don't want to believe it but I believe Isaac. Why would he lie about something like that?

And Crane's faction would be a good bet to find our ship. I don't want to tell mother and father. And I don't want that ship found. Headaches. I'm so sick of headaches. Sort the numbers. Add the numbers. forty-seven, thirty-three, seventy-one, One Hundred Fifty-One. Better.

"How many of you are in this colony?" Kanoa asks. We have made our way to the main area. The biggest tree was carved out in the middle to make room for our market and a training ground.

"Almost three thousand last I knew." I replied.

"Impressive." Kanoa responds. "Too bad they're not all soldiers," He muses under his breath. I roll my eyes.

We don't openly show our skills and abilities unlike another race I know of. One that loves showing all their cards right away or how I once heard Mordecai explain it. Dick measuring.

A couple children run by on a lower level. Probably off to more lessons. They're honestly just like human children, smaller versions of the adults. Learning about the cruel world awaiting them.

"So how did you get off the train?" Isaac asks.

"It was a scout group that saw me. Managed to pull me off the train without Neon noticing. I told them that we should wait around for you guys. Glad you were right behind us." They really are reckless. I realize.

"Over here is the classroom," I point. "This is where we teach the children and adults. The basics and how to fight if they want." I explain while walking onto one of our bigger fighting rings.

One of several situated around the main building. Off on a few circles I see small groups practicing their fighting and abilities with staves. Peering inside the building I am hit with a tad of nostalgia. A dozen small neighbors sitting in a circle. Listening carefully to an adult.

"Z, do your people prefer melee over ranged weapons?" Kanoa asks.

"We try our best to avoid ranged conflict. Melee applies to much more situations you may face in life," I explain.

"Still. Can't hurt to know how to fire a gun." Kanoa remarks.

"We use what we have." I say rather sharply. Suddenly the doors to the classroom open and dozens of children filter out, run around and play on the empty fighting rings. I feel one tug at my pants. I look down to see a child no taller than three feet. He turns and looks at Kanoa and Isaac.

Scared he hides behind me. "Um, hello." Isaac says awkwardly. The child puts two fingers on the back of their neck and taps twice. Remembering, Isaac does the same. They smile and run away.

"Oh, yeah I forgot." Isaac says, rubbing the back of his neck.

"You didn't cover your mark today." Kanoa says.

"They saw it so they consider you a friend." I explain to him.

"I'm still a friend even without it." Isaac remarks. "And people who are our enemies will brand themselves in order to get close. That one clearly hasn't been taught yet how to be careful."

"How do you guys not go crazy with every single one of you being able to communicate telepathically?" Kanoa continues his list of questions.

"It's just like talking out loud." I continue to teach. "If you're in a public place you'll hear a lot of voices. If you're having a conversation with someone you'll hear one voice."

"Yeah, but how do you separate talking with private thinking, then?" Isaac asks.

"It's similar to breathing. We don't consciously do it, but we know how." That's half true. It was something our race developed at some point. But it does take some effort to sort the verbal with the mental.

"If we want to think to ourselves we can. I guess it's like using a specific muscle." I sum up.

They both nod. Isaac looks lost in thought again. Why is it that he has our ability to communicate telepathically. It has nothing to do with the verve in his system we've learned. I wonder if he is able to communicate with anyone else of my race. As we walk to our next location we pass by a massive tree.

All of the bark is shaved off of one side to reveal smooth wood and on it is a beautiful mural of art. One member is there admiring it. As we pass, she turns around to reveal that it's mother. I'm a tad surprised.

"Oh, hello Norx." Isaac greets. "Mother." I nod acknowledging.

"Enjoying the tour so far?" Norx asks.

"Yes, we are." Isaac replies. "It's very impressive." Kanoa forces a smile.

"Has Z told you the story of the mural yet?"

"No, she has not. What's the story here?" Isaac gazes at me. I don't like them talking with mother and father. If they promise to find the ship or make any sort of plan it'll only expedite this painful eventual encounter. I turn to mother.

"Why don't you tell it? You are much better at it." Norx smiles brightly.

"Oh well alright. As you know, we are not from this planet. We came from far away. Our ancestors were brilliant scientists and engineers. They found ways to keep our world alive even after our sun went out. Their highest accomplishment was finding a way to continue to extract energy from our now dead sun." As she talks she shows different parts of the mural.

"What did they do?" Isaac asks in wonder.

"They designed a massive spherical cage, and built it around the star. It was comprised of millions of devices designed to capture and contain the lingering energy produced by the white sun." As mother tells this story she is moving around the mural, pointing out what each section means and how it represents that part of the story.

"What they didn't plan on was the discovery of-"

"Verve." Isaac finishes her sentence.

"The white sun's unique elemental composition created something.

Our best people couldn't understand what it was, for years," Norx remarks. "What else out there rapidly shifts from solid to gas, to liquid, then back again? The practical applications were seemingly endless."

"An elixir of life," I hear Isaac mutter. Kanoa elbows him lightly in his side.

"So if things were going so well what happened?" Kanoa asks. Norx smiles sadly, and continues.

"Well the substance wasn't in high abundance. The process of obtaining and purifying verve was rigorous. We thought we had decades of extracting but an argument began. Half our planet believed that continuing would cause the sun to explode again, this time finally finishing us. The other half believed that Verve and the white sun would last forever and this was god's way of saving us; praising us for our incredible ingenuity. Arguments lead to fights. Those lead to riots. Then wars."

"How and when did you leave?" Isaac asks. He is completely enthralled in mother's story.

"The half that believed we were pushing ourselves to extinction starting working to prevent that. Thus our ship was built. A completely self-sustaining ecosystem of sanctuary, capable of traveling the stars forever." Norx arrives to a spot on the mural that has their ship.

The thing that stood out is that it has massive sections and prongs jutting outward, creating a geometric wonder of shapes all attached to the main body.

"How many people did you leave behind?" Kanoa asks.

"My mother told me that our population was around twelve billion before the ship left," Norx says sadly.

"And you only saved a hundred-thousand?" Kanoa says in disbelief.

"They tried their best!" Norx defends.

"The ship was capable of holding two million. It would've been at max capacity if nobody attempted to sabotage it!" Norx raises her voice a little. This story always made me uneasy. Deep breaths. Sort the numbers, add the numbers. Sort the numbers, add the numbers.

"Not everyone wanted to leave," she continues. "Those who were on the other side thought leaving was abandoning god. You often feel the ability to do anything if it comes with the promise of eternal paradise," Norx is solemn.

"Is that what you, um, your people believed in? Eternal paradise?" Isaac asks. Norx shrugs.

"Nobody who really believed in our religion was on that ship. We are the descendants of our planet's smartest scientists and engineers. Not exactly faith holders. Any records of our beliefs and religion remain on our planet." Norx explains.

"So then Techno's are technically right. By going to your planet they may actually be able to prove the existence of god." Isaac says sitting down.

"If your religion has significant comparisons to say Christianity then that's hard to ignore." Isaac rambles off.

"You guys don't remember reading any religious books about one guy with long hair did you?" Kanoa asks Norx. She shrugs.

"So how did mentions of your religion get out when you arrived here?" Isaac asks.

"None of us were there. Who knows?" Kanoa says.

"It's been so many years now. If we were right then there is nothing waiting for us at home. They finished extracting the star for all it's worth and got themselves killed. Or the planet is prospering." Mother ponders. Or the planet got blown up by an anti-matter bomb. I think to myself. I exchange looks with Isaac.

"If you find your ship, and you go home and it's no longer there then what would you do?" Isaac asks. Crap.

"We found you. We will find something. Somewhere else." Mother says. "I for one would just love to see the ship our parents before us arrived in."

"Sorry you had to land on our miserable planet." Isaac shrugs. Mother smiles.

"It hasn't been all bad." She looks off in the distance where her kids, my siblings, who are part of the group at the school, run and play.

"I'll do what I can to find your ship Norx." Isaac says out of nowhere. I'm taken aback by that. What did we just talk about last night? I stare at Isaac whos too busy making friends with mother. She smiles and takes his hand.

"You are sweet. Be safe out there," she says.

"Let's head for the ground," I decide to jump in.

Together the three of us head for one of the biggest trees near the center of the whole community. There, a beautifully-built wooden spiral staircase carved into the tree that descends to the lowest and ascends to the highest levels of the colony exists.

Upon reaching the bottom, the ground is still ten feet above the ground. I pull a lever and a loose ladder drops from the last step. We climb, and I uncover another lever on the ground which pulls the ladder back up.

"We have the immediate area cleared down here. A makeshift wall of sticks and dead trees surrounds most of the area as well as most of the major trees supporting the houses,"

I show. To a historians' perspective, where we are is technically in the heart of Queens. As Isaac looks at the ground I am able to find bits and pieces of metal here and there. It's hard to believe such massive trees are now where such a big, industrial city was.

"I'm going to head back. If you both need anything this is the way back up." I show them how to operate the levers.

"Alright. Thanks, Z." Isaac says smiling. He doesn't mean to harm. But his ignorance can be so infuriating sometimes.

"Let's go see what remains of New York in this forest."

Kanoa leads Isaac into the unknown, unnatural ecosystem of eastern New York City. I need time to process all of this. Why is it so different? "Sort the numbers, add the numbers. Just sort the numbers and add the numbers." I mumble to myself.

CHAPTER 19

WAR & PEACE

"Where is that light coming from?" I notice a small beam of daylight penetrating the roof of the church.

"Not sure, It's got to be nighttime now," Kanoa guesses. "Search it first." Together we slowly and quietly check every possible hiding spot in the building.

It turns out exploring an abandoned city overtaken by nature makes time go by like crazy. Kanoa and I walked around this jungle for what felt like an hour or two, but was actually more like four. It's impressive how so much wildlife has grown on what used to be a major urban city. Every once in a while we made out old streets and concrete bits.

Some buildings are still intact, oddly held together by the vines and greens that have fertile ground around them. Once we realized that we were probably out here for the night due to not knowing the way back, we searched for a place to camp. We found an old church that we decided to hunker down in for the night.

I walk into a room off to the left side of the center area. It looks like an office. An old cast-iron bedframe lies in the corner. Shattered and splintered bookshelves lie in a dusty mess in two of the corners. The desk is still on it's feet.

A few books with a foot of dust coating them like a blanket are on the desk. I wipe away at one to see its reflective gold text. The Holy Bible. Suddenly, something creaks in the far corner of the room.

I point my gun towards it and slowly approach. It's cold in here. My breath fogs up, then fades. I try to steady my breath. I feel the familiar ache of pain my anxiety draws from. My hand shakes. My breathing skips. Suddenly, a rat pops out of a hole in the ground and scurries out into the main hall. I jump and catch myself.

"It's clear!" I shout from the priest's chambers in the back.

"Hey Isaac." Kanoa shouts back. "Come here!"

When I return, I am surprised to discover Kanoa climbing up a marble statue. She rests in the far back of the room where the priest presumably gave their sermons. It's a bit large even by church standards. Her head almost scraping the ceiling. He is trying to reach for something in her hand.

"Careful!" I shout.

He has already climbed a good fifteen feet by the time I got out there. The piece of statue Kanoa was holding for leverage suddenly cracks. Kanoa lunges for the hand and grabs it only for it to collapse under the weight. Kanoa lands with a hard thud. I duck out of the way of the large piece of marble. He groans as I race over.

"What was worth that?" I ask looking down at him.

He shuffles and reaches for something underneath him. He holds up a long thin sword. It's inches from my face. My eyes widen as I push it away from my face.

"You're lucky you weren't impaled!" I exclaim.

"That's all my luck for today." Kanoa holds his free hand up. I help him to his feet. He inspects the sword. It has a brass handle with a crest on the hilt. "That's a-" I begin.

"Katana." Kanoa grins ear to ear.

"Why would that statue be holding a sword?" And why a katana?" I look to the stained glass where I can clearly still make out a shape of a cross.

The Katana was invented hundreds of years after Jesus. And the statue does not look like any female religious figure I remember.

"Who cares?" Kanoa eyeballs the weapon.

"You realize it's rusted beyond belief?" I note the blade's color, a splotchy brownish-purple completely covers the sword.

Kanoa scoffs and walks to a clear area to sit. He removes his pack and rummages around. He pulls out a small bottle of liquid and the Thermo-Mitt. He uncorks the bottle and uses the dropper attached to the cap. He drips a couple drops of the liquid onto the sword. A small sizzle emits from it as he then puts on the glove. With a few wipes he eliminates the rust, revealing a shinning blade. He puts his tools away and looks over to a thick piece of cloth draped over a turned-over pew. With a swing he cleaves the decorative tapestry in half.

"Do you recognize that crest?" I ask as I cautiously watch Kanoa practice his new found sword skills.

"Nope." Kanoa continues to swing, cutting various cloths in half. The crest looks like a sun except cut in half with what appears to be an arrow. "Why would a steel katana be in an old catholic church?" I ask again.

"It's too light to be steel." Kanoa remarks as he tosses the sword upwards then catches it. He repeats this a few times. It appears to be incredibly light. I hold out my hand to see for myself. Kanoa catches the sword, looks at me, then continues to toss the sword.

"I'm going to start a fire." I say frowning as I walk towards our gear. Eventually, Kanoa comes over to get warm. He sits down with his new friend and sets it to his side.

Kanoa stares heavily into the fire. He rubs the metal penta-gon-shaped machinery on his shoulder, stretching his shoulder around. He seems discomforted.

"Why won't this work?" I ask holding up a makeshift GPS I've been trying to put together. Kanoa stays fixed on the fire.

"So you really just don't have your ability anymore?" I notice his fixation.

"Whatever I got hit with neutralized all the verve in my body. It's like I never had an ability." Kanoa says sullen.

"We'll figure it out. We got some smart people." I try to cheer him up. He finally breaks his focus on the fire to look at me.

"Verve changed my life. In more ways then I planned on." Kanoa says with a half laugh, as if laughing at his own situation.

"This is the only life you've known though, isn't it?" I ask.

"My parents were both in the resistance their whole lives.

They were born into it just like I was. Their parents, my grandparents were there when they re-wrote the constitution. I'm told they couldn't decide what was the biggest moment of their generation. Was it the arrival of alien life? The Third World War? The country's rewriting of their constitution? The rise of Mercia?"

"The wrong people were in seats of power when our Neighbors arrived," I interject.

"Has there ever been a right person?" Kanoa continues.

"My parents raised me on the teachings of the old world. The idea that someone could hold power over another is un-just. Absolute power corrupts. And it's the duty of the people to seek balance and stop abuses of power. No one is untouch-able. Everyone is subject to the laws of nature. Anyone who convinces themselves or others of anything else is corrupt."

"My father thought something of the same." And my mother thinks the complete opposite I realize.

"I was raised in resistance camps. One after another. Always on the move. My mother liked being a teacher. She educated all the kids in our group. Math, Science...War. She only ever knew war but she would tell me stories her grandparents told her about the old world. About how there were billions of people and how they all flew in airships."

"Planes. They called them planes." I smile slightly, Kanoa continues on.

"How sports and entertainment were everywhere and people actually spent time outside, in parks and at museums. I've always wanted to go to a museum. My mother said those were her favorites." I straighten my back.

"So how did they-" I begin. Kanoa already knows where I was going.

"I was sixteen. There was a mission. We thought we could unplug a industrial center for T.R.A.C.I booths. Over ten thousand people signed into slavery. We thought by forcing people out we could get more people to join us. I learned of a location from an informant about a control hub. We take that place, then we could shut down the entire building."

"But it was a trap," I connect the pieces.

"Job was grounded before it even started. I pushed to do that mission Isaac. If I hadn't pushed to do that mission my parents might still be alive." Kanoa spits into the fire.

"The place wasn't a vault. It was a fake, designed to lure us all in. The building exploded with almost a hundred of us inside. I was on perimeter duty. I saw the missile they launched at it. The initials I.H.L were displayed on the side of the silo."

"That's why you blame my mother..." I pause.

"Whatever happened to the informant?"

Kanoa looks at me. Now breaking his gaze from the fire. The blaze illuminating the intensity in his expression and eyes.

"He disappeared. I tried to track him down several times. It only drove me further and further away. If I hadn't found Crane around that time...I probably would be dead too." I swallow hard.

"Crane's a nice person isn't she?" I try to get the conversation back on a lighter note.

"The smartest among us. And probably the strongest if I'm being honest," Kanoa remarks.

"How come she left the Nether?" I ask. "I learned a few things when Caleb and I were there. Crane used to be a council member?" I press. Kanoa scoffs.

"Yeah, Crane was a council member. You've met them so want to take a guess as to what happened?" I toss a piece of wood into the fire.

"Difference of opinions?" I guess.

"More like ideals. Everyone wants the same thing. The Prexy dead or in chains. But the one thing people can't seem to agree on is who should wear the crown after she is dethroned."

"Why should there even be a crown?" I ask. "Is there going to be a war immediately after the one we are already fighting?" Kanoa doesn't reply. He stokes the fire angrily.

"As of now the board is at a stalemate. Nobody's moving until the Prexy is toppled." Kanoa is enraged.

"But there are a lot of pieces ready to move when the queen is toppled. More then we know. You've been at this for what? A few months? This has been my whole life Isaac. And the closest we got to peace was when I lost my parents. All I've ever known is war." Kanoa says.

"Maybe peace is closer then you think." I try to sound optimistic.

"Depends on your definition of peace," Kanoa answers. "It's late. Get some sleep Isaac." Kanoa gets up and finds a corner to curl up in.

I do the same, finding an old pew still holding together. I lay down on my back looking up the the rotting ceiling. Trees and branches intertwine through the old, soggy planks. The stained glass is splotchy and translucent. I eventually drift off into a restless sleep.

The next day Z gives us a more complete tour of her home. Their community is a network of treehouses that expands miles in every direction. At one end the furthest treehouse is more of a greenhouse. A beautiful display of hanging plants, flowers and crops. Amazing devices that automatically deliver water and nutrients. The greenhouse itself is built out of different various shards of glass and old buildings they scavenged from down below.

At another end is their armory. Z couldn't share much, other than that they have a small supply of verve. They seem to be well trained in weapons. Things like spears and darts. This must be where Z learned how to use her staff. Around noon we are back at the center hut. We are all outside enjoying the sun sneaking through. I am laying on the wooden planks enjoying the peace when I feel something hit my face. A pebble. I sit up and look to see Baix waving me over on the far side of the hut.

"What the-?" I look back at Z and Kanoa.

They are both napping. I look back at Baix who clearly insists I meet him over at the far side of the hut. His waving is a bit more frantic. Curious, I go to him.

"Baix? Is something wrong?" I ask.

"Would you come with me please?" He asks kindly.

I nod and follow him into a rear entrance into their hut. The back rooms are three bedrooms. Baix explains their two youngest share one and he and Norx share another. He stops in front of the third.

"This is Z's room," Baix explains. "Okay?" Why are we here I wonder.

"My daughter next to my two boys are my whole life," Baix continues.

"I understand." Where is he going with this?

"I don't know what occurred in the generations before us. I'm not sure who hit first. I'm not ambitious. I don't desire war. I'm just trying to protect my own." Baix is not getting to his point here.

"No one can blame you for that." I am unsure where this is going. "You've built a good thing here. Safe." His expression turns worried.

"But for how long?" There is a pause before he continues.

"I want to show you something." He walks into Z's room and comes back a moment later holding a journal.

"When we lost Z I thought I would never see her again. This was years ago. It was hard but we eventually moved on. When I saw her yesterday I was beyond happy. But also concerned." His hands are trembling slightly.

"Why?"

"You honestly have not noticed? Our species' eyes work a lot like your own. Different colors, but always passed genetically. What color are my eyes?" I gaze at him and notice see they resemble a tiger's, a soft orange hue fills up most of the space with the pupil in the middle.

"Norx's eyes are orange as well," he continues.

"That is odd." I say as I piece it together. For as long as I've known Z, she's intergraded with Verve so she is capable of making them flash that bright fluorescent blue.

But when she isn't doing that they are a light sandy brown with a tint of green. I've never really seen a shade like it before. Remembering now it's what caught my attention when I first met her. Besides the whole telepathy thing everyone else in that room on the Loft had bright orange, green, blue eyes. She was the only one with light sandy brown eyes.

"Something happened to her while she was gone. Last night she wrote this." He hands me the journal. I reluctantly take it and open it to find page after page random jumbles of numbers.

"What the-?" I flip through it. It's entirely filled with random numbers in different sizes and fonts, overlapping. After looking at it I realize it's only four different numbers repeating.

"Z tells us that she has been working with your group for the last few months. Has she been writing numbers in journals?" Baix asks me.

"I-I'm not actually sure. We've been pretty distant lately," I admit.

"Z is strong. Whatever she went through..." Baix reflects, and becomes quite upset. He then sighs and opens the door again to Z's room.

Now showing me inside of it. I am met with those same four numbers scribbled everywhere. On every wall, the ceiling, every viable surface. It reminds me of people who suffer from schizophrenia. My mother took matters into her own hands when it came to my science education. She personally hired a tutor to teach me about every mental and physical illness in existence. She really wanted me to become a researcher or a doctor.

"This is more then just journaling." Baix concludes. I agree. "We're working on bringing the people responsible to justice." I close the journal and hand it back to him.

"But what is it going to cost? We've already lost so much." Trying to keep my thoughts from spiraling I attempt to end this conversation.

"I'm sorry." I start to walk away.

"I trust my daughter. I trust her to make her own choices. She's chosen to return with your group for the time being. But I'm tired of the fighting. Of the hiding. Of the sacrifices. My community feels as I do." Still not understanding his point I turn back on my heels to face him again.

"What is it you want of me? Why show me this?" I ask.

"Z talked about you a lot these last two days. She's drawn to you for reasons she doesn't understand. Our species share a lot of similarities." I am beginning to get uncomfortable.

"Please make your point sir." I beg.

"I am simply asking you to keep an eye on her, as she has for you apparently. I know where your path leads. Your life-style is dangerous. I don't want to lose my daughter again."

"Isaac!" Kanoa shouts from outside.

I look at this man. This leader figure. In this moment he is nothing more then a concerned parent. Not something I am used too. Trying to be kind for all the hospitality they have shown us and out of care for Z I say.

"I will look after her. You have my word." I do mean that.

Something is tying us together and I can't quite figure it out. Now I need to figure out why she is obsessed with numbers. I head out to see Kanoa and Z are awake and standing. I watch as some hovercrafts roar by. Dozens of Neighbors appear and begin screeching and hissing.

"We're hidden right?" Kanoa asks. I shrug. Sure enough the hovercrafts pass by without issue.

"We're still good to head out this afternoon?" Kanoa turns to Baix who has joined us while looking overheard. He nods.

"Scouts will take you to the water line. After that, you are on your own." Baix says.

"You coming back with us, Z?" Kanoa turns to her. She looks down at the ground, nods, then lifts her staff and moves off to the area where she commonly practices her combat moves.

As the afternoon starts to set in Z, Kanoa and I find ourselves on the ground level facing a dozen or so neighbors. Z's family is there alongside several guards. Hillo and Nax run up to hug Z. They only reach up to her waist.

"Bye, bye Z!" They look up at her. She smiles and rubs them both on their backs.

"Nax, Hillo!" Norx shouts, and they go running back. Both of them grabbing one of her legs. Baix approaches Z.

"Take care," They hug warmly, and he stares at me during it. I sort of nod, in understanding. Not sure if Kanoa notices.

"Kind humans. Here I thought I'd never see the day." He smiles.

"We'll see what we can find out about that ship. I promise!" I shout back as we walk away. Together the three of us make our way back into the city.

CHAPTER 20

TERRIBLE SWIFT SWORD

It took the three of us a few days to figure out where Crane had relocated everyone. Enough time has passed that we need to move shop to stay out of the Prexy's radar. This new location is much further north, the furthest we have ever gone according to Kanoa. Cold temperatures and snowy weather are more present. We are closer to the coast. As we drive on abandoned roads, I notice more rocky coastlines and tall, thick trees.

"So where is this new base?" I ask, checking my GPS. Kanoa is at the wheel driving an old beat up truck we found hours ago. Z is in the back seat asleep. She passed out shortly after we found this ride.

"I'm told it's an old military base repurposed during the war. It's built right into a mountain on an island. It was a rebel base that burned all records when we lost. Only those that were there remember it's location," Kanoa explains.

"Your war or a war before me?" I ask.

"My war." Kanoa rolls his eyes. The sun is beginning to set, creating a beautiful golden glow on the icy water of the ocean to our side as we hurdle down these roads. My GPS finally is able to get a precise location.

"44.441578, North. -68.370194 West. I think we're in Maine. Or what used to be Maine," I mention.

"Ever been there?" Kanoa asks.

"No. I had a friend once think that Maine was part of Canada, and not America though."

"May as well have been ever since Mercia. Most things north of The Central Zone are either abandoned or wild lands," Kanoa tells me. "We should be getting close now. There's the mountain. Kanoa points ahead. A large curved mountain surrounded by smaller hills and mountains.

"How is it an island if we are driving to it?" I ask.

"Sorta island. It only connects to the mainland through this road here. Every other direction will take you to ocean." Kanoa explains.

"Easily defendable, I guess." I mutter.

"If Crane was able to fully activate the base then we will have eyes on the entire island. Every inch of it is monitored." Kanoa grins at the potential of it all.

"This entire sorta island?" I gawk as I look out the window. We are driving close to the edge of a massive rocky coastline. I look down towards the water.

"So where's the entrance?" I turn back in my seat.

"Good question," Kanoa holds up the GPS. "Crane says the entrance is at the top of the tallest point. Here, this road goes up."

Kanoa turns hard, slams through a withered security checkpoint that contains a small one-person hut. Two roads diverge from here but both immediately climb upward. We make our way to the tallest point. Finally, we reach the summit. Kanoa parks the car and we exit. I immediately shiver as the winds are rough up here. Snow covers the ground. The sun is just about to go down giving us a little sliver of light.

"That's a view!" I shiver. Looking to the horizon, I can see for miles. Kanoa is right. This is indeed a sorta island, stretching off in every direction for miles but always winding up becoming rocky coastline that gives way to ocean. I can see smaller islands far off in the distance.

"So, where is this entrance? I'm freezing." My teeth chatter as I head back to the car to grab something warmer. I wake Z. "Hey we're here. You might want a coat." I nudge her. She comes to, looks around. She steps out and moves her feet in the snow.

"You're cold?" She looks completely unaffected. I look back at Kanoa scanning the area with the GPS shaking even more than I am.

"Yeah." My breath fogs the air between us.

"Found it!" Kanoa shouts as he wipes away some snow around a medium-sized rock. There is a man-made flat stone platform.

"I think a podium used to be there. Like to display facts about the mountain." I waddle over. Kanoa draws a knife and softly carves a narrow square into the rock. He then pushes downwards, puts increasing pressure on it until it shifts, slides down a couple of feet. With a hard grind, it moves to the side out of sight, revealing a ladder.

"Pretty cool, huh?" Kanoa asks as I hurry past him and begin the climb. This tunnel looks like an old service pipe, however nothing about it is aged or rusty. The tunnel walls, the ladder, all look to be upkept and almost clean. We reach the bottom where an iron door holds court. It is thick, like one you would use in a prison. It chirps and clicks, then suddenly it slowly opens. Out pops Mordecai and Kate with smiles on their faces. Their wounds look almost completely healed. They are walking about without any limps.

"Good to have you back," Mordecai passes Z and I to find and hug Kanoa.

"Good to be back." Kanoa replies. Kate looks at me and signs.

"Almost died?" I smile and sign back.

"Did you?" She smirks. "So, a mountain in the frozen north. How long you think we have in this one?" Kanoa asks.

"Hopefully, forever." Mordecai says with a strange, happy look on his face. Confused, the three of us follow them into this new facility.

"Woah," I exclaim as we enter a perfect viewing area of the main part of the base; a circular dome room with a massive runway that tunnels out on one side. We are up in some walkway that reminds me a lot of nosebleed-level seating in a stadium. As we walk along the wall on a ramp heading down to the main floor, Mordecai explains.

"Anyone else who found this base, it would've been useless to them. Thanks to our gear and abilities we brought it back to it's former glory." Kate elbows Mordecai and signs something to him.

"You're right. We improved it," Mordecai brags. Walking down closer and away from the wall towards the ground level, the dome continues on further in. It splits off into five more tunnels, man-made no doubt, as they are braced and supported with weight-bearing beams and pillars.

"Tunnels one and two on the left is all housing. We're still counting and securing all the rooms but at last count we have five- hundred-and-twenty-eight beds." Mordecai points to the first tunnel a few hundred feet away.

"Beds, or rooms?" I ask, not really wanting to live in a broom closet again. Kate turns around and excitedly signs.

"Rooms. Bigger than our last spot."

Mordecai continues the tour. "Tunnels four and five have just about everything you could hope to expect. Kitchens, armory, storage, security and surveillance. We were able to reactivate sixty percent of the cameras across the island. We'll have to go out and manually replace the ones that are either gone or too damaged."

We've now made our way off the walkway ramp onto the tar runway. I look down the tunnel and see it end with a wall of solid rock.

"Don't tell me that opens." I am excited. "Okay, then I won't." Mordecai says rather bluntly. "It doesn't?" Kanoa asks.

"We're not sure. Clearly this is a runway for some sort of vehicle but we haven't been able to figure out why it goes straight into the wall. There's no divider, no source of power, or machinery. We're not sure yet how far that wall is compared to outside, or if it's even above ground. We had to hide our ship on the far end of the island and trek our way here."

"You mean ships?" Z tries to correct them but Kate and Mordecai frown.

"Nope. Ship. We're down to one." Mordecai says sadly. "Part of the reason why this base needs to be the last one, speaking of which..."

Kate and Mordecai both look like they remembered something as they stop. We stand in the middle of the runway, at a perfect distance from all five tunnels.

"What about tunnel three? Straight down the middle here?" I ask. Looking down it, I don't see much other then the continuing tunnel.

"That's where we are heading right now, unfortunately. I'm sorry guys but we don't have time for you to unpack. Crane needs to see us immediately."

Mordecai becomes rather stressed. Kates nods and they move quickly straight down tunnel three. We keep pace and as we race-walk down this tunnel I realize this hallway is rather short. We get to the other end of it swiftly and find ourselves in another large dome room, not as enormous as the first one but big enough to contain a football field. The first one could hold four. There is a platform raised up into the air at the far end with a podium on it.

"This is where whoever was in charge spoke to everyone in this base." Mordecai explains.

Together the five of us pass groups of workers and head up to the platform into the doors behind it. Inside is a conference room with a tired-looking Crane standing at the end. There are more doors in this room leading to who-knows-where.

"Z. Nice to see you. I'm happy you are okay." Crane says with a relieved smile. Z nods curtly.

"What did Neon have to say?" Crane looks towards Kanoa.

"We didn't exactly get a chance for a full conversation," Kanoa replies looking at me. I look anywhere else.

"Things went sideways, we wound up in the forest east of the city." Crane's eyes widen.

"The forest? How?" Crane asks confused. We go on to explain everything that occurred in the last few days.

"I see." Crane says. "So then how are they staying hidden if they are out in the open like that?"

"I was thinking about that on the way up here." Kanoa says. "Sweepers target light and heat sources to find enemy bases. They were able to snuff any source of light in under one minute in that entire community. Just like in the Nether."

"What about heat?" Mordecai asks.

"The snow..." I mutter. "Z you weren't cold outside were you?" Z looks at us.

"No." She says.

"Their cold-blooded. That explains why the Prexy is having a hard time finding them!" I exclaim.

"Poikilothermy. Impressive." Crane remarks. I can't help but notice Crane is extremely distant and distracted. Something is clearly on her mind.

"What's going on?" Kanoa asks also noticing Crane's demeanor. Crane nods to Kanoa to shut the door. He does so and she brings everyone in closer.

"I'm making an announcement tonight. We're low on resources. We're running on fumes here." Crane looks up at us. She looks visibly stressed. She sits down at the front of the table and rubs her temples.

"What about the ships? What happened to them?" I ask.

"Going this far north took a toll. We paid a price to get this far out of Prexy's borders. Matt is exhausted. He needs time to rest before he can produce any more verve. He's been working overtime for us. I don't want to push him past his breaking point." Crane continues. They pause for a moment, look down.

"I'm thinking about disbanding." She says flatly.

"What?" Mordecai says surprised.

"We have lost the most amount of people in these last few months ever. We know exactly why too. Governmental security is always at an all time high during these months. Maybe after the election and the Prexy goes into her scheduled hibernation we can reconvene but right now? We're barely hanging on." Crane finishes.

"You know how hard it was to get to the numbers we are at now. The vetting processes? If we scatter now we will not be at this strength again for years. Probably until the next election cycle! Then what? We scatter again?" Kanoa is visibly angry.

"I am not going to order these people to their own deaths!" Crane stands up, matching his anger. "This facility has the ability to sustain ten times our current numbers. We're far enough from Prexy's territory that we could realistically be free from her influence indefinitely.

"Our people know what they signed on for. Every one of us is ready to give our lives if it means the Prexy's downfall!" Kanoa shouts. "What's stopping The Prexy from expanding? We don't run Crane."

"We are all out of moves." Crane tries to end the conversation. "I'm sorry." I attempt to butt into this conversation.

"What about the Nether?" I speak up. All eyes turn to me. Kanoa scoffs. Mordecai and Kate look uncomfortable.

"Don't they want to work with you?" I continue. Caleb joins in.

"Crane. You know what they have." Crane holds up a hand. "I have no interest in working with those hypocrites," Crane replies.

"Aren't we both on the same side?" I ask.

"It's not that simple Isaac," Mordecai interjects. "The Council of the Nether seek for the dismantlement of the Prexy's government, yes. But what they want to instill in it's place is just as bad." Crane explains.

"Okay? What do they wish?" I ask.

"Every single member of the council has a different idea on how a country should run. If the Prexy falls and the Nether takes control then this land would be split evenly amongst them. And that can only lead to future wars. The last thing we need is more borders then we already have." I take a seat, lean forward.

"So that's why you left?" I conclude.

"I've been a leader out of necessity. I do not wish to be a ruler or leader of a country.

Their methods are controversial and shady. They don't care who they have to lose or what they have to spend in order to win. I value life. They don't." Crane finishes. It feels like there is more but I decide to let it go.

"The Nether is on the climb," Caleb jumps in. "When Isaac and I were there I clocked their arsenal. Cogs also clued me in. They currently have a dozen Verve producers. They've been focusing on weapons primarily. Their numbers are bigger then ours. I think they are close to a thousand."

"So, well over doubling us. Great." This information clearly frustrates Crane.

"But they do still want to work with you," Caleb adds. Crane sighs loudly. "Even if we work something out that still leaves us horribly out-numbered to the Prexy." Crane looks to Z.

"Do you think your people would be interesting in being a part of this?" Z looks to me and I speak up.

"They believe that their home world is returnable. Z's father seems to be their leader. They wish to find their original craft that brought their ancestors here." Crane and the others take this new information in stride, and process it quickly.

"Is that enough motive for them to join the fight?" Crane asks.

"It might be. It's their decision," Z says. "But I'm not comfortable with lying to them." Crane walks up to Z

"Then don't." Crane says bluntly. Z nods.

"Okay. Here's the plan. Z, I would like to talk to your community. I want some of you to also head to the Nether in the meantime to arrange a meeting. On our terms. This will take a few days. Caleb, we're going to need some doors." Caleb sighs.

"I'm going to need the rest of the Verve Matt was able to create." Crane nods.

"Okay, we head out soon. Everyone get some rest."
One by one everyone files out. Z flashes me a look of anger.
Where on earth is that coming from? It's not like we weren't
going to talk about that. Mordecai leads Kanoa, Z and I to
the sleeping chambers where we all pass out before our heads
even hit the pillow for blissful dreamless sleep.

CHAPTER 21

THE PRICE OF LIFE

The next few days are filled with the routine I have gotten used to. Learn the layout of the base. Stock and count supplies; what remains of them, anyway. After I finish my duties I peek into where we set up our T.R.A.C.I booths. Some are currently in a simulation while they are being monitored by techs in the adjoining booth. I feel a hand place on my shoulder, startling me. I turn to see Z standing there carrying two staffs. They look to be from the room we established as a practice studio. She tosses one of them to me.

"Let's train." She says. I look back into the room knowing I'll only get into trouble if I set foot in there.

"Sure," I agree. Together we head to the area.

The smell of sweat and iron hits my nostrils as I walk into the room. A gymnasium sized room with workout equipment take up about half the space. There are three different sparring rings sectioned off for hand-to-hand combat training. Other then the two of us the room is mostly vacant. Save for a couple individuals bench pressing and running on a treadmill on the far end. Z walks into the ring right in the center of the room. She takes a ready position. I follow suit. Z takes the offensive and rushes me.

With fast motions and by quickly adapting athletic movements, I am able to parry or avoid most of her attacks, but the occasional jab and whack get through. Whenever one occurs it triggers Z to start a conversation.

"You're improving." Z tries to be supportive.

"It'd help if I actually chose a weapon to get good with." I spin the staff and go on the offensive, attempting to land a hit on her. She blocks my advances with ease, moving with acrobatic-like agility.

"Focus. Steady your breathing." She takes back the offense. I attempt to do exactly that but she effortlessly increases her speed, moving exponentially faster until she whacks me hard across the back of my head. I didn't even see it coming. I drop the staff and fall to my knees, rub my head.

"Ow!"

"You're hesitating." She stands over me.

Usually my training has been with Kanoa or sometimes Mordecai, or even Kate. Z and I still feel at odds. Why did she want to do this?

"And you still seem angry." I sweep her legs from underneath her, causing her to tumble, giving me time to grab my staff and get up. She greets me and we resume our fight, this time both increasing our power and speed.

"I do not condone what my mother has done." I lock up with her face-to-face.

"But you protect her." She returns.

"How?" I retort.

"She's a mass murderer Isaac. She wants genocide. The extinction of my race. And she wants yours plugged in and controlled for the 1% to abuse." She grimaces and then says what she really means.

"You had a chance to kill her and you threw it away." She powers over me and pushes me off of her.

"I am not a murderer!" I shout to her. "And my mother is certainly not going to be my first kill!"

"So who is?" Z fires back. "You're not a child anymore, Isaac. You're a solider. And you're the only one here who hasn't killed anyone." Z breaks off from the circle and jumps onto a nearby stack of mats. A good five or six foot straight jump.

"You say that like it's a bad thing!" I shout up to her. The sweat pools and drips off of me. I use my arm band to wipe my face. A mistake. By the time I look up again Z is already back down and attacking again. I manage to take the brunt of her attack and push her off. Resuming the standoff.

"If you are not able to react when needed one of us could die instead." Z rushes me again. I match her movements, step-to-step, in a beautiful display of mirrored actions. I dodge, parry and counter her advances.

"I'm not the only one with some issues though, am I?" I hiss. Our staffs clatter loudly as they make contact. It becomes a strength match. Trying to push each other back. Z looks at me with shock. I've distracted her. I step back and she stumbles forward. I place my staff by her feet. She trips and falls, bouncing her head off the ground. She sits upright.

"What do you mean by that?" Z asks, looking angrier.

"What's with the numbers?" I ask her holding out a hand to help her up. She looks shocked for a moment then smacks my hand away. She jumps up and attacks me with a blind fury filled assault. Signs of recklessness. I'm able to counter with ease. With each clash of the staffs I push further.

"How long have you been drawing numbers like that?" I lock in again.

"That's none of your business." Z grits her teeth.

"Does Crane know?" I continue.

"This isn't about me!" she replies.

"You're the one who still hasn't accepted he's not going home," she says spitefully.

"I think this is a good enough reminder that I'll never get back what I lost!" I stop in my tracks, turn and part my hair behind my head to show the tattoo.

"So get it removed then! You've had plenty of opportunities. Get contacts. Your marks are fixable!" Z shouts back.

"Unlike yours?" I match her volume. She drops her staff and walks up to me.

"What did you say to me?" Breathing heavily. This isin't just a sparring match. We're digging into each other. Pushing one another until we find our breaking points. I wonder if I've reached hers.

"Why are your eyes different?" I say right to her face. Inches away. She clocks me square in the jaw, and I stagger backwards. I found it. I drop my staff to cradle my face. She slams the staff to the ground and screams.

"I don't know!" Tears form in her eyes. "Ever since that man...I've had those numbers buzzing around in my head, that I can't forget. I have headaches all the time and I sometimes feel like I'm not even there. My family, Isaac? I recognize them but it feels like they are complete strangers to me! I don't feel like myself! Not since The Loft."

"Do you remember how you wound up there?" I ask.

"No. I woke up there with splitting headaches and periods of blacking out. They didn't get better until-"

"Until we met." I finish her sentence. How did I know where she was going with that?

"When I saw you that day the headaches stopped. For a while anyway. Then I discovered you could talk to us like how our species does."

"So what are you saying, Z?" I say catching my breath.

"My eyes aren't normal but they are mine. Whatever happened to me, made me who I am today. And I don't hate myself!" Z screams, tears fall down her face.

"Okay. I'm sorry! That- that makes a lot of sense. Maybe I feel like I deserve it. I don't know!" I sit down against the wall.

"My life before I woke up here was shit. My mother was always gone. My dad was always sick. I've never had any control over my life. I took advantage of my friends and never considered their feelings. I just needed to control something in my life. Removing the tattoo. It's expected of me. To me, keeping this tattoo is the first time I made a decision for myself." Z sits down next to me. She becomes fixated on my face.

"That decision makes you a hated man in the eyes of your own people."

"Maybe I feel like I deserve that." I look up to the ceiling.

It's true. It's how I feel. Ever since waking up in the future all I have been able to do is focus on what I left behind. The unfinished arguments. The stupid, petty, shitty things I did. Knowing that all of those people are long dead without any resolution for me feels like hell.

"You still haven't figured out your power, have you?" Z asks me with a thin hope in her voice. She's changing the subject. Did she just see something with my eyes?

"I don't think I have one, Z! I think it was just some odd reaction to Verve. Whenever it happened." I say.

"However we are doing this isn't verve. My eyes would be changing, but their not!"

"C'mon. Were not done yet," Z insists. She stands back up, throws my staff into my lap. I sigh and rise. We resume sparring.

"You're special Isaac. Whatever happened to you between when you were frozen and now, clearly it was for a reason. You are meant for something big. You need to accept that you are never going to be the same again. T.R.A.C.I is not real. You have to let it go." Z is trying to hit all the trauma targets in one session clearly.

"You can live entire lives in the time it takes for us to have this conversation." I argue.

"And people who log centuries of time within T.R.A.C.I are the quickest to lose their minds." Z fires back.

"If I can log hundreds of years living whatever life I want before I go crazy I'd consider that worth it!" I shout.

"Do not go gentle into that good night!" Z says. Surprised, I drop my guard and she delivers a hard final blow to my sternum. As I fall hard on my back, she looks down at me.

"What did you just say?" I cough. Z, confused, helps me up.

"What?" Z is confused.

"Those words. That phrase." My mind swirls. "Just something I heard once." Z replies. Suddenly Crane appears holding a backpack in their hands. They toss it to Z.

"We're ready." Crane says. Z throws her staff aggressively at me to catch as she walks off.

"Was that....a poem?" I say to myself. I drop the staff and run to join them.

I follow the two of them back out into the main hanger area where Caleb, Mordecai, Kate and Kanoa are all waiting. All of them except Kanoa are packed for a journey. Crane turns around and whistles to alert the entire hangar. People stop what they are doing and walk towards Crane, forming a small crowd.

"Okay. You all know the drill. Kanoa is in charge while I'm gone. If all goes well we will have access to some much needed supplies soon. We should be back in a few days. That's all." Crane dismisses the crowd. Some leave but a few stay to watch the unique method of departure. Crane turns to Caleb.

"You sure you can handle this?"

"I've got enough juice on my own without Verve." Caleb smirks. He looks to an open area and focuses.

The familiar crackle and smell of ozone appears as a semi-translucent blue vortex of energy grows until it's big enough for people to pass through. Peering over the crowd I can see the town square within the Nether. Mordecai and Kate step through and give a thumbs up as the portal dissipates.

Caleb drops his arms and takes a few deep breaths. He then focuses again to open another door. This one leads to Z's colony in the forest. Caleb drops his arms much quicker and sucks for air a lot harder. Z and Crane throw his arms over their shoulders and hurdle into the portal before it closes. With a puff and a spark the energy fades away and everyone resumes their duties and chores. I approach Kanoa.

"They'll be fine," he says. "Think we will actually meet with the council in the Nether?" I ask.

"Yeah. And that's what worries me." Kanoa says. "There's a reason Crane is hesitant to work with them. It's beyond ideologies. There's bad blood between them," Kanoa continues.

"Does Neon have any part in it all?" I ask. Kanoa snickers.

"He wishes. He visited the Nether from time to time. You meet a lot of people down there. A lot of backgrounds, a lot of stories."

"I'd like to find that guy. Give him a piece of my mind. That verve chick too." I remember the horrors I saw within his basement.

"The rats will do what they do best. Jump from one sinking ship to another. They'll survive. It looked like that was his main headquarters that got raided by I.H.L. He'll be in the wind for a bit. We don't have to worry about him for a while." Kanoa walks off. As I head off on my own I rack my brain trying to remember where I've heard that phrase before.

CHAPTER 22

UPGRADE

Things start to move quickly after that. Well, for everyone else, anyways. I'm stuck here learning about our final head-quarters. We apparently are in what used to be an old military base located in the mountains of Acadia National Park. A pretty remote place before the world blew up. The views from the top are amazing. It's nice to get a better look when the temperatures aren't negative.

Crane, Caleb and Z went to her people's base to talk. Mordecai and Kate went on Crane's behalf to negotiate at The Nether. Caleb can open doors for himself and usually one other person all on his own without the aid of additional verve. But to open multiple portals in one day for several people takes a lot out of him even using it. The plan was for the three of them to get to know Z's people, then travel to The Nether to round everyone up and use some of their verve to bring them all back.

Until then? I get to explore this extensive bunker. My father would've had a field day here. I guess it was built in the 1980s but was one of those super secret bases for end-of-the-world scenarios. It never really got a chance to be used...until now.

After a few days, as I am walking around the base, passing by people every now and then I eventually run into Kanoa.

"Hey," Kanoa waves at me. "Come here." I walk over.

"While Crane's gone you and I are going on a field trip."

"Where? How?" Kanoa gestures to follow him. He leads me to the room we've set up our T.R.A.C.I booths in.

"Wait, really?" I am thrilled.

"Don't get excited," he says. "What are we doing?" I ask.

"Another Lesson. One I can only teach in there." Kanoa says flatly.

"Okay, fine." I head towards the loading bay.

"Hold on, I promised Garrett we'd stop by the shop first." Kanoa is a little annoyed. I already had one foot in the booth when he said that. Dejected I climb out and shuffle back over to him.

"What insane inventions has he come up with this time?" I laugh a little.

"All I know is he wants to see me about that katana I found." Kanoa replies.

Together we head to the workshop, where five people quietly mill about a makeshift lab. There are lots of boxes and scattered pieces of machinery and various bits and bolts. One of the scientists, lanky and pale. Short brown hair standing straight up. It's either hair gel or grease. He's typing away furiously on a desktop.

Another is almost a polar opposite. A husky gentleman with a full lumberjack beard. His hair a long black web tied into a messy bun. He types away furiously on a desktop. The other two are both women. One older then the other. Her hair, shoulder length and gray while her younger partner has blonde hair tied up in a ponytail. A stripe of aqua blue runs through it like a river.

They are both busy organizing the boxes and building their workspace. The last one holds a clipboard and looks over to us as we enter.

"Kanoa! Just the man I was waiting for. Oh and Isaac, perfect! I have things for you as well!" He greets us excitedly.

"Nice to see no matter where we go you're always tinkering, Gurt." I say, amused.

Garrett or Gurt as his nickname has been decided is an overall happy person with short red hair frizzed to no end. His ocean blue eyes provide a wonderful contrast to his looks. He is dressed in some of the crew's normal gear but also dons dirty smudged jeans, and casual builder attire. He quickly leads us over to an already cleared area designed for testing weapons and gear.

"Thank you again for providing me your weapon. I understand you've become quite attached to this sword." Garrett grabs it off of a counter.

"You didn't break it did you?" Kanoa can't hide the worry in his tone.

"How often do I really break things?" Garrett asks smugly. Kanoa raises an eyebrow.

"You're right, never mind. Point is, I didn't break this one. And I think you'll like the modifications I've made to it."

Garrett hands the sword to Kanoa. At first glance, it seems like nothing has been done to it. I peer in and see two rows of strange symbols that I don't recognize from hilt to tip on both sides of the blade. Kanoa notices as well.

"You stylized it?" Kanoa is unimpressed.

"You think so little of me. Do me a favor and jerk your wrist inward towards you." Garrett instructs.

Kanoa does and nothing happens. He again looks at Garrett unimpressed.

"Um, oh wait!"

Garrett races back to the counter and grabs something off it. When he re-approaches Kanoa, he has a small device that looks like a portable USB in his hand.

"Do you mind?" Garrett asks as he inserts the device into Kanoa's shoulder patch.

"Now try again." Kanoa flicks his wrist, and the shoulder patch hums. The symbols on the left side of the sword glow a bright verve blue.

"You can now apply the stun serum normally in our guns by a hit or swipe with your sword. It only needs to be triggered." Garrett beams.

Kanoa's eyes go big with excitement and swipes at a nearby box. A blast of the cold energy erupts from the sword and lands with a splat onto the box.

"Woah." I remark.

"How come only half the symbols lit up?" Kanoa asks. Garrett smirks again.

"Flick your wrist the other way." Kanoa does and the blue symbols dull. The other half of the sword's symbols light up a bright red. Suddenly the sword erupts into a steady stable blaze.

"A flaming sword?" Kanoa grins from ear-to-ear. Garrett nods.

"Just be mindful around explosive things, please. We have a few of those in here." The other scientists look tense.

"How do you turn it off?" I ask.

"Switch hands." Garrett instructs Kanoa. He does so and as soon as the sword leaves his hand the red symbols fade. The flame around the blade does as well.

"The handle scans who is holding it through biometric readers. It syncs up with your shoulder patch and tunes to the verve dormant in your body so you are the only one who can activate the sword's ability, Kanoa.

We're still not sure how to rid your body of the toxin so you probably won't be shooting fireballs anytime soon."

"Thank you Garrett." Kanoa is genuinely happy. He sheathes the sword and shakes his hand hard. Garrett readjusts his glasses and turns to me.

"Isaac. You still haven't really committed to a weapon of choice have you?"

"Not really no." I say. Still haven't killed anyone yet.

"Well until you do I think I have something you are going to love. This is my latest achievement." Garrett says excitedly.

"Our latest achievement!" one of the scientists from the other end shout.

"Yeah!" a second tech yells. Garrett rolls his eyes.

"Our," he repeats. He grabs a small case, flicks the hatch and opens it. He pulls out a dozen thin, flexible rings and stacks them on the table. He then takes out a bracelet and two 128 oz soda can-sized tanks.

"What on Earth is this?" I ask, completely stumped.

"A potential means of transportation. If it works." Garrett continues arranging and setting up the device.

"If?" I am concerned.

"If you don't mind," Garrett holds up a black harness with the soda cans attached to the back. I take it from and awkwardly slip it on like backpack straps. I clip it in the front.

"Now the bracelet."

Garrett holds out a thick metallic ring that looks different then the ones still on the table. He attaches it onto my left arm and suddenly a holographic keyboard and dial appears there.

"Woah!" I am impressed. I move my arm around. The holo-panel is displaying on my arm so it looks and feels like a remote attached to my arm.

"That's not the impressive part." Garrett snickers. As do the other techs.

My face turns read realzing that's probably dated technology.

"Now the rings." Garrett gets visibly more excited. The other techs are now interested to see this play out, and join in to watch and offer advice.

"This isn't going to roast any of us is it?" Kanoa asks cautiously.

"Hopefully not." Garrett grabs one of the rings on the counter. He twists it apart like opening a pill bottle. It splits into two halves.

"This half goes on the body. A safe non-irritant glue but will weather any condition out there. We're going to start with four, okay Isaac?"

"I trust ya Gurt." I say in an unsure tone as he places the first ring on the palm of my left hand, then another on my right one. Next, he positions one on each of my feet.

"Okay, now what?" I ask.

"Everyone, step back." Garrett instructs. Kanoa and the techs all move behind the counter.

"Not really instilling confidence Gurt!" I start to get nervous.

"Isaac. Type activate on the keypad." Garrett shouts from his hiding spot.

I look down at the bright holographic keypad and type on my own arm. The ring halves on the table chirp and shoot toward me. I hold my hands up to protect my face and feel them attach to the spots on my palms, twisting into place, reforming themselves I lift one foot up at a time and the rings twist and lock back into their original look.

"Woah!" I repeat, looking into my palms. I now have circles on my hands.

"Don't look right into the rings please!" Garrett shouts as he walks over with some incredibly thin transparent wire.

"I need to attach them to your power source."

He runs and tapes the wire from each hand and foot ring to the soda can pack on my back.

"Okay! It's all connected. Fuel canisters are full. When I get back to the counter type launch then turn the dial to four." Garrett instructs me then races back behind the counter.

"Launch...four..." I repeat to myself.

I type launch then turn the dial to the number. With a brilliant burst of energy, a rocket-like thrust of power erupts from the rings on my hands and feet. The momentum shoots me up a few feet! I hold my hands out to try and stable myself only to cause the thrusters to send me flying backwards into the wall with a hard thud.

One of the techs shoves a sofa under me as I turn the dial back to zero. The thrusters shut off. I peel off the wall and fall a few feet onto the mattress.

"Ow!" I am annoyed.

"Cool." Kanoa says.

"Okay, maybe not four." Garrett mutters as some techs nod and scribble onto notepads.

"Let's try it at two." Kanoa looks at me from the ground.

"You okay?" He holds a hand out. I grab it and get to my feet.

"I think so. What the fuck do you have me rigged to, Garrett?"

"It's supposed to be a way to fly." Garrett goes back to his huddle, conversing with the techs.

"So, like a jetpack?" I look at Kanoa. He shrugs.

"Okay!" Garrett claps his hands.

"Let's try again." This time Isaac, keep it at two and keep your arms at your sides. I gather myself and stand back at my starting spot.

I take a deep breath and turn the dial two notches. I quickly put my arms at my sides and the thrusters slowly come
to life, gaining power gradually. It begins to lift me off the
ground and I do my best to stay balanced. I'm able to stay
upright for a few moments a few feet off the ground before
stumbling back down. I turn off the thrusters.

"There's definitely a learning curve." I pick myself up
back onto my feet.

"We're hoping to eventually make it so they cancel out our
natural gravitational pull without combustion energy." Garrett
jots down notes.

"So we can what? Walk on air?" Kanoa asks.

"Basically. We'd be practically impossible to catch at that
rate." Garrett helps dismantle the dev   ice, removing it from
me.

"Imagine running from someone only to hop into the air
like there's a staircase." He starts to pack it all up.

"Sorry, still in testing." I brush myself off.

"Still super cool already. Can't wait to see it when it's
done." I say. Kanoa walks up and shakes Garrett's hand.

"Thank you Garrett, again." Kanoa says.

"Give them hell out there." Garrett replies with a sort of
half-chuckle as he returns to his colleagues to begin more
tests on their inventions.

We both head back to the room and prepare to dive. As I
get comfy in the tube I see Kanoa nod to the techs that will
monitor us. Curiously, I slip into position and allow the machine to transcend me into beautiful cyberspace.

CHAPTER 23

AND STILL I CHOOSE TO LIVE

As the world forms around me I find myself outside in a city alley. It doesn't look like New York or The Central Zone or anywhere I know. I see skyscrapers and buildings although some of them are clearly broken down and destroyed. I peer out and see cars going by and people walking past.

"They won't interact. We're watching a memory I constructed in T.R.A.C.I." Kanoa is behind me. I turn to face him as he walks calmly onto the street.

"I'm not sure what state or city this would've been to you but for Luke and I, it was home." Kanoa admires the view.

"Luke?" I ask.

Suddenly, two kids run right past us. I don't recognize either of them. Both have very scrappy builds. One has black short hair and the other sports shaggy long blonde locks. They're both carrying food and scraps of metal. Some older guy shouts at them from a few yards back.

"That was us," Kanoa smiles. "Like I told you, we've been on the run our whole lives. And we were better off then most kids. We had our parents."

The world deconstructs and Kanoa and I fly into another programed memory. This time in a run-down hotel that is clearly abandoned. There are a bunch of people huddled into a room. A man, mid-forties and a woman of similar age are standing near the front of the crowd near a whiteboard.

"Okay, this supply warehouse supposedly holds years of rations inside. It's protected by Military and I.H.L soldiers." The man explains drawing a depiction on the board.

"Even after taking what we need the remaining value inside that warehouse could feed half this city's homeless population for six months," The woman continues. People seem to hum and nod in agreement. Moving through them, I position myself closer to the front.

"Kanoa! Luke! You two will be leading us this time!" The man shouts to the crowd. I watch as I see Kanoa in his late-teens and who I can only suppose is Luke step forward. They're patted on the back and cheered by the crowd as they come forward.

"Those were my parents." Present-day Kanoa points them out to me. "They lead us through countless missions helping and aiding the poor and un-defendable in the city. We tried our best to inform and educate the public. Try to convince them not to sign themselves into indenture or military service. We saved hundreds. But thousands fell every day." His mood turns somber as he remembers.

"You never had a childhood." I think about the implications and get hit with a pang of guilt. Kanoa shakes his head.

"It's not like many had the past to compare it to. Mercia did an effective job of re-writing history. A corrupt power awarded to the winners of war. But Luke and I had the old world to dream about. Thanks to our mother." Again, the world around us fades and rebuilds itself into what appears to be a deep underground hideout;

old rusty rooms with pipes and cogs. I see an even younger Kanoa and Luke, they can't be older than ten, being tucked into poorly constructed...I can't even call them beds. They are made of cardboard.

I watch their mother, a woman with a sweet face. Orange-red hair done up in braids that are falling out. They look like they haven't been tended to for a few days. Lips dry and cracked. The room we are all in is uncomfortably hot. Beads of sweat form on her face and drip onto her kids sleeping bags. Her attire suggests she's marching off to war. All black combat light armor. Not for tucking in children.

If she was wearing anything else you would see another ordinary citizen, a mother. She does not look like someone running a resistance. She curls some clothes into makeshift pillows to tuck under both of their heads.

"Get some sleep okay boys?" She readjusts some picture frames so they face the two boys. The photos appear to be different locations of the world. Lush jungle forests. Mountain ridges that expand for miles. I think I saw the Grand Canyon in one of them.

"But I'm not tired." Luke complains.

"Well what if I tell you boys a story my mother told me?"

"A story about the before world?" Young Kanoa perks up looking at the photographs.

"Yes, shhh. Lay down." She sits between them, crossing her legs on the floor. "Once upon a time there was a world that was filled with life. More humans then you could count and they loved going outside."

"C'mon mom. There's no way," Young Kanoa interjects.

"It's true," she continues. "People would leave their houses and go on hikes and adventures in their cars, driving from one side of the continent to the other. Some would sleep at night in little fabric pouches outside called tents.

Others would spend days laying nearly naked on towels at places called beaches!" Both Kanoa and Luke laugh at that.

The memory goes quiet as if someone pressed mute. I turn to Kanoa watching the memory with me.

"She told us everything her parents remembered and experienced. Her visions and dreams of the world before kept me going in our world today. Watching all those people die or get barcoded and locked into slavery or just atrophy away in their booths. I hated it." The memory continues to play out now silent. I look back at Kanoa.

"I get it. But why are we here? Why are you showing me this? You already told me what happened to your family. I'm sorry for what my mother did."

"I told you how my parents died. We're not here because of them." Kanoa turns to face me with the most serious look I have ever seen from him. We shift again, this time to a city sidewalk. It's night and raining hard. It's a weird sensation to be standing in a downpour but not getting wet. It's much like how I imagine a ghost would feel.

"Where are we now?" I shout over the constant slamming of water.

"When our parents died, Luke and I went our separate ways. He blamed me and I couldn't argue against it. I still hadn't forgiven myself. I was leading that day." Kanoa shouts.

Headlights approach. The car pulls right up to the curb and out steps a much older Kanoa. In fact, this one doesn't look much younger then the real one. He pulls out a wet piece of paper, reads it, then scans a nearby structure. It is a terrible, disheveled excuse of an apartment building. The memory of Kanoa walks inside and we both follow. He makes his way to apartment 9-B, and bangs on the door.

"Luke! Luke are you in there?" Memory Kanoa shouts. Locks turn and chains move as the door slowly opens.

A woman in her late teens answers the door. She is ghostly pale with neon pink hair completely frizzled.

"I'm looking for Luke," Memory Kanoa says.

"What's it worth it to you?" She slightly slurs her words, under some influence. Whether it is drugs or alcohol, I can't tell. Memory Kanoa huffs in annoyance and pulls a hundred out of his wallet. She takes it and stuffs it in her bra.

"Third room to the left." She staggers out of the way.

Kanoa hurriedly pushes past her and runs to the room. Inside he finds the entire bedroom has been outfitted to support an intense T.R.A.C.I Booth and Console. Kanoa looks at the display and it reads: Autopilot.

The logs say he's been under for over two months straight, living completely off of the nutrient IV system. Distraught, Kanoa hits the emergency eject button. The machine clicks and puffs of air rise as the pod slowly brings the human inside out of hibernation.

"I've told you about mental degradation from T.R.A.C.I but have you actually seen it yet Isaac?" Kanoa, here in the present, asks. I just shake my head, growing increasingly uneasy.

"It's not talked about because The Prexy doesn't want to admit it exists. And why should she? The only cases that occur are ones where the subject is pulled back into reality. Most people prefer to die in their booths. Makes it easy to clean and resell for a discounted price." Kanoa says sullenly. I return my attention to see a gravely, thin, pale-as-a-ghost, long, greasy man stumble out of the booth onto the floor. Luke. The younger Kanoa, in the memory, rushes to him while the real one watches on with me.

"Luke. Shit, Luke. What the fuck?" Kanoa gets down on his knees and holds him up.

"K-Kanoa? Wh-Why are y-you here? You're supposed t-to be in Ambronesia. You and Aurora have been talking about visiting that new island system forever." Luke barely keeps his composure. Every word is a long drawn out slur.

"Pause it." Kanoa looks up to the ceiling. The entire memory freezes. "Look at his eyes." Kanoa says.

"Kanoa, I-"

"Look!" He shouts loudly, startling me. I walk over slowly to get a better view. Bloodshot doesn't even begin to describe what is wrong with them. They are a horribly deep red, purplish color with dark black veins bulging outward from his eyes, but they go all the way up to his forehead and outward to both cheeks.

I would've been disgusted at that alone if I wasn't transfixed on his pupils. They aren't round. Instead, the left one has taken the form of an x and the right is now a plus shape. It is equally terrifying and fascinating.

"Resume," Kanoa instructs. The memory does.

"Luke. What are you talking about? Who's Aurora?" Kanoa tries to help him to his feet. Luke laughs weakly.

"Yeah, right, man. Like you don't know your own wife. I only went to your wedding and to every one of your children's birthdays. Aurora is a sweet woman. We really lucked out on the wives, man. Why did they ever marry idiots like us?" He tries to play-punch Kanoa's shoulder but misses entirely.

"How many years have you logged in T.R.A.C.I?" Kanoa is horrified as the realization comes over him.

"Hmm?" Luke is barely able to stay conscious. Kanoa leans him against the booth, then gazes at the console. I look with him and my eyes go wide at the stat log.

"Total Immersion Time for T.R.A.C.I Account User CC-8769241: 584 Years. 7 Months. 12 Days. 2 Hours."

"Five hundred years?" Kanoa is terrified. "Luke, you've logged over five hundred and eighty years of life on your brain? It's only been a year since Mom and Dad!" He shakes him angrily.

"Mom and Dad? Oh you haven't heard yet. They finally broke down and bought that cabin mansion in the mountains. Guess Dad finally wore down Mom, huh? We should visit there this winter. Have a nice big family Christmas with all the kids." Luke stares off into space, not making any eye contact with Kanoa.

"Luke." Kanoa slaps him. "This isn't funny man. Snap the fuck out of it! We're not married to anyone. Mom and Dad are dead. And it's my fault. I know that Luke It's my fault!" None of his words are getting through to him. His head bobs around to the rhythm of Kanoa's shakes. Luke is barely conscious.

"I remember this room. It's a part of this nightmare I keep having." Luke's head rolls around awkwardly.

"It's a shitty nightmare, man. The world sucks. The government sucks and you got our parents killed. Good thing that's just a dream right?"

Kanoa lowers his head. There seems to be no emotion on his face. Some anger. But other then that Kanoa goes stoic. Reactionless, he let's go of his brother and falls onto the ground. He leans against the wall in the room and slides down to sit. He just stares at his brother. Luke turns his head to the T.R.A.C.I booth.

"That thing. That's the thing that wakes me up. I wanna wake up." Luke uses every muscle he has available to crawl his way back into the booth. A single tear manages to break free from Kanoa's face. Luke manages to get to his feet for a moment before his whole body seizes up and he falls hard onto the ground. Kanoa stands up and walks over to look down at him.

Luke's strange, deformed eyes roll back into his head. He twitches uncontrollably and gasps for air. Kanoa looks around and yells out into the hallway.

"Whoever is conscious and can dial a phone, call for help right fucking now!" He walks back over to him and sits down next to him. Holding his head in his lap.

"I'm not going to let you fucking die you hear me? Not you too." Luke's eyes bleed and his thrashes come to a halt. "Luke?" Kanoa puts his head against Luke's chest. He lays him down and tries to perform CPR for a minute before standing up.

He takes a few deep breaths and walks over to the window and punches it out entirely. Cutting up his hand in the process. No screaming, no crying except a few breakaway tears. Out of nowhere memory Kanoa begins laughing. His sanity clearly reaching a breaking point. He laughs his way out of the room, leaving his brother on the ground. Some furniture crashes out in the hall. I can hear fists being thrown.

The woman who answered the door screams. I try to go out to investigate but real Kanoa stops me by placing his hand on my shoulder. He just looks down, away from me. Regret and guilt covers his face. Memory Kanoa slams out of the apartment and back into the street. Suddenly everything goes black.

I feel the pull of the system waking me. I open my eyes. Kanoa stands over my pod. Looking at his knuckles I can make out the faint scars from that day still present on his hands.

"My parents died because of an impulsive, arrogant decision I made. My brother died because I wasn't there for him when he needed me most." His glare is emotionless. He holds a hand out to help me up and out of the booth.

"What happened to the people in the apartment?" I ask not sure if I even want him to answer.

"They lived. But they wished they hadn't. I blamed them because they were right there. They could've done something. But after awhile I realized I was the one to blame. I regret my actions that day." Kanoa states firmly.

"That's why you've restricted my access."

I finally understand. That's also why they forbid auto-pilot dives. I conclude. Time can really run away on you.

"After Luke, I researched everything I could about the long-term effects this technology has on your brain. It's starts with headaches. Then visions. You slowly develop an addiction to the system. Basically escapism to the extreme to the point that eventually you spend so much time in there you can never again tell what is real and what is fake."

Now I am unable to meet his gaze. "I'm sorry." I say.

"For what?" Kanoa asks me. That catches me off-guard. I realize I don't have a reason.

"If you don't have a reason to say sorry then don't say it." Kanoa lectures. "I showed you that because I don't want what happened to him also happen to you. You deserve better then that." Kanoa sticks his hand out for me to shake. Before I can accept it, the door opens. Caleb enters.

"Guess who's back! And guess who needs to get moving!" Caleb looks at both of us. Crane walks in behind him.

"We have an audience. Time to negotiate." Crane says. Kanoa nods and looks to the tech booth. "Adam! You know the drill. Shelter and hunker down until we all return. If we're not back in a week then move to Plan B. "Yes sir!" The tech says.

"Good luck, guys." I say. Crane looks uneasy. I find out why immediately.

"Oh yeah. They want to talk to you Isaac." Caleb says as casually as he can muster.

"Me?" I am genuinely surprised.

"Apparently it got slipped to them that you're the doctor's son. I believe you've already made introductions with them?" Crane asks.

"Uh yeah I have." I wonder what on Earth I have to bring at this kind of meeting.

"Great then let's go. They're waiting for us." Crane says.

"Wait, like, right now?" I feel blindsided, as Kanoa already has a pack and is walking out to the hanger.

"No time like the present! Got to love teleporting off of excess Verve!" Caleb displays a decent handful of Verve in individual containers. The ever-strange substance forms into solid, liquid then gas over and over again. I grab my pack and meet them in the hanger. As Caleb uses his power to begin opening the door, I am kind of excited to be heading back to the nether. But why am I wanted there?

CHAPTER 24

HYPOCRITICAL HUMANITY

———

"Well this is certainly a historical event already. All of our leaders, back together again under the same roof! Alongside guests from beyond our planet!" Allahara beams.

The room that I had first met him in now has a gigantic circular table elevated a few feet off the ground, supported by staging. The six council members only took up a little under half of the wide surface. The other half seats Crane, Kanoa, Mordecai, Caleb, Z and myself. Baix and Norx are also here along with three others that I assume to be delegates or generals from their community.

The room is filled with guards from each respective side behind the table back towards the wall. I can see Markus and Cogs protecting the council and Mercedes and Kate along with a few others with us.

"Everyone in this room is here because we have something in common. We all wish for the demise of Madam Prexy." Allahara starts. He gives a big speech welcoming us all and how together we can be a fantastic force to be reckoned with.

"Save the politician speech for your voters who put you in that chair Al," Crane speaks up. "You're not trying to win votes right now."

"With all due respect Madam Crane you accepted our invitation. The least you can do is hear him out," one of the older council member says; an older looking woman.

She didn't speak much when I was here prior. Her snow white hair was now coiled into buns on either side of her head. Her wrinkled skin contained in a rather regal uniform. She must have pounds of jewelry weighing her down. Thick jeweled and ringed necklaces as well as bracelets hide any indication of frailty she might have. Crane huffs and slumps back into their seat.

"Though I suppose our colleague is right. There's really no need for small talk. You know what we want. Join back into the fold here Crane. Your intellect is invaluable." Crane holds up a hand and stands.

"Our position is simple. We are low on resources, including Verve. We've heard that you have an impressive stockpile you've been protecting. We would like to share in it."

"That stockpile is for members of the nether!" Another councilmember speaks up. It appears that most of the council of the Nether is somewhere in their seventies. Except a couple of them like Al. His young age makes him stand out. I wonder if that's normal. Allahara holds up his hand to silence him.

"That sounds like a simple proposal to me. Join back up and you all may have the same access as anyone else here."

"Crane?" Mordecai turns to them. She can be seen folding her arms and gritting her teeth. It is rather simple. But I guess there's more to joining back up than I'm seeing.

"Perhaps now we listen to what our neighbors have to share and offer." Kanoa chimes in looking over to Baix and Norx.

"Yes, lets." Allahara turns excitedly. Baix, who has since been as still as a statue, slowly rises.

"My name is Baix. I am the leader of a community of more then three thousand. All we want is the return of our ancestors' ship. It is our property and our birthright." He nods his head and sits back down.

"Fascinating! What would you do if said ship was returned to you?" Allahara grows more intrigued.

"That's our business, thank you." Baix retorts. Norx lays a hand on her husbands arm in an attempt to comfort him. Also in a way to convey to him to be careful with your words. Allahara leans forward in his seat. Pressing over the surface of the table.

"Come now, we're all allies, aren't we?" Al presses. I can't get a read on his intentions. He's either curious or demeaning. If he's aware of it is another thing. Baix and Norx look at each other with uncertainty in their eyes.

Their guards take a step forward towards their chairs and almost in unison the rest of the guards in the room take a single step forward. No weapons raised or anything. Everyone around the table keep talking as if nothing happened. Was I the only one who noticed that?

"We are allies with Crane. They saved our child from one of The Prexy's sky prisons." Baix clears his throat. "However we are open to expanding our alliance." Al smiles.

"Good. Otherwise I'm not sure why you're even here." Allahara says bluntly. His attitude baffles me. He flips flops from calm, collected and proper to that of a child. He doesn't look that much older then me. How did a guy like this get elected?

"They're here because they can help us. And because we owe that to them!" Crane's voice crackles with thunder.

"Do we now? I don't recall owning anyone, anything!" Allahara matches their energy. We're getting into a shouting match at this point. Kate looks up to the ceiling with an ironic audible sigh.

Kanoa rubs his temple and Mordecai cracks his neck in effort to get more comfortable. It's clear there is another conversation going on underneath their words.

"After what you people did to us?" Baix joins in the volume contest. He jumps out of his seat away from his wife startling her. All the guards in the room take another step forward. Caleb sees my concern over this and gives me a silent gesture to stay calm. I guess this is really how it normally goes.

"I am not responsible for the sins of my ancestors. I truly am sorry for what your people had to endure but I am the wrong person to shout at if you are looking for restitution." Allahara fires back.

"This is going nowhere. They're all yelling like children," I whisper over to Caleb.

"Welcome to politics," he whispers back.

I guess I can't be too surprised at these leaders. The leaders of my time weren't exactly squeaky clean. In fact I remember a quote from my father.

"Vote for the lesser of two evils."

"We're all focused on further steps up the staircase. We should be discussing The Prexy and what we've been able to figure out." Kanoa speaks up growing annoyed himself.

Allahara sits back down and smooths out his robes. Baix follows suit as does the guards.

"Where is the son? The child?" Allahara asks.

Suddenly, every face at the table turns towards me. Not ready for the sudden large amount of attention, I shift in my seat, lean forward on the table and awkwardly give a half wave. "Hi." Allahara lasers in on me.

"I've been informed that you have connections to the Prexy's second in command. In fact you are her only son. Is that correct?"

"It is, sir. I was born in 2006. She froze me and my father and we didn't awaken until a few months ago. She kept all three of us young through cryogenic technology." I wonder what he would've done if he had learned that when it was just Caleb and me here earlier.

"And where is your father now?" A new council member speaks up. This gentleman I don't recognize. He wasn't there last time. This man has been calmer then his cohorts so far. A middle aged gentleman with a salt and pepper beard matching his short hair. I swallow hard.

"He's dead, sir. Cancer. Weeks before the announcement of the cure." I try to remain emotionless. There's a few side conversations and mutters finally ending in that same council member saying,

"My apologizes." He nods in respect.

"Thank you, sir." I do the same and lean back into my chair. Silently wishing for all the eyes to shift back towards each other. I focus on Z who seems to be the only one not looking at me.

"Okay, look," Allahara tries to re-energize the room after my grim response killed the flow. "I agree with Kanoa. None of this matters if The Prexy remains on the board. Our intelligence suggests both her and the doctor are planning on going back under after the elections. No matter what we've tried, we are never able to locate their pods while they are hibernating."

"Right. Our only attempts can be while she is awake. If we miss this time around we will have to wait an unknown amount of years with her reign continuing. We might all die out before she decides to come back." Mordecai contributes this morbid concept.

"The fact of the matter is, even if all of our combined strength at this table here is utilized, we will still fall short of the size of her army.

By last count, the number of IHL Soldiers and Prexy Guards are close to hitting seven digits." Salt and Pepper speaks up. He must be in charge of surveillance and or military. Must be why I didn't see him last time. I conclude.

Shock and anger fill the faces of everyone in the room. Nobody was expecting those kinds of numbers pitted against us.

"A million soldiers?" Mordecai becomes baffled by the sheer size of the obstacle in our path.

"That's too many!" Kanoa says aghast.

"We're simply outmanned. We need more people." Caleb's voice stays calm but he is also clearly at a loss for a plan.

"We need another uprising!" Allahara states in a too-matter-of-fact tone. Suddenly the room explodes in argument. Mainly between Crane's people and the council. Baix and Norx look back and forth sheepishly.

"That's the dumbest idea I have never heard." Kanoa shouts.

"It's also the closest we ever got when we could destabilize the country." Old Lady Jewelry rebuts.

"Quiet!" Allahara shouts. The room settles. Once it does, he sits.

"We believe if we can ignite the nation again on a large enough scale then we can cause enough unrest to shake the election and keep the Prexy from going under sedation. That will at least buy us time." Allahara explains.

"We advertise and seek out new people all the time. Using proper channels to stay safe." Crane stands on her point. Allahara replies.

"However the vetting process simply takes to long and we have to keep changing it whenever a mole gets through." Mordecai and Kate hesitantly nod in agreement, checking their wounds from their previous excursion. Crane clocks this and goes quiet. Caleb looks down at the sound of that.

"What if we could hack into the main T.R.A.C.I Hub?" Allahara proposes.

There's some stillness, as everyone wonders where he's going with this. "What if we made a video and found a way to broadcast it to every single active T.R.A.C.I user in that moment?" He continues.

"A mass cyber hijack..." Crane ponders the possibility.

"If we could get into the main server room and use the right administrator credentials we could project a video in front of everyone's visor that they couldn't click away from. No secret black market online meetings. No vetting process. One massive wake up call." Mumbles of thought and agreement begin to fill the chamber.

"They'd have to either watch it or leave their booths." Kanoa realizes. Everyone from Crane's side begins to lighten up at this idea.

"And what would the video say?" Crane's eyes narrow a bit. Regaining her focus on the subject.

"Well, in much better-written words, but, essentially...join us and defy the Prexy. A promise for a better future." Allahara proposes.

"Join you. So, the Nether." Crane locks eyes with Allahara. The stare down doesn't last long, and Crane is the clear victor as Allahara nonchalantly waves his hand backwards, metaphorically cutting through the thick air in front of him.

"We can include that there are others," he adds. "People already working to take her down. The more resources we can prove we can provide, the more people should take to the idea." Allahara and Crane both clearly continue to try and read each other, but are now locked in a stalemate as both have masterfully crafted non-chalant gazes, even if there is clear fire in both of their eyes.

"What's stopping us from doing this?" I ask. A frustrated sigh comes from Allahara.

"The administrator hub is under the strictest security the Prexy holds. It's on a quantum computer locked in a satellite that orbits Earth. To perform this kind of hack we would have to manually upload it and that's not even considering the kind of firewall protection it has once you're there. First problem. How to get aboard an orbiting satellite."

I look to Crane and get a stern facial response that tells me to shut my mouth. I decide to not press my luck.

"Even before that even we'd need access to the computer network to even have a chance," Allahara concludes.

"Let's say we did have that," Crane keeps their poker-face strong. "What would be the next step?"

"To find the admin passwords to get us into the hub, then find a way into space." Allahara's tone suggests that he is already abandoning the plan.

"The boats top out at MACH 2 but can't survive outer space." Kanoa frowns as he offers these facts.

"Our spaceship is!" Baix perks up! He has been quietly absorbing the dynamics of the room, and the ideologies of how to attack the Prexy. But now he finally has something to contribute.

"I honestly don't know where they are keeping it. I'm sorry." Allahara responds in a surprisingly genuine tone.

"What if I used my ability?" Caleb chimes in from out of nowhere. Everyone turns towards him, Crane's expression is one of sheer shock at Caleb's offer.

"Have you ever attempted a jump from that distance?" Salt and Pepper asks.

"No. But if we can find enough information about it. Photographs. Video of inside of it, and have a good enough guess on where it'll be at a given time-"

"It's suicide." Crane cuts him off.

"You say that like we're not living every day like we can't die at any given moment," Caleb fires back.

"We have a way into the doctor's computer." I blurt out half-regretting it as Crane turns their fiery stare at me. I could tell they wanted to use their ability to shut me up but they are showing incredible restraint.

"We established a hidden link a few months ago at Oakwood." I continue. I'm getting too excited at this idea. Caleb could get us up there. We just need enough Verve. They have enough. We could do this.

"At the very least we can pull the schematics and passwords for the admin hub satellite then make a more informed decision and plan." The words keep falling out of my mouth, uncontrollably.

"What our colleague is forgetting is that to be able to pull that much info, I would need help and time to browse through the doctor's files. We would need to make sure she was not at her computer so they can't trace us." Crane says attempting damage control.

"Then let me in a T.R.A.C.I booth and allow me to contact her. You can encrypt our location, do whatever you need to do to protect it. She will talk to me." I find my voice. Again, the room goes silent.

"I see no issue with this plan." Baix says.

"Nor do I." Allahara adds. "Crane?"

We all look at Crane who I think is ready to beat me to a pulp. Kanoa shares a similar look.

"Use the son to distract the doctor to pull the satellite codes and schematics. We'll go from there. We're done here." Crane hops down a good seven feet to the ground and walks out of the room. Kate follows them as the meeting abruptly ends.

People quickly engage in the planning stage of setting up an encrypted T.R.A.C.I booth for me and talk about proper hide ports and contingency plans. I exit with Caleb to greet the rest of our crew on the building steps outside. But not before getting stopped by Allahara.

"Oh hello sir." He produces a watch and offers it to me. I recognize it as the uniform watch that everyone here wears. The one that protects our heat signatures.

"I wanted to thank you and properly welcome you to the Nether. I think we finally have a real shot at checkmating the queen once and for all. I had a good sense about you." Allahara says beaming with hope.

"Oh um well y-your welcome sir." I can't focus as I see Crane staring daggers at me from the entrance.

"Sorry sir please excuse me." I say taking the watch from him and nudging past him.

"I don't even know where to begin." Crane begins. She is extremely pissed off.

"I have the right to share my ability." Caleb says.

"Not to sacrifice yourself for something we don't even know will work! You have never pushed yourself that far. And you!" Crane now turns to me.

"Isaac, that was one of our biggest secrets that you just told the entire council! What if a guard in there is a spy? Did you think about that?"

"No. I didn't." I say sheepishly.

"And you finding a way to put yourself back into the T.R.A.C.I program completely disrespects and undermines my authority as a leader.

"What do you want from me, Crane? I am trying to help, to do what I can to end this ridiculous nightmare I woke up in. I'm sorry you had some falling out with those people, but from what I can see they want what we want.

We can work with them!"

"You've spent a few months here. I grew up in this time. Don't try to tell me what I should think about the world I know." Crane notices the watch in my hand and swipes it from me. She holds it up to my face.

"You are right Isaac. This isn't your world!" With that Crane heads into the center of town. Mordecai and Kate follow looking displeased. Kanoa sighs and joins them. Caleb and I sit on the stairs looking out into this underground metropolis.

"You regret any of that?" I ask Caleb.

"No, not really. That's just Crane. She doesn't like it when others step on her toes. What about you?" I sigh.

"I've never been known to make anyone happy. Guess it's just a part of me." I feel a hard punch on my shoulder.

"Ow! The fuck was that for?" He laughs.

"You are way too cranky and dramatic. What you did in there took balls. It's a good plan. It's realisitc. They just need to all get over themselves." Caleb says smiling.

"Well, I am the oldest man on Earth. Maybe that comes with wisdom." I chuckle and rub my shoulder.

"I have weird taste in friends." Caleb stands. "C'mon. Drinks are on me tonight. We need to figure out how the fuck I am going to open a door seven miles above me."

CHAPTER 25

CONFLICTING OPINIONS

———

Neon's temporary base is an old manufacturing building nestled neatly in the heart of The Central Zone's red light district. Right in the smack dab epicenter of a group of abandoned buildings. It used to produce the previous generations' VR headsets. The government doesn't really care what happens to places once they are done with them. As a result there are entire blocks' worth of areas to hide from the law.

"Gather around," Neon exclaims, as he enters the lobby where a few dozen people are standing. They form a small crowd around him. "The mission is a resupply. Thanks to some recent intel we have three warehouses that are suspected to be abandoned by the Prexy. They might be filled with resources we desperately need." The crowd chatters amongst themselves about this mission.

"What kind of resources?" Someone from the crowd shouts. A heavily tatted individual with neon green hair adoring half of his head. The other half shaved bald. Not really muscular.

"Weapons, rations, if we are lucky, some verve. We need to regain our strength," Neon explains. Scrape steps next to Arthur. "You better be right about this."

She says to Arthur as she keeps her focus on Neon. Arthur appears to be in his own world. Spacing out and couldn't be bothered with the information being shared. Neon continues to hold court, all eyes on him. He draws a diagram on a whiteboard.

"The plan is to split into three groups. Each one will take a warehouse, loot and grab as much as you can and bring everything to the docks. From there we can load everything up to bring back here. The warehouses are right on the water with easy access to the open channel." He draws a basic layout of the area and the docks on the whiteboard.

"We'll hit the warehouses simultaneously. The sooner we're in, the sooner we're out. We'll hit them tonight. Examine this paper taped to the board to find out which team you're on." Scattered mumbles and grunts fill the air as everyone crowds up on the whiteboard.

Neon flips it over to where everyone's name is written down in one of three columns. As people find their name they split to three different areas to pair up with their working partners for the job. Scrape finds her name. Annoyed, she stalks over to Neon.

"Don't put me with him," Scrape pleads.

"They were all assigned randomly." Neon says.

"It's the furthest one. Don't trap me with him for that long." Scrape continues.

"What is your issue with him?" Neon asks.

"Something's off about this guy. I don't like him." Scrape explains.

"Well then. If he tries to kill you, then kill him first. He got us in these doors, we need what's in them. Suck it up." Neon heads off to their collection of vehicles. With a heavy sigh, Scrape approaches her group to discuss their plan.

Sometime later after the sun has fully set, the cold winter air blows gently in the night sky. Slushy, muddy snow in pushed-up piles create makeshift walls along the roads. Chunks of ice stick to the harbor like barnacles. The other two warehouses are a couple of miles away. Scrape, Arthur and a group of a dozen thieves hide shivering outside of the massive warehouse.

"You sure these storage facilities are abandoned?" Scrape asks Arthur.

"She stopped patrolling this section of the city heavily months ago. There hasn't been a bit of business since." Arthur explains snapping out of his daydream.

"So then how do you know-" Scrape is cut off by Neon's voice coming over a radio.

"Warehouse one in position. Warehouse two in position. Warehouse three?"

"Moving into position now." Scrape replies. "Travis, you're up," Scrape whispers.

A tall man in his late-twenties with a buzz-cut, thick glasses. Gaunt and scrawny. He's carrying a tablet with four individual screens arranged in a grid like pattern. Each one is displaying different information. He sneaks his way up to the warehouse door. The door has an electronic keypad requiring an eight-digit input.

"The codes need to be submitted at the same time. That'll start our clock." Neon's voice emanates from the radio. Travis punches in the code provided to him by Arthur. The four panels all chime in sync and display

"Awaiting Confirmation". He hovers his finger over the activation button. "Warehouse three ready." Travis says.

"Warehouse one ready. Warehouse two ready." He hears over the intercom.

"Right on the hour. Fifteen seconds." Neon orders.

Everyone waits anxiously as the timer ticks down.

"Three, two, one. Now!" Neon hisses through the radio. All three codes are entered at the same time and with a confirmation beep the warehouse doors begin to rise up.

"Let's move!" Scrape orders. The dozen thieves hurry into the warehouse. "Greg, lights," Scrape orders.

An older male, late-thirties with already gray hair steps forward and with a flash of verve-filled blue eyes he forms a shining ball of pure energy in his hands. With a toss he throws the miniature sun into the air where it hovers and illuminates the area before them. Looking in, there are dozens upon dozens of crates.

"Holy," Travis mutters. "It's a motherload!" Greg says. Scrape walks around, starts reading off some of the crates.

"You were right. There's enough supplies here to get us back on track. Call the boats!" Scrape shouts.

The warehouse has water access built inside it for easy unloading and onloading access. Two small fishing carriers arrive and park. People move cargo as fast as they can. Some use enhanced abilities to hasten the process. After a half an hour, the boats are packed to the brim.

"Send them off! We have time for another run!" Scrape orders. Neon agrees over the radio.

"All or nothing."

They wait, organizing more cargo crates for easier transport. Once finished with that task, the crew takes a break, while waiting for the boats to return. Scrape approaches Arthur, who has not eased up in his stance or expression this whole time. He has been watching outside by the docks.

"You gave us a good tip. Thank you," Scrape says. Arthur doesn't reply. He keeps staring out at the ocean.

"Look I get the whole 'woe is me' brooding thing. But you come off as slightly creepy, man."

Scrape now joins him in his sea gazing.

"You talk too much." Arthur keeps his focus on the water.

"Call it my gift. Another one, that is, anyway." She smirks. Suddenly voices on the radio start going crazy.

"Abort! Abort! I.H.L. presence at warehouses one and two. They are making their way to you!" The radio screeches. Everyone moves quickly to get their things packed up and to carry whatever extra they can bring along.

"You said these spots were clear!" Scrape aims her gun at Arthur. He calmly raises his hands, almost as if he doesn't care what just came over the radio.

"I thought they were. Someone must've tripped an alarm." Arthur says with a monotone expression.

"Or you set us up." Scrape says turning the safety off her gun.

"Arthur's poker face gives away to a little bit of surprise and anger. "Now why would I do that? I'm here for the same stuff you guys are. I was fired by those pricks!"

A boat's horn blares as it returns. The captain waves his arms frantically for his allies to board. Several of the thieves jump into the water to swim towards it. A few of them fill their pockets with product that they believe is waterproof which causes them to have a harder time swimming. Some abandon this attempt shedding their clothing in order to arrive safely to the ship. One of the grunts runs up to Scrape and Arthur.

"We got to get out of here! What's going on?" The grunt asks, confused.

"I wouldn't." Arthur warns Scrape. She fires the gun. The metal bullet stops midway in the air as Johnson concentrates on it. With a turn of his neck, he turns the bullet. It fires right between the eyes of the surprised grunt. With a thud, the body hits the floor, already dead.

Scrape, angry and shocked at the loss of her friend, quickly unloads her clip at him. Arthur stops all of the bullets and uses his hands to pry the gun from her. Addison's body locks up and is lifted a few feet in the air.

"Now what should I do? You're putting me in a difficult position here." Arthur says with no emotion. Scrape tries to use her ability to speed away but with no ground beneath her feet she is left struggling midair.

"What the hell do you want?" Scrape exclaims, she spies the remainder of her allies start to climb aboard the boat. They are oblivious to her plight.

"Nothing you can provide me. And now you've made up your mind about me. Neon, however, may still be of use. Can't have him turning on me now." Arthur moves the frozen bullets and Scrape over the water. The sounds of sirens and helicopters begin to slowly grow.

"Warehouse three, they are converging on your location now! Get out of there!" Neon says from the radio on Scrape's hip. Arthur brings her towards him to grab the radio before returning her above the water.

"Copy," he says before using his ability to crush the radio into pieces. He tosses it into the water.

"Killing people is not going to bring back whoever you lost." Scrape is now actually worried for her life.

"How do you know I lost someone?" Arthur asks, intrigued.

"I recognize the look. You're grieving. Trust me when I say killing people does not make it any better. You will always have that pain. Is that what whoever you lost would've wanted?"

"His name was Damien and he would've wanted to live!" Arthur screams. "I don't care what happens to myself or others. So long as I can correct the misjustice in this world.

And I guess you are next on that list." Scrape spits towards him.

"Fuck you!" Arthur cocks his head and the frozen bullets turns and fire all at Scrape.

Half a dozen bullets rip into her torso, legs and head. Blood drips into the water, Arthur let's go of his hold and Scrape's corpse falls into the icy cold black water. The noise of vehicles growing louder, Arthur sees the boat is already a good mile away.

He focuses hard and begins to levitate his own body up over the water. In fifteen minutes, he is able to catch up to the boat, now safely away from the police-swarmed warehouse. People watch in amazement as Arthur flies his way back onto the boat.

"Wish I could do that." One of the grunts mumbles.

"Headcount!" The captain shouts back to the remaining people on the boat. Everyone looks around.

"There's only eight of us on board, including you captain." Travis says.

"Our team had twelve..." The captain slams the steering wheel.

"Fuck. Where's Scrape?" He shouts back.

"She told us to go on. That she would try to hold them back." Arthur says. A couple of them are struck dumbfounded by the probable loss of their leader. Others are hit with sadness and anger.

"Fuck. Well, hunker down. We're gonna have to be out for a while before we can return to base. Wait for Neon's orders," the captain explains. Arthur sighs and finds a spot on on the boat to lay down on and enjoy the free boat ride. After three hours on sea the remaining thieves return to the base where Neon awaits. He is clearly upset.

"What the hell happened? One moment we're fine, the next we have half the I.H.L. on us!" Neon complains to the now much smaller crowd.

"Infinite Horizons Laboratories has some of the most cutting edge tech available on the planet. I warned you all about the potential of silent alarms. I was not privy to every meeting about the companies security while working for the loft. Anyone of us could have tripped one without our knowledge." Arthur admits flat out. Everyone looks at him shocked.

"What?" Neon is baffled.

"Of course I wouldn't have had no way of knowing. It's clear I was never fully trusted in my position with The Prexy after all now." Arthur says casually.

"But you knew that was a possibility!" Travis speaks up. Arthur turns to him.

"So did you!" They stare each other down. Neither one is backing off. "And what would you have done if you've known? Look around here. Clearly we needed the supplies. For what we managed to get I consider that a worthwhile trip!" Arthur claims.

"We all knew." Neon says defeatedly.

"We lost ten people. Our numbers are now under fifty!" Greg chimes in.

"So now everyone gets better gear." Arthur retorts. There is a mix of reactions from this. Some scoffs, other's sigh and shake their head. A few grumble in agreement.

"Where's Scrape? I don't see her." Neon says.

"She didn't make it sir." The grunt who was driving the boat says. Neon has a look of sheer anger as he turns around and punches the whiteboard hard. It tips over and clatters loudly to the ground.

"Everyone unpack and unload the cargo." He orders as he storms off.

As the remaining members of Neon's squad slowly, quietly go about their chores and business, Arthur can't help but let a small smile break though his face. He walks over to Neon.

"With what we managed to get we'll still have the strength of a force twice our old size." Arthur says standing behind a hunched over Neon. He stands up straight and turns to face him.

"With what we have now we can find Isaac and probably Abigail as well." Arthur concludes. Neon holds up his hand as to indicate to pause. He steps toward him.

"I'm not going to war with The Prexy. That's your fight. That kid however. He's still an accessible wanted figure." Neon's tone is direct and commanding. Clearly flushed with anger but trying to keep a sense of professionalism about him. Remembering his conversation with Scrape right before this mission he eyes down Arthur. Wondering what really happened out there.

"Maybe you'd feel better if you saw what we managed to acquire thanks to their sacrifices." Arthur says in an an attempt to cheer him up. They both head over to one of the crates they managed to steal. Neon grabs a crowbar and with a grunt he pries open the crate revealing the contents within. Arthur and Neon peer over to look inside. Arthur smiles first with Neon's hesitancy causing a few seconds of a delay before succumbing to a grin.

"That's enough to make an army." Neon declares.

CHAPTER 26

HOLLOW WISHES

It only took a day for The Nether to set it all up. It wasn't hard to send off an invitation to Abigail. With my help, they made sure to word it in a way that she knew it was coming from me - virtually untraceable. As I climb into the chamber, Crane shakes her head and walks away. Kanoa comes up to me as I lay down and he takes my hand.

"Isaac. It's not real. It never is." I nod my head, agreeing but staying silent. I want to believe him. I want to learn from his experience. But the promise and power of creating your own reality is just so addicting.

"If we detect a trace we will pull you out in a moment's notice." Kanoa continues. "Remember. Keep her as busy as you can. Talk about whatever you can. Kate will need as much time as you can give us."

I know The Nether council and Baix's group are all in attendance for this and my POV is being displayed on big monitors within The Nether, so it feels weird knowing that I am basically doing some odd TV show for a bunch of people in my old house.

"Don't get emotional kid," Kanoa finishes turning his back and walks away from the booth.

"Says you." I sigh. As the chamber closes and I feel the familiar process of entering the program I close my eyes and after a quick, sharp pain I am back in my childhood home.

It's a perfect recreation. As I walk through the hallways and rooms of my old house, checking every little detail, I can't help but feel like a ghost or some sort of echo. The real house has long since been demolished, I'm guessing, either through time or war I have no way of knowing.

But T.R.A.C.I does a good job at reading your every thought. It's too easy to get lost in these digital worlds. As I go and sit in the living room I hear my friends talk to me though an ear piece. They are monitoring this simulation from the outside.

"So, this is where you used to live?" I could tell it was Caleb.

"Yep. Small little cozy area in the woods. Two floors, a basement and a wood fireplace. It was simple." I reminisce. My mother wanted to live in the city but it was my Dad's family home. He somehow won that argument. It's uncanny, even the carpet feels the same. I walk over to the fireplace and look at the framed photographs on the mantle.

My mother and father eating at their favorite local diner. Another one of when my father proposed to my mother when they were vacationing. They were at the Grand Canyon. One photograph however I don't recognize. It's of a gentleman in a police uniform. He looks young. Fresh out of the academy.

"What the?" I mumble. Leaning in I see his name on his badge. Ramirez. I look away sharply and step back from the fireplace.

"We're sending her the password now Isaac." Caleb says. A private T.R.A.C.I simulation is usually used for friends for in-between matches of games or to host virtual parties with guests all over the world at once. But you need the password to log in. The password we sent her was 'Dorothy'.

After about fifteen minutes I hear the alerts that someone is connecting to the server. Watching with utter fascination as a bright white silhouette in a humanoid shape materializes in front of me. Slowly, bit by bit it forms into the woman I know as my mother. She opens her eyes and looks around until locating me.

"Hi, sweetie," she says with a somewhat genuine tone. Not letting my guard down I keep my distance.

"Hi, Mom." My tone is rather flat.

She walks around. We are both in the living room which has an old tube TV right by the front door and a window. Two couches, one faces the TV and one is angled to the side of it. The fireplace is on the free side and in the back of the room is an old desk with an ancient computer tangled within it.

"I remember the last time I was here," she says.

"Yeah I do too. That was when you kidnapped dad and froze him against his will." She turns to me with an unnaturally sullen expression.

"I just wanted more time to help him," she says quietly.

"It wasn't what he wanted." I catch myself, try not to get angry.

"I see we are in a private lobby hosted on your end. Is this where you torture me for information?" She stares back daggers.

"You would know all about that, wouldn't you?" I retort. She simply hums in understanding and begins to walk upstairs. The staircase being in the direct center of the house, leading up to four small rooms; three bedrooms and a bathroom. She turns to the left and opens the door at the end of the hall. I follow her.

"This was your room. You had blue walls and the cutest treasure chest for all your toys," she reminisces.

"I remember." I look around my old childhood bedroom. I grew too big for it but we loved this house too much. I made it work right up until I was eighteen. Abigail sits on the bed, looking away. She turns to me with some tears beginning to break away from her eyes.

"You're doing great Isaac. Keep her talking." Mordecai says.

"Will you tell me where he is buried? Please?" She asks as the tears fall from her face.

"How do you-" I stop myself, remembering who my mother is. Of course she knew. Somehow.

"Scotland. The Lighthouse. You can visit him if you'd like." I lean against the door across the room. She chuckles slightly.

"Now that is definitely what he would've wanted. He loved that place. So did you, always climbing over rocks." I walk up closer now feeling a bit more safe.

"I'd rather not talk about him anymore, please." She looks hurt by that.

"Fine." She brushes herself off and stands. "Then why don't we talk about why we're here. What do you want?" I hesitate for a moment. "I promise this is not being recorded on my end," she says harshly.

"And I should believe this because?" I press her. She heads back downstairs and out the front door. I follow her. Outside we had a small grassy yard before the tree line to the forest all around the house met us. No further then fifty yards. They set the weather to an overcast cloudy day. The moisture in the air is heavy.

"Because I know the kind of people you are with. And yes, while the Prexy wants nothing more then all of their heads on a pike, and despite what you think of me, I'm trying to keep you alive Isaac.

"She would kill us both if she found out who you were."

"So why don't you quit?" I throw back at her. She sighs, frustrated.

"Still such a child Isaac. Haven't I taught you better? Our abilities in this world must be utilized to their highest form. I've single-handedly brought us both into an age where anything is truly possible. We are our own gods. We have the power to create our own universes. Live by our own rules!"

"And killing people is just a means to an end?" I tack on to her speech.

"For our species to continue to survive, yes. Could you imagine what the world would look like right now if we didn't have T.R.A.C.I? Utter chaos and breakdown of total civilization. At least with T.R.A.C.I the populace is controlled, complacent, dormant. Allowing the bright minds to build our way towards a better future."

"You mean the ones able to afford a T.R.A.C.I booth? What about the millions out there homeless and starving?" The wind begins to pick up now. They're getting close out there.

"They can walk into a government building and get a job right now if they want it!" Abigail shouts.

"You mean they can be slaves if they wish? Not that it's really any different then the average joe you have hooked to your product. It's not healthy. It's not right, mom."

"It's all we have at this point," she says sadly. Almost with a defeated tone in her voice. Not something I am used to seeing from her.

"For now." I say quickly then instantly realize I fucked up. She brings her full attention to me and quickly approaches.

"What do you mean for now? What are you planning?" She becomes increasingly alert; agitated.

"Isaac..." Crane says in a tone that almost matches my mother whenever I was young and I was tip-toeing into getting in trouble.

"You know Dad awoke and was conscious for a few moments before he passed?" I try to hard detour the conversation. Luckily it does the trick.

"He did?" My mother is intrigued.

"Yeah. He asked me about my dance. You know the one you kidnapped me from. Away from all my friends."

"And if I recall, I remember a certain anonymous donation that put a lovely portrait of you in the school for many years," my mother counters.

"What happened with Clara, mom?" I finally get to my biggest question for her.

"Who?" She looks genuinely confused.

"Clara Hall. She was from my school and she disappeared around the time you guys took over. Please don't lie to me right now." My throat tightens. My mother sighs deeply.

"I heard someone from your school was digging into what happened to you. Yes, I remember a girl. I remember learning how she tried to bomb the constitutional convention." She adds in almost trying to defend her decisions.

"What did you do to her mom?"

"Nothing. At first," she starts. "We caught her and I had her on ice next to you and your father for a few years. I thought she'd be nice to have with you whenever I chose to wake you, but-" she hesitates again. "But what?"

"There was an attack at the facility you three were in. I tried to save her." She walks right up to me and places both her hands on my shoulders.

"No..." I begin to realize.

"I was barely able to save you and your father," she continues.

"So she's dead. You kidnapped her and now she's dead just like dad!" I grow furious.

"Neither of those deaths are my fault!" She matches my fury. The wind picks up harder now. I suddenly hear the chime of the cowbell we always kept hanging from our porch. I knew that was the signal. They are about to pull me out.

"Wait!" I shout off to the side completely forgetting to keep them hidden.

"Wait for what? What's going on, sweetie?" My mother asks, looking around.

I feel the familiar pull. The hypnotic, jerking sensation as I am ripped out of my childhood home much like waking from a dream. The image of my mother outside my childhood home fades and I am in the booth within the Nether. I jump out as Kanoa, Crane, and Z approach.

"I needed more time!" I shout at them as Caleb, some council members and Baix's group also come closer.

"We didn't." Crane says. "You got it, Mordecai?" She shouts back towards the tech booth fifty feet away.

"The entire schematics and logins of the main T.R.A.C.I satellite!" He shouts happily.

"We need to review it and draw up possibilities on how to invade it." Allahara says.

"We will review every possibility," Crane reaffirms. Allahara nods. "Thank you Isaac, that was very helpful." Crane says montone as everyone begins heading back towards the council chamber building. I sit on the ground with my back against the machine. Caleb and Kanoa stay and look down at me.

"She kidnapped her too. And got her killed." I don't make eye contact with either of them. I hear one of them sigh.

"C'mon," Kanoa holds his hand out to help me up.

"Let's drink."

"If you're buying, I want in." Caleb grabs me by my other arm as I take Kanoa's hand. Together, the two of them hold me from either arm over the shoulder as we all walk to O'Halloran's.

"Just don't ask Hal for his signature drink. Don't think you could handle another one of those." Caleb remarks, trying to lighten the mood.

"I can." Kanoa says confidently trying to make me laugh. I try to smile but fail to do so as all I can think about is our last show we did together.

In a laboratory, Abigail steps out of a similar T.R.A.C.I booth. She removes the gear and ponders. She remains deep in thought until a younger scientist, a woman with short blonde hair shaped into bangs and thick glasses, comes stumbling into the room.

"Madam Secretary," she corrects her posture.

"Well?" Abigail asks expectantly.

"You were right. They had a tracer attached to your network. They've been able to spy and steal from your computer for what I can tell at least a few months."

"And why did they feel the need to distract me now?" She inquires.

"They stole access codes and schematics for the main T.R.A.C.I satellite." The scientist looks horrified. Abigail calmly stretches her arms.

"Hmm. Interesting." She smiles.

"We need to respond at once!" The young scientist exclaims.

"Oh we will darling. But best not disturb The Prexy with this. I've dealt with more serious situations before." Unsure of what to say, Laura stays silent.

"You know I have so few loyal companions around here. I'm glad I can rely on you Laura." Abigail smiles.

Laura adjusts her glasses.

"I'll never be able to repay you for what you did for my father. Thanks to you he is cancer free." A couple tears try to break away from Laura's face before she wipes them away.

"Do me a favor doctor and fetch me my rolodex. I need to arrange a few things. We will handle this incursion swiftly." She orders. Laura heads out of the room.

"Doctor. Keep this between us for right now." She nods and heads out. Abigail then plays back the recording of that simulation. Filmed from her first person perspective. She stops the recording on the shot of Isaac when she had both hands on his shoulders.

"Now Isaac, it's time for you to come home." She says to herself smiling.

CHAPTER 27

NEXUS LOG 10.23.32

———

The command room is quiet. Three dozen people each at their own station, standing up glued to the giant screens at the front of the room. Three gigantic monitors high up display different angles of a rocket getting ready for takeoff. In a tinted booth behind and above these people stand two figures. A younger Prexy and Abigail, are also glued to the monitors.

"Everything is set?" The Prexy asks, not taking her attention from the screens.

"Every precaution and test has been run over ten times now. There is a 0.001 percent chance of failure." Abigail says.

"And in that 0.001 situation?" The Prexy breaks her focus to look at Abigail, who responds without hesitation.

"The rocket is on the other side of the globe. If the contents of that rocket explode we are on the furthest and best continent we could be on." Abigail takes a deep breath.

"So we will survive?" The Prexy wants reassurance.

"You really do not care that are incinerating our last ally in this stunt. Once Australia learns what is really inside that rocket we will have effectively burned our last bridge."

"We don't need bridges. No country will challenge us after our little demonstration of our advancements. We alone hold the populace of the aliens and therefore are the only manufacturers of verve-powered weapons." Abigail shakes her head.

"It'll seep out into the world, if it hasn't already." Abigail argues.

"Then I guess it's a good thing we are going to wake up to some impressive walls." The Prexy turns back to the screen. The countdown begins. The two of them hold their breath as everyone in the room joins in the counting.

"Three...two...one!" The rocket ignites and roars into the atmosphere. Cheers, high-fives and hugs fill the room as the two women let out huge sighs of relief.

"Congratulations," The Prexy says, while holding her knees, hunched over.

"For what? Not blowing up half of Earth?" Abigail sits, feeling a little light-headed herself.

"It'll reach it's target in twenty years. Assuming the self-defense mechanisms onboard keep asteroids away we will have won this stupid war.

"By blowing up an entire planet? All that research, knowledge, and culture." Abigail says eyes wandering around to the unknowing scientists and techs.

"They brought this on themselves by invading us. Hey, I respected your wishes. You and I are the only ones who know what was really on that rocket. And you are the only one with the research and schematics on how to build an anti-matter bomb."

"And....?" She says looking for more of an answer.

"And I will never again ask you to build one for us. I am aware of how much it cost you. Cost us." The Prexy looks out onto the floor of happy, cheering scientists and workers.

"We made history today you and I."

Abigail feeling a pang of regret.

"Something like that should never have existed." Abigail's eyes lock onto The Prexy's.

"And it never did. The technology will die with you." The Prexy is clearly annoyed. Abigail nods.

"You realize that technology could utterly change the very foundations of-" Abigail interrupts her.

"What of these resistances I'm hearing of?"

"They're small and unorganized. We're stomping out any sort of organization we see. I've drafted plans to take effect while you and I skip this decade. We will wake up to T.R.A.C.I hubs and walls protecting our borders nearly a mile high and super soldiers per your design. I.H.L. will lead the production." Abigail smiles at that. Her business has a profitable future ahead.

"We really will have the chance to push humanity into the ranks that they were once in." Abigail gestures to screens monitoring captive neighbors.

"Space travel, immortality. Thanks to you we can be there for it. So let's go and wake up in the future shall we?"

"I'll meet you in the cryo-chambers." Abigail smiles as The Prexy walks down to shake hands and congratulate the eager workers below.

A chirp rings out from her phone in her pocket. Abigail reads it and begins quietly slipping out of the room. She makes her way to an operating room. Sterilized instruments and robotic arms welding different tools stand still in the room awaiting commands. Abigail who normally is the most at ease in the operating room right now feels stress. She closes and locks the door behind her. She begins turning on and testing the equipment.

"Custom procedure" She mutters to herself as she inputs the instructions on the robots.

She takes off her lab coat and folds it neatly on a nearby table. She hops up and lays down on the operating table. She takes a rectangular chunk of rubber out of her pocket. She then takes out what appears to be an SD card contained in a translucent white case and sets it down in front of the machines.

"This is your item you are attaching to my rib. Confirm." The robot scans the item and chimes successfully. A robotic arm moves a screen to face her.

"Anesthesia?" The console asks.

"No."

She places the hunk of rubber in her mouth. Too big for her to accidently swallow but perfect for biting down on. She secures it in place. She hits a few buttons and restraint straps move out of the table securing her arms and legs to the surface.

"Beginning procedure." The robots announce.

Abigail's pulse quickens. She realizes in this moment she is not in control. She watches helplessly as one of the arms lifts off her blouse revealing her bare torso. The machine makes an incision near her 6th rib on her right side. She winces in pain. Groaning as the machines carefully, methodically attach this item to her rib. After a half hour she sits upright.

"Procedure Complete" The machine chimes.

"Perfect" She says now beginning a hard wipe of all the machines data and memory banks. As she is finishing up there is a knock at the door.

"Hello? Who is in there? This OR was reserved!" An angry male voice rings out startling Abigail.

She closes out all the computers and composes herself. She turns off the lights and unlocks the door. Outside a similar aged gentlemen. Sandy blonde short straight hair. Horn rimmed glasses match his lab coat and binder.

His expression immediately shifts from anger to nervousness.

"Oh Doctor Ashter. I'm sorry I must have the wrong room." He fumbles looking over his notes.

"No not at all. I was just checking up on our equipment." She says hurrying past him. "Room's all yours doctor."

"Doctor Ashter!" He shouts at her now having made a bit of distance. She reluctantly turns around.

"Yes?" He looks down at her side.

"You're bleeding." She looks down and realizes the robots only put one layer of gauze over her wound. It has already bled through her lab coat. Not a lot but enough to notice.

"Went too close around a corner." She says grabbing some more gauze from a nearby medical cart.

"Good day doctor." She says continuing her path.

"Good day" He mumbles confused.

The cryochamber location is in the deepest floor of the whole facility. Blackstone is used to keep temperatures cold and unforgiving. Abigail arrives and passes through two security guards and a retinal scan to enter. There the Prexy has already undressed for the most part and is just about ready.

"Abigail. Your late. I was about to go into the future without you." She says. Abigail sighs and begins undressing herself.

"Like that's an actual threat." The Prexy notes the now heavier bandage.

"When did you do that?"

"Few days ago. You should see the other guy." She says smirking. The Prexy still appearing quizzical leans back into her chamber.

"Goodnight Doctor." She says.

"Goodnight Madam Prexy" The Prexy nods and steps into a large metal and glass cylinder. It slides to a close. Several wires and IV's snakes their way from the machine into her skin.

She winks at Abigail as a tube enters her mouth and the cylinder fills with a bright blue fluid. Before Abigail steps in she side-steps towards a computer.

"Computer locate. T.R.A.C.I fridge number three." She speaks. The computer chimes.

"Fridge three located." An automated voice reports. "Inventory?" Abigail speaks.

"Inventory is currently four thousand, four hundred and two out of five thousand," The computer reports. Abigail sighs in relief.

"Power off." She orders and the computer shuts off. She walks over to the cylinder and nods to the techs and guards in the room.

"See you in a decade gentlemen." They salute her and she steps in. The door slides shut and as the IV's and liquid consume her she whispers to herself.

"See you boys soon."

CHAPTER 28

QUANTUM IMMORTALITY

Abigail walks swiftly and orderly down the hall, passing scientists and businessmen. She turns a corner and arrives at a set of double doors. Two heavily armed guards nod and let her pass. She enters. The Prexy and Dr. Kim sit across from each other at a conference table. The room has massive windows overlooking the massive metropolis they reside in.

"Ah, doctor. Thank you for joining us." The Prexy says relieved. She is wearing an all black power suit with solid, silver bracelet cuffs on both wrists. Her skin is covered in makeup to hide her aging. Her silver, long hair is tied into professional-looking Dutch braids. She seems relaxed which Abigail and her both know is a rare commodity in this line of work. Dr. Kim is in his lab coat. He has several documents on the table in front of him. He looks giddy. Like a child on Christmas morning. Ready to jump out of his chair.

"What brings us all to the top of Prime Center?" Abigail huffs, taking a seat at the table next to Dr. Kim.

"We have developments." The Prexy stands and pushes the button on a remote. All of the windows slide shut, encasing the room in darkness. A bright holographic screen appears in front of them. It shows schematics for a building.

"Thanks to Dr. Kim's miraculous breakthrough, I believe the conditions are finally lined up to launch operation Final Destination." The Prexy is upbeat. Abigail's eyes widen.

"Operation Final Destination?" She is surprised. "How many successful trials are we at?"

"I have two dozen consciousnesses contained within crystal port hard drives," Dr. Kim reports.

"And they are able to sync into a T.R.A.C.I server?" The Prexy asks. Dr. Kim nods.

"That's it then. We have everything we need, Abigail." The Prexy steps forward towards her. She has a look of hope and happiness which is unbecoming for her.

"Everything we've worked for has been leading to this," The Prexy says grabbing her arms. For a moment Abigail is reminded of her and Freida back in school together.

"With current estimations, we can have the facility up and running this time next year." Dr. Kim exclaims.

"We can finally end this nightmare we've been in for the last two hundred years." The Prexy adds on.

"That's amazing." Abigail stares at the screen in wonder. All she ever strived for is too create more time. And now she is staring right at it. The ability to have infinite time. Kim continues.

"The structure will contain the latest, most advanced T.R.A.C.I servers and provide secure hermetically-sealed storage for the crystal consciousnesses. Now usually to operate T.R.A.C.I servers you need someone running it on the outside. Solo-Dives are possible but you lose track of time the easiest that way. But with the latest developments certain individuals who transfer their mind to a crystal port, and have the right skillset can operate a T.R.A.C.I server from within." He moves towards the projector pointing to various charts and graphs.

"It takes a certain I.Q level and mental fortitude in order to perform such a task. Too manage the source code of an artificial reality." Dr. Kim explains.

"You both scored proficiently on the aptitude tests so I strongly believe you both would be capable of running simulations while under. To you both it'll simply feel like a never ending lucid dream. Able to shape the universe as you see fit." He concludes.

"We should make announcements immediately!" Abigail says, now growing excited. "We can finally tell the world we have a cure! We can finally end all this pain." The Prexy and Kim both grow sad.

"About that," The Prexy says. As if Abigail just spoke about someone who died. "The process to transfer a mind into a crystal port is extremely costly."

"It requires pure, unfiltered verve. We can't use any manufactured verve created through abilities. Only natural verve from their planet works," Dr. Kim demonstrates by playing through a couple videos outlining and showing the process. During the surgical procedure they used natural verve. It's chemical components and purity aren't that vastly different. However only the subjects that received natural verve survived the process. Abigail is shocked.

"How much do we have left?"

Kim hits a button and the screen displays the current amount of pure verve left in storage.

"Enough for five thousand units." The Prexy says sadly. Kim swallows hard and turns off the projector. The lights come back on and the windows let the sun back into the room.

"Five thousand? We're on a planet with nearly ten billion people and we can only save five thousand of them?" Abigail grows angry. The Prexy sighs and looks at Dr. Kim.

"Could you give us a minute?"

Dr. Kim nods and gathers his things. Once he leaves the atmosphere grows in intensity. Abigail is fuming.

"Do you remember junior year of college?" The Prexy walks over to the window and looks down to the smaller skyscrapers.

"Remember when I came to you crying that I failed my biology exam?" Abigail joins her at the window.

"I do." Abigail's eyes adjust to the sun.

"Do you remember what you said to me?" The Prexy looks to her friend.

"One day we'll run everything, everyone else doesn't matter. We decide what we're worth." Abigail recites.

"We can be gods Abby. We can live forever in a world of our own design. We can finally have everything we've ever wanted." The Prexy attempts to hug her. Abigail allows it but doesn't hug back.

"I gave up everything, for you. For this!" Abigail gestures and moves around the room. "All on the idea that we were going to save humanity!"

"And we are. To some. You better then anyone should know. Not everyone can be saved." The Prexy puts both her hands on her shoulders. "This is happening, Abigail." The Prexy walks back over to the end of the table and hits a pager.

Dr. Kim reenters. "Doctor Ashter. I'm putting you in charge of hosting the event. We will sell all available spots to the highest bidders. Our investors will be excited to learn about this opportunity. Dr. Kim, you are overseeing security. Elections are a month away."

"I'm sorry?" Abigail says flabbergast.

"Security is my department!" The Prexy turns to Abigail.

"Yes however I need you to play host to our benefactors and showcase to them what awaits for them if they continue to pledge their support."

"Have Kim do it! It's his breakthrough!" She is growing agitated.

"Our benefactors know you. They don't know Kim. Besides I want someone closer in their age range. No offense... to either of you." Abigail scoffs at this. She is only a year younger then her.

"Are there any new developments on the resistance?" The Prexy turns gears to Kim. Abigail bites her tongue.

"...No." Dr. Kim says. Abigail stays silent.

"Great. Polls are looking good. One fifth of the population has already pre-voted for me to stay for another term."

"How much did you offer them this time?" Abigail asks.

"Two years of Premium T.R.A.C.I Service." The Prexy smirks.

"Perfect, then." Abigail retorts. "I just have one last question. We haven't been able to study the long term effect this has on human psyche's. Going through this procedure is clearly one way. How will we secure ourselves within the facility and stay safe?" Abigail asks.

"The facility will be underwater, powered on combined water turbines and solar panels. The chamber that will hold the servers and crystal ports will be sealed away through robotic commands and machines. We are keeping a small crew responsible for building the facility, to avoid possible leaks. Once the facility is done and all members have been processed and transferred, the remaining people with knowledge of the facility will "conveniently retire," The Prexy finishes.

"Worthy Sacrifices. We should erect statues dedicated to them once inside." Dr. Kim says. The thought of those men and women's lives having no effect on his soul.

"That is all. Thank you." The Prexy dismisses both of them. Dr. Kim leaves first. Before The Prexy leaves, Abigail stops her.

"Freida. Can we speak again. For a moment?" Abigail beckons. She turns around. "I'd like to request an additional spot in the facility." She locks her focus onto her.

"Abby once were in there you'll have all the space you can use. You can continue to experiment and do whatever you wish." Freida remarks.

"I want to bring someone with us. Into our cure." Abigail says doing her best to remain monotone and serious. Quietly hiding her desperation.

"May I ask who? The value of one of these seats is several trillion dollars after all." Freida now growing curious. Abigail doesn't use her name unless it's something serious.

"If you are going to call back to our days in college then I'll do the same. We've come a long way Freida. Can I just ask this favor from my friend without inquiring further?" Freida stares at Abigail for a moment.

"You're responsible for their compliant delivery, Doctor." Freida nods her head and Abigail nods back. Abigail smiles.

"Thank You." Freida heads back into the hall almost immediately swarmed by her bodyguards. Abigail remains in the conference room and looks over the city.

"Fuck," she says in a half-whisper. "This changes things."

Over in the Nether at the same time a similar conversation of future plans is occurring. Allahara along with Crane's and Z's people discuss over a work bench with a computer and a whiteboard with dozens of diagrams and math scrawled all over it.

"This changes nothing." Allahara says to the group. Crane stays silent and Baix hums in agreement. "The satellite that carries the main server vault orbits Earth at over seven thousand miles-per-hour." Allahara continues. "If we want any hope of infiltrating it we will need to move when it stops. It halts for fifteen minutes once a month for self-diagnosis."

"So, the only way we can get in there with that short a window is by using your ability, Caleb." Allahara finishes.

"I will need several detailed photos of the interior." Caleb replies looking over the whiteboard.

"We have plenty." Mordecai says. He taps the worker at the computer. He hits a button and several photographs begin to print out of the connected printer. Caleb takes them and begins studying them intensely.

"Once inside we will log into the system and upload a video encouraging people to stand up and fight. We will shoot it in the next few days. The election is next month so we only have one chance at this beforehand." Allahara shifts back to the group. Everyone looks at each other waiting for someone to speak up next.

"He can't go alone." Crane speaks up. "With that distance he will be severely weakened. Even with the assistance of Verve. How will he return?" Crane moves over to Caleb and tries to take a few of the photographs. Caleb holds them away from her.

"I can hold the door open as long as I don't step through it. That'll help me conserve strength. I'll stay on the ground on this end." Caleb lets down his guard for a moment. Crane snatches a photo from his hand.

"So who is going to go? We will need someone able to hack into the system and broadcast the video," Crane asks. Caleb snatches back the photograph. Mordecai steps forward without saying anything. Kate tries to stop him but hesitates. Crane nods in approval.

"Forgive me but I insist someone on our end goes as well," Allahara says.

"That should be fine. It looks like like a big enough craft." Crane pours over the photos with Caleb.

"I'll do it, Councilman." Markus steps up.

"I can support him in there." Markus says.

"When is the next service stop?" Allahara asks the tech. He replies

"It's in two days sir." Allahara cracks his neck.

"Okay then. We should prepare to be ready for it then." Allahara orders.

"We need to film the video. We'll get started on it right away." Kanoa says gathering a small group of both Crane's and Allahara's people to plan out the video.

"I'll get some hands and supply all the gear you'll need. You have free use of our services and supplies." Allahara seems excited. Eager to pitch in. Could this be genuine? No clue.

"We wish to be there. To support." Baix speaks up. Allahara nods in agreement. People start dispersing, I look for Crane. I find her talking with Caleb apart from the groups.

"Crane! What can I do? I want to help," I say running up to her.

"You're sidelined for this one Isaac." Crane doesn't even look up to meet my eyes. Caleb does. He looks at both Crane and I.

"What?" I am surprised.

"You can be there to watch but I don't want you anywhere near this. If I could I'd send you back to base right now. But we can't expend the manpower or vehicles." Crane decides now to look up at me. Caleb is deciding to stay out of this by staying silent. Fine.

"Why?" I am agitated. Crane looks around and pulls me close.

"Are you even considering the fact that everyone in this underground city now knows you're the doctor's son? Do you have any idea how much risk you are putting yourself in? I don't condone what she did, but I understand why."

"You are a target. And you don't even seem to care. Or about how it might affect those around you." Crane looks at Caleb as if to make a point. Caleb just ignores it. He seems really fascinated by that same picture he's been on for a few minutes now.

"Why the hell did you even save me then? Just for some sick pleasure? Some savior mentality?" I blurt out. She sighs and turns around with a look of hurt and sadness.

"Are you kidding me?" Caleb says before turning around and heading off with her. I regret saying that. That wasn't fair. She's been nothing but accommodating and kind to me. To this day she has been such a hard person to read. But she didn't deserve that. I think about running after them but decide against it. I'll catch them sometime tomorrow.

CHAPTER 29

A GOOD PERSON

———

It's kind of exciting, you know? We are opening a portal on Earth into space. I am a little bummed I'm not going through it. But it's still cool to watch. For the last two days, Kanoa led the effort with Allahara to shoot the video. I catch glimpses and moments here and there.

Crane worked with Caleb to prepare him for the furthest door he's ever opened. Z is staying with Baix and their group. I was allowed to assist Kate and Mordecai to prepare him for the jump. I read off some documents provided to us.

"So according to this, the interior of the satellite is pressurized. Even factoring that in, you still need to be ready for a massive shift when stepping through that door."

"So my ears are gonna pop. Okay," Mordecai says rather confidently. Kate smacks him behind his head. She signs to him rather angrily.

"Pay attention!" I read her signing, trying to keep up with it.

"Ah, she's just jealous. She's always wanted to go to space." Mordecai chuckles. Kate huffs and continues signing.

"I'm going to be fine." Mordecai reassures her. I continue reading the documents.

"You'll instantly be thrown into zero gravity. You'll need to maneuver through being weightless to the console." My eyes trail the document. In a matter of hours I have had to familiarize myself with the entire layout of this structure and become an expert on space and zero gravity. It's proving to be a daunting task.

"I can run a simulation in T.R.A.C.I" Mordecai says. Kate grabs his face with one hand and turns him to face her. She signs a long and complicated message. I'm able to understand a few words but she is moving too fast.

"It was my choice." Mordecai responds. Kate stomps off back towards the town square. We both watch her head down towards the crowd. An awkward few seconds pass before I end the silence.

"So you guys-"

"Have known each other a long time." Mordecai finishes donning the makeshift suit we've scrapped together over the last thirty-six hours. It's supposed to help with the massive adjustment to high altitude.

"What do you think?" He tries to get a look of himself.

"How long?" I say turning back to face him. He stops admiring and walks over to me. Mordecai places a hand on my shoulder. The suit made his hand exceptionally cold, catching me off guard a little.

"We care for each other Isaac." I brush his hand off.

"Yeah I get that it's just-" He interrupts me again.

"Have you ever known someone who you couldn't explain why but trust them wholeheartedly? You know if push came to shove you'd want that one person standing behind you for whatever comes?" I look around.

We are standing in an open area somewhere near the heart of the Nether. Some people are walking by. I look back towards the courthouse.

Z and her people stand around the staircase.

"A girl from my old life. She looked out for me. More then my mother did back then." I say looking back to Mordecai.

"What about you and Z?" Mordecai asks.

"What about us?" I'm flustered at that. I don't think of Z like Clara. Z is literally a different species then me. I don't have feelings like that. Sure I like her as like a friend. And I do trust her..

"You guys still fighting?" Mordecai makes his point. I sigh in relief.

"If you can call it that. It's different you know. She's different." Mordecai laughs at this.

"Isaac. She's from another fucking planet. No shit she's different. What I'm asking is, are you guys good? She really was attached to you up until this last month or two."

"Yeah, when she found out about the possibility of her home world being gone she sort of blamed my mother and to an extent, me." I look over the distance at her.

"Damn, blamed for the possible destruction of an entire planet." Mordecai tries to poke fun into it. He sits down on a concrete slab and gestures for me to sit down with him. We stare at the underground marvel of this city.

"It doesn't matter. I'm more concerned with her then she is with me." I say. Mordecai shakes his head and laughs even harder. What did my mother's people do to her? Why is she drawing numbers erratically?

"What's so funny?"

"I say the same thing about Kate." Mordecai smiles. "I wouldn't worry about it man. She'll forgive you. Just give her time." Now it's my turn to laugh. I jump off the slab.

"I've had enough time." I hold out my hand to help him up. The suit is a tad heavy. Won't be a big deal up there but down here it's a bit like a scuba divers suit. Awkward to move in.

"Not me. I haven't had enough time. I've got plans. For her and me. I'm gonna build her a log cabin. Somewhere near water. That's why I'm doing this. Because I want more time with her."

"Crane trusts you. Kate trusts you. I trust you. Just please don't die." I say in a half serious tone. It's a dangerous mission but there is no one better for the job. Kanoa offered but Crane and I both know he's a leader who's needed down here.

"Only when tomorrow starts without me." Mordecai says upbeat as he waddles his way over to Kate. From a far she still seems upset and shoves Mordecai almost knocking him off balance. A scatter of laughter erupts from the area.

We didn't get a lot of sleep. It's nerve-wracking for so many reasons. But sure enough, the morning came as the large LED's on the ceiling told us, and everyone met in an open meadow in The Nether. It looks like a field where football was played. There is a massive crowd. I think the entire populace is here. I notice Hal and several others milling about. I decide to hang far back, to watch from a spectator stand on a high area on a hill.

Kate is the only one who wants to watch from here with me. Mordecai and Markus stand in the field with Caleb. Crane is there next to him. Allahara is out there as well alongside a few of the council members. I see Z off in the distance with her parents and their bodyguards.

"Are we ready to begin?" Allahara asks.

Caleb nods, then takes off his jacket to reveal a massive harness around his body with two massive cannisters filled with verve strapped to his back. A lot like that thing Garrett is tinkering with. They begin wheeling out a stage like platform with an circular arc frame on the back side onto the field. I take out a pair of binoculars to get a better view.

"What the hell is that for?" I say partly to myself and to Kate. If she is responding I'm not watching her signing. I'm sure she's just as confused as I am. I watch as another circular frame is brought out from another direction. No stage just framework. It's quickly assembled to create a semi-circle like pathway that is twelve feet tall and wide.

The stage one is positioned fifty feet away from this door. Caleb heads towards this one and steps up onto the stage. The backing on it releases several restraints. I watch as a couple workers begin securing Caleb to the device from the waist down. He needs use of his arms to use his ability so they are securing everything else.

A pad is positioned to give him something to lean back on. By the time they are done. You would think his bottom half is all statue. Nothing is moving even an inch. Kate taps me on the shoulder. I look away to see her signing.

"You heard people call it a support device? Well from the looks of it, I think it's meant to keep him from falling or flying if it's too much for him. I bet that other device is where he is going to throw the portal. Gives him something to focus on." I return to my binoculars. Kanoa steps forward and hands Mordecai a simple flash drive.

"You know what to do. You know how long you have. Please don't get distracted by the beautiful view." Mordecai chuckles and Markus steps forward.

"I won't let him."

"Good man!" Kanoa slaps them both on the shoulder. "On my count!" Kanoa shouts. "The satellite will be stationary in one minute!" There are a lot of murmurs and side conversations in the crowd, but it quickly grows silent as Caleb takes deep breaths. I smell the familiar scent of ozone as the air crackles. If I'm smelling it from here I can only imagine the intensity down there. The verve packs on his back glows.

Caleb closes his eyes to brace himself. He takes deep breaths trying to focus and calm himself. He raises his hands and the bright fluorescent hue of smoke appears and slowly grows.

"Thirty seconds!" Kanoa shouts louder. Kate grabs one of my hands to hold. I look down at her. She didn't need to sign for me to understand what she is feeling. I squeeze her hand back. "Ten, nine, eight, seven, six, five, four, three, two, one!" Kanoa shouts. Caleb unleashes an unholy scream that startles a lot of us and the blue smoke widens to reveal a small interior of a space shuttle.

"Holy shit," I whisper.

"Caleb! Are you okay?" Crane shouts.

"I'm fine. I'm fine. I can hold this." He takes deep breaths. The verve on his back slowly disappears, like a canister being drained.

"Window's open. You've got fifteen minutes!" Kanoa shouts. Mordecai and Markus look at each other and nod. They walk towards the portal. The crackling of electricity shoots out in every direction. A loud thrumming sound beats in rhythm. Causing mild shockwaves to pulse through the ground. Together they both walk into the portal. As soon as they do they fall and contort to a zero-gravity experience. It looks bizarre from our end.

They give a thumbs up from theirs, begin air-swimming deeper into the structure. For a few moments everyone's quiet. The portal makes a considerable amount of noise but Caleb indeed is able to control it as he positions himself into a more comfortable position. Crane checks on him every few minutes.

"I wonder what the view is like out there." I wonder. "You can let go now Kate I think they are going to be fine." Kate doesn't let go.

Instead she grips me harder, and surprises me with a hug. Her knees buckle and she collapses.

"Kate, are you okay?" I am alarmed as I help her to the ground. Suddenly everyone around me drops similarly. I watch as a sea of people suddenly buckle, drop and shiver uncontrollably on the ground. Allahara and the councilmen, Z and her people, Even Crane, next to Caleb, drops.

"Crane? What happened? Are you okay?" Caleb manages to keep his concentration on the portal.

"She's fine. Just a little cold." A female voice rings out. The voice steps in front of Caleb.

"Cogs!" Caleb shouts. "What the fuck!"

I look down at Kate. She has begun shivering uncontrollably. Her watch shakes off revealing a small syringe on the backside of it.

"The watches!" I say hushed. Cogs triggered everyone's emergency dose somehow. Everyone is frozen except for me. If Crane hadn't... I immediately take out a pair of binoculars and watch what is happening down on the field.

"All this time, Cogs? After everything?" Caleb shouts over the viscous vortex holding open the door. Cogs proceeds to tie up Crane. Binding her arms behind her back, tying her legs together then proceeding to finish with a complete hog tie. She picks her up and tosses her into the portal. Her restrained body tumbles into zero gravity, flying deeper into the space station.

"Sorry, Caleb. There was never a chance against The Prexy. Don't worry, I made deals for some of you." Cogs takes out a white hexagonal device and rolls it on the ground. It produces leg stands and begins flashing and spinning.

"If you know what's good for you, you'll drop this door right now." She looks around for someone. Grunts in annoyance then steps into the portal.

I drop the binoculars and scramble to my feet.

"Kate. I got to go help them!" Kate, unable to sign, stays shivering on the ground. I run down the hill. It takes no time to get over to Caleb jumping over piles of frozen people.

"Caleb!" I shout.

"Isaac! They took Crane! They took her into the door!" Caleb tries hard to keep his focus. Tears beginning to break from his face. I frantically look around. Z is nowhere to be seen. I spot Kanoa nearby. He's stunned, on his back, thrashing around. I run over to him.

"I-I-Isaac. W-What are y-you doing?" He says. Teeth chattering so hard they might shatter.

"Not sure yet." I grab his pistol and head back to the portal.

"No, Isaac!" Kanoa shouts, unable to stop me. I stop in front of the portal. I can see a bit further into the space station now. It goes on for awhile. Nobody is in view. They must be in another section.

"Keep it open as long as you can Caleb!" I shout back to him. He nods in agreement. The canister is already half empty. I take a deep breath and jump into the portal.

CHAPTER 30

A CHANCE EVENT

———

There was no preparing for the immediate experience of being firmly on the ground then suddenly transported miles above in space. My stomach lurched as my ears popped worse than I ever have experienced. The effect of no gravity wasn't helping at all. I find a railing and grab it to steady and orient myself. There are multiple sounds of computers beeping and chiming. Steam hisses from various pipes. A truly eerie place.

"Literal freaking space" I mutter. I slowly make my way through the craft, looking for signs of Crane or Mordecai. Turning a few corridors that go in all directions, I hear arguing above me. I look up to see a small rec room. Crane and Mordecai are tied up together. Mordecai looks bloodied and bruised. Crane, now shrugging off the effect of the ice pop, thrashes angrily in her binds.

"I told you, I didn't see the kid. We'll have to accept half the reward!" Cogs shouts.

"Fuck!" Markus shouts louder.

"What is it?" Cogs asks.

"The escape pod only holds two people. Only one of us can take Crane to the Prexy. One of us will have to head back through Caleb's door." Cogs and Markus are now visible. They are on the far end of the room distracting each other.

"I'm not going back through that way! I.H.L is about to be all over that place. We wouldn't get through them all!" Markus whines. I glide down, or rather, up the tunnel to the room. Crane and Mordecai make eye contact with me. Their eyes immediately widen. I get to Crane and remove her mouth gag.

"Isaac? What are you doing here?" She hisses angrily.

"Making it my world." I respond. I cut her binds, free her. We both then work together to quickly free Mordecai. He is not looking good. One eye is quickly swelling shut. He appears to have a stab wound in his back from a blade. Specks of blood are pooling and floating in the air harmlessly.

"Take him back to the door. I'll take care of them." Crane orders.

"Crane there's two of them," I whisper back. Crane looks back at me with unprompted confidence.

"Then it's a fair fight." She heads up a different tunnel into the station. I help maneuver Mordecai back towards the door. Partway there, however, he pushes off of me.

"What?" I ask, letting him go.

"I'm finishing this mission." He holds up the flash drive.

"Bastard took me by surprise before I could upload the video. I just need a few more minutes," he says groggily.

"I don't think that's a good idea, Mordecai." I am concerned. He smiles grimly.

"Too bad you're not in charge." He flies off back down the tunnel we came. Unsure of what to do now, I awkwardly float back to the docking bay. The portal is still there, thank goodness.

"Isaac!" Caleb's voice rings out. Coming through the portal, it sounds discorded, as if interrupted by static; like a bad phone connection.

"I don't have much longer!"

"Just hold on a-" My breath halts as a sharp pain enters my shoulder blade! My muscles tense as I am thrown back into the space station. A now bloodied Markus stands before me and the door.

"Thanks for making it easy to find you!" he shouts. I grab a railing to stop myself from flying backward any further. The pain from my new wound throbs terribly. I feel the wet spot on my back grow larger.

"I don't appreciate the struggling!" He shouts.

He advances towards me. I reach for the pistol with my one free hand but instinctively cover the wound instead. Suddenly a gust of a spray that resembles white paint shoots down the tunnel with tremendous force blinding Markus, causing him to stumble backwards.

Crane drops into the room holding a fire extinguisher. Once used up, she uses it as a melee weapon. She bashes Markus' head. He groans, tries to grab Crane. They lock together in struggle, spinning uncontrollably towards the direction of Caleb's door. They pass through it and land with a hard thud on the ground. Before I can see anything else the door closes. The portal is gone. I'm now frozen in shock.

"What happened?" Mordecai flies into the room.

"The door closed. We just lost our only way off this space station." I'm paralyzed with fear.

"I got the video uploaded. Job's done. And that's not the only way off this tube of metal." He says applying a makeshift bandage to his eye, now swelled completely shut.

Together we make our way back to the recreation room where the escape pod is. The area is how you'd expect it it be; some couches, a pool table, a dart board. Some mini-fridges. A jukebox. Even a TV. Nice digs. The room also has a kitchen and bathroom area walled off into smaller rooms. As we enter an automated voice starts up.

"Artificial gravity engaged" We land on the ground, dropping only a foot. Cogs drops from the tunnel above us directly onto Mordecai. They both tumble into the kitchen and begin a primal fight of fists and weapons.

I aim the pistol, try to get a shot on Cogs. I set the gun to stun, hold my breath, and fire. They both throw each other out of the way causing the blue energy to smash into the window in the kitchen. The freeze effect causes spider cracks in the glass. Alarms blare!

"Cabin pressurization warning. Sealing off site of breach." The kitchen locks down. Walls shoot down and out of the walls sealing off the kitchen from the rest of the rec room. The only way to view into it is a porthole-sized circular window where the doorframe once was.

"Annoying bastard. You're costing me more money then you can count!" Cogs grits her teeth as she stabs Mordecai, twisting her blade further into his back. Mordecai howls with pain and uses his last bit of strength to return the favor by sticking his knife into Cog's side. They lock into each other into a strange stalemate, try to overpower the other. I run up to the window.

"Fuck, Mordecai!" I watch helplessly. Mordecai gazes at me then back at the cracking window. It's big enough for both of them to go through. He looks back at me, I already know what he is thinking.

"No don't! Mordecai! Don't!" I try to quickly learn the wiring and coding behind this door. I frantically look for a panel to open.

"Isaac! Tell Kate, I'm sorry. She was right. We ran out of time." He pushes off the kitchen table with his feet holding Cogs and crashes into the fragile window.

"You...murderer!" Cogs shouts right at me before her breath and the air escapes from them both.

They fly into space, instantly gone. Mechanical arms drop down into the room and release a shiny sliver of a thick putty material over a dispensable frame large enough to seal the hole.

"Re-pressurizing cabin. Routine maintenance completed. Resuming programed course." The satellite says as the doors seal shut. The divider removes itself. As I gaze through other windows, I can tell we are now moving again. The satellite makes more noise but I can only hear a faint ringing in my ears as I clutch my head and begin to scream.

I didn't know if it was anger, or sadness, or both. I wrap my arms around my knees and sob into my lap. I cry for what feels like hours. Eventually I am so tired and wrecked from this I fall asleep there in the satellite.

I wake up upside-down. After collecting myself, I decide to tend to my wound and look for the escape pod Cogs kept talking about. As I explore I find supplies and materials. I could survive up here for maybe a month. But who knows what's happening in the Nether right now. Eventually I find a shuttle meant to be taken to the ground. I climb into it and try to teach myself how to fly this thing.

"I think I'll die trying if I attempt this." I say to myself.

"Greetings!" I hear a different automated voice chirp up, startling me a little. "Welcome to The Main T.R.A.C.I hub. Are you returning to the ground?"

"Um...yes." I say uneasy.

"Ground course selected. How many passengers?" I look at the passenger seat.

"Just one." I swallow hard.

"One. Please fasten your seatbelt we will be leaving short-ly," the machine instructs. I strap into the craft. It seals shut and begins a countdown sequence.

"Three...two...one..."

And with a hard thrust it moves at an incredibly fast pace. I look out the window. The satellite I was just inside grows progressively smaller while Earth grows bigger and bigger.

"Please don't be like my boat." I say to myself. As we approach the atmosphere at an ever increasing speed, I have trouble breathing. Really not the best time for an anxiety attack. I try to steady my breath but I can't stay clam. The craft feels like it's going to rip apart any minute and burn in the atmosphere with me.

"Elevated heartrate detected. Administering air sedative." The machine speaks.

"Wait! What?" I exclaim. Suddenly the air hisses as the shuttle fills with a light smoke. "No that's okay! Cancel! I'm fine!" I try to move my head away from the gas. I have no chance though, of evading anything in here while cannonballing towards Earth. Despite my best efforts I inhale the sweet smelling mist. My arms and legs go numb and my head feels heavy as I fall fast asleep.

CHAPTER 31

OFFLINE

It happened at 9:47 AM on November 17th, 2119. There were two-hundred and thirty-three million accounts logged into T.R.A.C.I at the time of the broadcast. People just starting their day, sitting down at their desks, beginning quests to raid dungeons or slay dragons. Everyone was living their perfect virtual lives. A T.R.A.C.I broadcast isn't like one on a television. When your visor is taken over by a message, you are halted in your tracks from whatever you were doing. When the broadcast began two-Hundred and thirty-three million people froze in place, forced to watch.

"Hello." Allahara greets the viewers. "My name is Councilor Allahara. I am here today to bring you a message. Your world is false. You may already know that. Or you may not. Either way. you need to know the truth. Our world is in danger. Our real world. Our desperate need for this resource you call T.R.A.C.I is finite, despite what The Prexy proclaims. We can no longer hide in the shadows while our planet is dying. It's time to wake up."

Allahara then begins to walk through the streets of the Nether. Showing only the good stuff. Kind business owners. Entire families with children.

"I represent a group of individuals who you may recognize from these posters." Several wanted posters of members from Crane's group and The Nether appear.

"Many of you may consider us terrorists. Perhaps now, given this platform, you can learn the truth. We seek to bring the world back to what it used to be. To bring people outside to celebrate what we already had as a society but have since lost by locking ourselves in metal boxes away from the sun and plugging wires into ourselves to live a fantasy, a false life. This cannot go on forever."

Allahara stops at a staged up version of a T.R.A.C.I booth. The door opens to reveal what someone who is in the program looks like from the outside. A comatose patient with several IV's going all throughout him.

"Consider this an official declaration. A promise. That if the Prexy does not resign, if she does not give up her seat of power and properly document and declare high T.R.A.C.I usage to be corrosive and unhealthy then we will not stop. We will not rest until her tyrannical reign is over. We won't lie to you. To bring her down may bring down the very product all of you have grown to love. T.R.A.C.I may disappear forever. This is not our initial goal. But you need to know what this technology is doing to you. T.R.A.C.I is killing you. You don't need it. You are stronger."

The man in the booth suddenly wakes up and steps out of the booth, he is pretending to rediscover the world.

"You have value out there in the real world. You can have superpowers. What you know as element 144, we call verve. We've been studying it and we can report that it is safe to integrate with as long as it is handled properly. This is how you can obtain powers. Why don't you look at what verve can give you in the real world?"

The video now shows moments of various members using their abilities. Kanoa shoots fireballs from his hands. Crane's impressive telekinesis. Mercedes uses her freezing ability. Kup's resizing skill.

"We are here to be honest. And the truth is, powers are not always guaranteed. In fact there is a chance you will either have no affect or even be disabled in a way if your body cannot regulate verve. But we took this chance to broadcast this message because we are willing to bet there are more out there who share our ideals. You must be sick and tired of feeling sick and tired whenever your memberships run out, forced to sell your soul for another two weeks of usage. Re-join the world. Help make it a place worth waking up for. Stand up and fight. We can build a better world together. Not under oppressions but democracies."

Throughout the video, several shots of T.R.A.C.I booths containing people growing sicker flow. Footage of I.H.L soldiers painted in a negative light. They also showcase examples of over usage in T.R.A.C.I systems.

"Find us. Find sanctuary. Find peace." Now the video shows a simulation of a busy park and outdoor scenery, a beautiful luscious green area with a live festival.

"We plan to change history for the better. The Prexy's days are numbered. We are all under her control. We live in her world, her dream. It doesn't have to be this way. Wake up and fight. Wake up and live. Wake up."

And as he said. Everywhere all at once. At 9:53 AM on November 17th 2119. All Two-Hundred and Thirty-Three Million accounts were manually logged out. The visor blinks a repeating message. All T.R.A.C.I Servers Offline.

CHAPTER 32

ABSOLUTE POWER CORRUPTS ABSOLUTELY

With a loud thud Arthur storms into Neon's office, finding the man hard at work packing up the office.

"What the fuck happened!" Arthur slams his hands on Neon's desk. Neon, expecting this, stops what he was doing and closes the door.

"Things went sideways. Someone tipped off the Prexy about The Nether. Whoever didn't get grabbed has gone deep underground." Neon replies.

"And the kid?" Arthur asks.

"My contact told me he is presumed dead." Neon says.

"Thought you'd be happy." Arthur groans in annoyance until composing himself.

"What about The Secretary?"

"Probably under extreme protective procedures. You did see that broadcast, yes?" Neon throws his hands up.

"So what's our next move?" Arthur asks. Neon scoffs.

"Take a look around! Everything is going to shit. The world is being flipped upside down. I'm trying to land on my feet." Neon says. He quickly shoves several items off a shelf on the ground into a storage bag.

"You going somewhere?"

Arthur grows more agitated.

"Take a look outside! I've never seen a public reaction like this before. I'm going underground myself; wait till this shit blows over." Neon is obviously in a bit of a panic.

"You're running." Arthur scrutinizes the office for the first time since entering, notices it is much emptier than it used to be.

"Until a time we can build back up, we need to scatter. This is growing bigger then The Central Zone. Bigger then us." Neon says.

"I thought there was no such thing." Arthur retorts.

"Grow up. There's a war going on out there. We are a couple dozen thieves. Self-preservation is our code." Neon says.

"We had a deal." Arthur grows angrier.

"Fuck off. Your deal got my people killed. We're leaving now." Neon throws his bag over his shoulder and makes his way towards the exit. Arthur steps in his way and uses his ability to force him back to the other end of the room. Neon is surprised.

"So you got an ability. Lucky you. Then that makes us even more square then. Leave!" he demands.

"You promised me the kid and the Secretary!" Arthur shouts.

"And I have no idea where either one is now or even if they are alive!" Neon shouts, frustrated.

"Then you are of no more use to me then." Arthur says in a dry monotone.

"Good, I'm glad we see eye to eye now." Neon heads back towards the door. As he is about to walk out his muscles lock into place and his body is lifted a foot in the air. The door closes in front of him. Arthur extends his hand, controlling his ability. He spins Neon back around to face him.

"What the fuck are you doing?" Neon gasps.

"You run an illegal business. I only worked with you because I thought you could help me get closer to who I am after. But now you are worthless. Just another wrong for me to right. More justice for me to bring this fucked up world."

Arthur continues to monologue. As he does so Neon manages to reach into his bag and grab a small round device. He presses a button and hurls it at Arthur. The device chimes and a blue gas erupts from it. Arthur is caught off guard. As he inhales some of the gas his connection to his ability is interrupted. Neon drops to the ground and scurries out into the hall where his people are packing up shop.

"Run! Leave! Get out of here-" His cries are cut short as Arthur shoots a crimson round through the back of his head. Neon's eyes flare red for a moment as the blast exits through his forehead, leaving behind a smoldering fiery bullet hole. Neon drops to the ground lifeless.

Two dozen criminal witnesses draw their weapons and fire gunpowder bullets at Arthur, but thanks to his power, no bullet ever reaches him. They drop harmlessly to the ground, having lost all momentum. The criminals expend their ammunition, then gaze in terror at how they did no damage. Some of them closest to the door try and make a run for it, but Arthur slams the doors shut and bolt locks it from afar.

Others try and make their way to a window to climb out only to be brought down hard on the pavement, yelping or groaning in agony. Only the rare few who are also enhanced try to fight. Greg summons balls of light and hurls them at Arthur in an attempt to blind him. Another grunt whose name Arthur never bothered to learn takes a huge breath and unleashes a hurricane force gale in his direction, trying to knock him over. Unfazed, Arthur lifts them, then brings them in close.

"Unnatural," he says before snapping both of their necks simultaneously.

Looking around, Arthur notices a matchbook, and swiftly acquires it. He lights one and runs it along some of the curtains, proceeding to other flammable objects in the warehouse. The fire quickly grows and spreads. As dark smoke fills the room, the remaining thieves cough and cry out for help. Arthur levitates himself and a box up through the roof by creating a hole then re-patching it before coming to a rest there.

He watches the building burn from afar. After thirty minutes the roof unable to support itself collapses. The fire now licks the sides of the building, which is consumed entirely. He decides to do one more sweep around the area to make sure everyone is dead. He turns the corner on the far end when suddenly a body crashes through a window above him and lands with a hard thud next to him.

A very badly burned survivor. Glass shards cutting into his face and chest. Most of his clothing and gear has burned away. His skin is red, blistered and bleeding. Coughing and groaning in sheer pain he rolls onto the cold snowy ground at Arthur's feet. Arthur kneels down to get closer to him.

"Why?" The grunt asks.

"Why not?" He says smiling. "Who can stop me? Nothing matters anymore."

"You're not a god." The grunt, who doesn't look or sound older then eighteen practically whispers.

"Oh? Now I never thought of it like that. No, maybe not. But I'm something real close to it. I just believe in an eye for an eye," he says.

The kid passes away moments later. Arthur looks around. There would have been I.H.L and Government forces here the moment they noticed the fire. But upon looking around the city it quickly becomes apparent that they have their arms full with a population uprising numbering higher then they expected.

As several other fires erupt across the city horizon, Arthur gathers the items from the box he saved, then levitates over the buildings making sure to avoid any I.H.L trucks. He eventually comes across a massive group of civilians engaging in a sort of make-shift fight club. A crowd surrounding two different groups of individuals fighting to the death. Curious. Arthur lands down near it and makes his way into the crowd, who scream and cheer loudly. He pulls one of the spectators to the side.

"What the fuck are they fighting about?" Arthur asks the stranger.

"We captured some soldiers. We're showing them we're not going to be locked out of our hard earned T.R.A.C.I booths!" The stranger says.

Arthur looks into the crowd to see men and women wearing uniformed gear that reminds him of his time he worked on The Loft. As the crowd punches and kicks the life out of them, a memory flashes through Arthur's head of Ramirez. Anger builds up in him as he shoves his way into the fighting ring. He uses his ability to push everyone away from the horribly injured guards. Everyone stops cheering. An eerie silence fills the air as they watch in wonder. The soldiers cough and groan, clutching their torsos. One of them, a man of similar age to Arthur holds up his hand.

"Thanks," he says.

"For what?" Arthur asks. Raising both of his hands he picks up all four soldiers and levitates them in the air while simultaneously telekinetically choking the life out of them. Arthur then addresses the crowd.

"Your angry! I understand. The ones in power have used their influence to control us for far too long! Now we have a chance to take it all back! But if you run into every fight you see you won't live to see the new world.

"These people represent a regime that needs to end. But ask yourselves, if they fall who takes their place? If it's not us then it'll be another oppressive leader and history will repeat itself. You need to be smart. You need to organize. The future of this shit world only has a chance if it's left to the people. Not a small minority given absolute power. Checks and balances. Let this be the beginning of the war to take back our lives."

Arthur flicks both his wrists and all four guards necks snap. He drops their lifeless bodies to the ground. The crowd stunned, mouths agape in shock. Someone deeper in the crowd speaks up.

"Big words for someone who looks like they can crush whoever they want," Someone shouts. Arthur frowns.

"I do not desire power. But I have it. Follow me and together we can dismantle this empire by taking out their number one resource!"

Arthur then using his ability causes hundreds of state of the art energy blasters to come flying out of the box and into the hands of this angry crowd.

"Which is?" Someone else asks.

"Madam Secretary. Otherwise known as The Doctor. She is the one responsible for creating this evil technology. We take her down and The Prexy has nothing left to defend her. Who is with me?" Arthur shouts to the crowd.

Everyone looks around for a moment. Looking at each other, waiting for someone to make a move. Then one person steps forward. Then two, then four. Eventually most of the crowd surrounds him as a few outliers walk off hands in their pockets.

"What would you have us do first?" One of the crowd members ask.

"We need to gather more people. Grow our ranks."

"What about the broadcast? That guy said there are groups like us already formed and working towards this."

"And they failed to explain what they would do after The Prexy is off the board. It sounded like someone who wants her job to me!" Arthur claims. People mutter and nod in agreement.

"We'll do this the right way. We will set up a proper democracy. A country your children can be proud of and grow up safe in!" Arthur gets on a roll. People grow more excited and cheer. What nobody notices though is an induvial with verve blue eyes and a shaven head slowly making his way to within reach of Arthur. He suddenly screams,

"Usurper!" And lunges at Arthur with a shiv. He is caught by Arthur's ability inches from his neck.

"Usurper?" Arthur asks. He spins him around to see the brand of a Techno on this guy's neck. He smirks and whispers something in his ear.

"Yeah, you're right." Arthur replies as he snaps the guy's neck. He tosses him onto the pile.

"I once knew a techno months ago. A real low-life. I blame him for the death of my son and my friend," Arthur addresses the group again.

"I don't know if he is alive but if he is then they will answer for their injustices! This war will claim many lives as we will fight anyone who stands in our way!" He stares at the Techno. Several people boo, hiss and kick the lifeless body, spewing their own hatred toward Techno's. Everyone claps and hollers in agreement.

"Let's go!" Arthur orders. Arthur begins leading the group of strangers down the streets, using his ability to move fire and rubble out of their way. The group grows larger as more people emerge from alleyways to join the fight. Some I.H.L and government soldiers attempt to halt or disperse them.

However they are overpowered by the mob mentality lead by Arthur.

"Hey, what's your name? Or what should we call you?" One of the guys walking at his side asks. Arthur thinks for a moment and grins.

"Call me...Balance."

CHAPTER 33

TOMORROW

───

Sulfur. That's the first thing I notice. Sulfur and ammonia. The stench is overpowering. It feels like a pound of it was thrown in my face. I rub my nose and sit upright. My whole body feels strangely fine - not exhausted or lethargic. I can't feel any of my previous injuries. It's odd.

"Good morning!" Dr. Kim says. I look around. An older asian man sits at a table in the center of the room.

"Who are you?" I step out of the bed.

"Funny. I have the same question for you." Dr. Kim keeps his focus on me. "You can't even be in your twenties yet." He says mostly to himself, inspecting me.

"I'm not really in a sharing mood right now. Where am I?" I scan for windows or doors but there don't appear to be any.

"Earth. Lucky for you. Imagine our surprise to see our satellite pod return with someone inside, especially when we had no one up there in the first place." Dr. Kim says.

"Ah. Fuck. Yeah that would be a doozy for the pricks not in the know." I say.

"Oh good. I love when they have attitudes." Dr. Kim says with a strange confidence.

"I'm not scared of you. I'm not scared of whatever the Prexy has to throw at me!" Dr. Kim smiles, and takes out a controller. He presses it and intense painful shocks course through my body causing me to collapse onto the ground.

He lets go of the button and the pain subsides. I cough in agony. I have no collar. No restraints on me. Where did that pain come from? It felt deep within.

"You can avoid a lot of pain if you just tell me who you are, and how you got up there." Dr. Kim says solemnly.

"Fuck you. I don't care what you do to me." I look up at him now walking up to me. My face level with his boots. He kneels down and grabs my hair painfully making me face to face with him.

"You will." He says before letting me go.

"You will remain in this room until you've had a change of heart and decide to be more talkative. Get used to your accommodations. Remember, we can always make it more unpleasant. I won't be lenient for long. It's the hunger that you will feel first, really messes with the brain. You'll be more compliant to do whatever, just to eat." Dr. Kim stands up I watch his body de-materialize in front of me.

"I'm in a T.R.A.C.I simulation." I mutter to myself. I walk to the table and pick up the gun.

"You left this here moron!" I shout to the ceiling.

Why give me a gun in here? Why give me an out? I take some deep breaths and reassure myself that I'm under. I did indeed see him dematerialize. Besides they need information from me. They wouldn't give me a way to die that easily. I close my eyes and place the gun to my temple and pull the trigger. Darkness. Only to wake up again in the same room, in the same bed. Looking around this ugly room I see the same gun back on the table with a vase with a single rose in it.

"What the fuck?" I say horrified.

As Dr. Kim awakes in his booth he steps out and heads over to a bank of monitors overseeing the flower room. An alert pops up for an incoming holo-link. He accepts it and a holographic version of The Prexy appears.

"So?" She asks.

"He's stubborn. He has an attitude. It won't take me long. He's a kid." Dr. Kim confidently wipes his glasses before returning them to his face.

"A kid got inside a multi-trillion dollar satellite and hacked into the servers to show a pirate broadcast nationwide calling for my head. I don't care who he is. Extract every bit of information he has. I want this one off all records. Keep your team to a minimum. No restrictions. Do whatever you have to. I have to go quell this growing fire."

The Prexy disconnects from the call. Dr. Kim turns off all the monitors just as Abigail enters the room.

"We need to talk." Abigail says sternly. She appears distraught. Her lab coat hastily thrown on and her hair frizzed beyond what clips and bands can reign in.

"Were in the middle of a crisis, doctor." Kim picks up some folders and carries them over to his desk. Abigail is the last thought on his mind at the moment. He couldn't be bothered with her. He too is understandably stressed out. Out in the corridor the sounds of dozens of hurried footsteps pound through the halls.

"And I'm wondering why." Abigail begins to circle Kim. Preventing him from leaving his office. Kim tries to go to the side and Abigail steps in his way. "I've been doing this for a long time Kim." Abigail picks up a decorative glass bauble from his coffee table in the center of the room.

"The Prexy and I. We have a complicated relationship."

"I'm not sure I follow." Kim says confused. Abigail turns the item over inspecting every ounce of surface on this sphere.

"She and I, we're both control freaks. We like to know everything that's going on. I've gotten pretty good at detecting when she is trying to spy on me. I know because I used to do the same to her. You know, before she became ruler of the world."

"If you are insinuating-" Kim begins. Abigail cuts him off.

"I am providing free advice. You don't get to our positions without crossing the moral line. We all have our skeletons Kim. Whatever she asked you to try and uncover from me, stop." Dr. Kim is silent. Calculating, he tries to figure out what to say. Abigail sets the bauble down and continues to speak.

"I never liked politics. That's her game. But I learned how to cover my ass quick. I suggest you learn the same."

"Are you threatening me, Abigail?" Kim sets down the pile of folders on his desk and approaches Abigail.

"I'm not your enemy. But I'm not your friend either. We're co-workers and we need to work together. Freida was right about that much. We have a huge problem on our hands. They were in the control hub on the satellite. What's the status of it? Is there anyone on it right now?"

"There was a conflict on the station. Security shows five different personal on board at one time. Here are the stills we were able to grab. Now two are unaccounted for. But we believe the other three were jettisoned." Abigail studies the photographs and her heart sinks when she recognizes one of their faces.

"Jettisoned?" She asks.

"The logs recorded multiple instances of the cabin depressurizing. There was a window break among other things. Current scans of the system show no heat signatures. There is no one on the satellite now. They must've gotten sucked out into space. It appears no one survived."

"Hope it was worth it to them to play their stupid little video." Kim says nonchalantly. Abigail looks dazed as she repeats.

"No survivors?" Her voice catching. Dr. Kim meets her eyes dead on.

"None. Now if you'll excuse me, the Prexy is calling a meeting soon. This video has circulated over fifty million times. It's already having nasty results. It's looking like another civil war is about to kick off."

As Kim again grabs his folders and shoulder shoves Abigail to the side to exit the room, Abigail's glance drifts. She walks through the facility as though she is walking through fog. Hurried scientists and soldiers run by her anxious and worried. Her security detail trails behind her trying to talk to her.

"Madam Secretary? Is everything all right?" her head guard asks. She doesn't respond. She walks for an hour around the base until arriving back at her office. She stumbles inside and bolt locks the door shut behind her. She hits a button that displays a sign out front.

"Do Not Disturb." The light of a slightly exposed window is all that illuminates the area. She walks over to her laptop where a communication log shows Cogs and Markus in communication with her. She closes the laptop gently. Then quickly grabs it and hucks it out the window. The sound of glass shattering is brief as bits and pieces along with the chunk of technology whooshes to the ground.

She falls down onto the ground, catching a glass beaker on her way down. It shatters in her hand. She winces slightly at the sharp tear of the broken glass digging into her palm. She opens her hand and looks at it. Deep crimson pours out as the familiar smell of iron hits her nose. She clenches her fist, burying the glass deeper into her skin and drops her head into her arms. She quietly sobs.

Dr. Kim rushes up and down different halls to get ready for his meeting. He is suddenly stopped by a lab tech of similar age, but with short blonde hair.

"Dr. Kim, I completed that deep dive into Dr. Ashter's history." He says, catching his breath.

"And?" Kim asks expectantly.

"There really didn't seem to be anything out of the ordinary. She had a couple hundred humans on ice for her cryogenic studies before she began working on T.R.A.C.I." The tech says.

"So another dead end. Sorry, but I'm a bit busy at the moment." Dr. Kim tries to push away.

"There was one thing." The tech adds. Annoyed yet curious, Dr. Kim turns on his heel again.

"Yes?" He says impatiently.

"I'm not sure. It might be nothing. Some of her subjects... she would pay regular visits to. In fact, I noted two distinct test chambers that she always checked in on. She spent a lot of time with them, actually." The tech seems baffled. Intrigued, Dr. Kim moves closer to the tech. "It was odd." The tech finishes.

"Send me the data." Dr. Kim instructs.

"It's already sent to your office." The tech beams. Kim hurriedly races back and pours over the info. It's mostly CCTV footage that was copied and archived onto some ancient servers. Kim fast forwards through hours of footage and watches Abigail sit, eat lunch, stare and sometimes talk to two specific test subjects.

"Eighty-Nine and Ninety..." He says to himself.

"Computer. List all test subjects either dead or missing." Dr. Kim orders. The computer begins to list numbers.

"Stop. When was test subject ninety lost?" The computer chimes alive.

"2024. No records or footage available. Presumed dead," the computer confirms. Even more confused, Dr. Kim asks.

"When was test subject eighty-nine lost?"

"Missing from Oakwood Facility August 4th 2119." The computer declares.

"Three months ago? Is there any footage?" Kim asks. A CCTV camera displays the visual record of the basement storage premises. Kim watches as several armed mercenaries make their way through and search for a test subject.

"Turn up volume." Kim orders. He watches in amazement as one of them resizes an entire booth with a verve ability. Then another grabs the now shrunken pod and places it within a suitcase.

"Jesus, just trust me Dad." The kid in the video says.

"Dad?" Kim repeats, noticing something, he shouts

"Pause!" The computer does as the video focuses on the young man in the picture.

"Zoom in and enhance." Kim instructs. The dim blue light in the storage room illuminates his face just enough to get a clear picture. "Display current flower room subject." Kim barks. The screens split to show both the security footage and the livestream where he is walking around, still inspecting the room. As the realization dawns on Dr. Kim. An evil smile grows across his face.

"I think I just found your skeletons, Doctor Ashter." He says maliciously.

EPILOGUE

Kanoa's eyes shoot open as he sits upright fully alert. Looking around all he can see for miles is sand dunes. The sky is dark. Looks to be almost sunrise, as the sun is beginning to rise in the horizon. Wind blows sand into his face. Instinctively he puts his arm up to protect his face. A pounding pain emanates from his temple. He winces in pain as he puts a hand to his head.

"What the fuck?" What happened?" He says out of breath. The last he remembers is Isaac running into the portal. Then gunfire and an earthquake. He slowly rises to his feet to try to get a better view. He can barely make out a few buildings way far off in the distance. Now focusing on his more immediate surroundings he finds a few items from out of his backpack. After a moment he looks over the closet sand dune and on the other side he finds a man face down in the sand. He rushes over to him and flips him over.

"Oh fuck. What the fuck Caleb? What the hell happened?" Kanoa says still trying to catch up on his breathing. He checks for a pulse and puts his head on his chest.

"Okay good you're alive." Kanoa talks to himself. "Okay well get your shit together man. You need to tell me what the fuck happened! And get us out of here!"

He tries to shake Caleb awake. It's then that he notes the burn marks on Caleb's arms. Lines of painful black and red color reaching all the way up to his elbows.

"Dammit. Fuck." Kanoa shouts. The sun will rise soon. Taking in his surroundings. He clocks the closest man made landmark. About ten miles from them. "Okay" Kanoa says embracing the situation. He begins talking to the unconscious Caleb.

"Here is the situation. We are both in a desert. I don't see anyone else. We have no water and the sun is going to rise soon. The Nether is probably under attack. And we are not there to help." Kanoa says this trying to believe it himself. He punches the sand. "Dammit Caleb what did you do?" He shouts. No response.

"You better hope I have enough energy to get us there. For both our sakes." Kanoa groans in annoyance. He takes off his jacket and rips it into strips. He fastens a makeshift sand mask for him and Caleb. Rips his pants into shorts and uses more cloth to wrap his head where it is pounding.

"What did you get us into you little shit?" He mumbles as he picks up Caleb and slings him over his shoulders fireman style. He begins marching, the foot trail in the sand behind him blows away with time. One slow step after another to the unknown structure in the distance.

ACKNOWLEDGMENTS

The journey of book writing is not and should never be walked alone. I crossed this checkered flag thanks to my friends and family who support me everyday. I feel extremely fortunate to have such a strong support system. My angelic mother, my heroic father and genius sister I am thankful for everyday.

Thank you to Alan Zatkow who keeps me on track and focused on what's best for my writing. Thank you to Alyson V. Peabody who's creative visions strengthen my own. And thank you to Mercedes Philbrook who put up with more of me then even I would want to.

I also would like to take this opportunity to thank other creative individuals who inspire me every day. Matthew Mercer and the Critical Role team. As a critter I thank you for the endless hours of Dungeons & Dragons and the inspiration to world build. To Ian Hecox, Anthony Padilla & the Smosh team. Thank you for making me smile & laugh on my hardest days.

This book was made possible thanks to the combined efforts of the community and sponsors who believed in me and this story. Thank you to those who supported the creation of this story. You made my dreams come true.

Elizabeth Allen
Michelle Allen
Sean Allen
Marino Barcos
Jess Beers
John Berube
Dawson Bishoff
Jacob Braz
Krista Butler
The Cole Family
Eric Daigle
Kyle Dow
Kelly Fernald
Andrew Freeman
Caitlin Friel
Danielle St Germaine
Guillermo Alex Gomez
Robert Groat
Tenzin Gyatso
Kylene Hall
Cole O'Halloran
Garrett Hamlin
Daniel Haskell
Madison Hemingway
Jody Henderson
Alyssa Herling
Teresa Hillgrove
Emily Rachael Howard
Stephanie Janette
Lee Kapaun
Evan Kenney
Mark Kenney
Marvin Kenney

ACKNOWLEDGMENTS · 317

Peter Kenney
Stephen Kerr
Emalee Landers
Alyssa Limeburner
Ryan Lowry
Sarah Marchant
Kelly McAllister
Caitlynn McCauley
Kylie McCranie
Kelsey Mehuren
Atreus Morningstar
Katelyn Oster
Danna Oxman
Terran Oxman
Carter Patterson
The Patterson Family
Alexis Philbrook
Katelyn Ploss
Katie Ploss
Alexis Racioppi
Breanna Slone
Ed Varney
Caleb Wallace
Mercedez Whitmore
William Karl Wilson
Jaime Wiltshire
Kim Woods
Kirsten Woods
Olivia Wright
Andrea Yoshioka